Beyond the Rhine

Contents

Contents i
Beyond the Rhine ii
Prologue 1
Chapter 1 7
Chapter 2 19
Chapter 4 41
Chapter 5 52
Chapter 6 61
Chapter 7 71
Chapter 8 85
Chapter 9 97
Chapter 10 109
Chapter 11 120
Chapter 12 135
Chapter 13 150
Chapter 14 171
Chapter 15 181
Chapter 16 195
Chapter 17 205
Chapter 18 219
Epilogue 226
The End 228
Glossary 229
Other books by Griff Hosker 233

Beyond the Rhine

**Book 10 in the
Combined Operations Series
By
Griff Hosker**

Beyond the Rhine

Published by Sword Books Ltd 2017
Copyright © Griff Hosker First Edition

The author has asserted their moral right under the Copyright, Designs, and Patents Act, 1988, to be identified as the author of this work.

All Rights reserved. No part of this publication may be reproduced, copied, stored in a retrieval system, or transmitted, in any form or by any means, without the prior written consent of the copyright holder, nor be otherwise circulated in any form of binding or cover other than that in which it is published and without a similar condition being imposed on the subsequent purchaser.
A CIP catalogue record for this title is available from the British Library.

Cover by Design for Writers

Dedicated to the brave men who served in World War 2. They died so that we had our freedom. Let us never forget that.

Prologue

London January 1945

Liverpool Street station was heaving. I had never seen as many people in one place for a long time. Gordy and Hewitt were at different stations heading home. We had all landed together and then split up. A leave was not to be wasted. We would be back at the sharp end soon enough. I had one eye on the departures board and one eye on the entrance. Susan was supposed to be meeting me so that we could travel to my home together. It had been short notice. Yesterday we had been in Antwerp but Major Foster had pulled strings and we had been brought by an R.A.F transport to Croydon. We had managed to get to London and I had bought tickets for the train. We were going home. I had sent a message to Susan's office but I was not certain if she had received it.

London was still a war zone. The bombers of the Blitz had first been replaced by the doodlebug, buzz bomb and now the even more deadly V-2 rocket. It was more terrifying as it came down vertically giving no warning. They could not be shot down and the devastation they caused was horrific. Air raid sirens could not give a warning and people would be walking through the streets when the deadly missile landed. Major Foster had told me of one V-2 landing in the central square in Antwerp just as a convoy was passing through. Almost two hundred men had been killed or wounded. Herr Hitler had some terrifying weapons; this was one of his worst. The fear showed in the faces of the civilians. They no longer carried their gas masks but they still twitched at unexpected bangs. It would take some time for them to get over that fear. Death could strike and hit anyone!

Our train was due to leave in six minutes. I had Susan's ticket. If she did not make it then we would have an hour or more to wait for the next one. I saw a hand wave above the heads of some sailors. I knew it was Susan. I hurried towards her. The sailors saw me coming towards them and an Able Seaman with a cigarette hanging from his lip shouted, "Ey up, someone is a bit keen"

The sailor next to him turned around and, seeing Susan, grinned, "And I don't blame him! Must be all the fruit salad on the Major's chest!"

They parted to allow me through, "Thanks, lads. It will be a short leave!"

"Make the most of it eh sir!"

"I will do!" I swept Susan into my arms and kissed her. The sailors all gave a cheer. I held her close and whispered, "I wasn't certain you would make it."

She put her mouth close to my ear, "I would have gone AWOL if they had tried to stop me."

"Come on then, let's hurry. The train leaves in five minutes!" I grabbed her hand and we ran.

As we reached the barrier I plucked the tickets from my battledress and held them for the ticket collector. "Just in the nick of time, sir! The train is full. I think you will have to stand."

As we passed through I said, "So long as it gets us home I don't care!"

It was a train with a corridor and the ticket collector was correct, we had to stand. Luckily it was not a long journey. Mum and Dad had bought our house in Essex because it was relatively close to London. Nor did I mind that Susan was pressed close to me. I could have happily inhaled her perfume all the way to Essex. After cordite and explosives, it was a most welcome change. She bombarded me with questions. As she worked in Combined Operations she normally knew what I was up to. This time she did not. My last mission had happened almost accidentally. We were supposed to have been training American and British soldiers but we had become embroiled in the battle that was now known as the Battle of the Bulge. It had almost gone disastrously badly for the allies but the Americans had managed to hang on and what turned out to be the last German offensive of the war had failed.

When she heard that I had been wounded it was as though she had suffered the wound herself, "You must be more careful!"

I laughed, "You sound like Mum. It isn't as though I go out of my way to get wounded. It is war. Besides, it was a minor one."

"You know what I mean. You are a major now. Surely you don't have to be in the thick of things all the time?"

"But I am a Commando. That means behind the lines."

"Not every Commando unit does that."

I said nothing for she was right. My section had specialist skills. While Commandos now fought as regular troops, we did not.

I changed the subject, "Hopefully Mum will be at the station. Major Foster had a phone call put through to her."

"Well if not then we can walk!"

I nodded out of the window. It was sleeting, "In this weather?"

She laughed, "I thought you Commandos were tough!"

"Not when we are on leave."

She coughed and I asked if she was unwell. She nodded, "I had the flu. All the time you were in the Ardennes I was lying in bed. They took me to the hospital. I had three weeks there. It was not a very pleasant Christmas! They let me out on Boxing Day. I have only been back at the office for a few days. You know it is strange; when I went into hospital the office was a happy and cheerful place but since I have been back it is like working in a morgue."

"It is always the same after Christmas. People are down and these V-2 rockets don't help."

"Perhaps." She did not look convinced. She smiled. "Still you are home now! Even the office and the weather can't spoil that!"

Mum was at the station waiting for us with the shooting brake. She hugged us both, seemingly oblivious to the sleet flecked rain. "We hoped you both might be here for Christmas! We will have Christmas now!"

As we ran to the car Susan said, "I only have a three-day pass."

"Then we will pack as much into the three days as we can eh?" As she sat behind the wheel Mum added, "Your dad is coming home later tonight. He is flying in to R.A.F. Rocheford. One of the lads will run him over from there."

"I thought he was in the Middle East?"

"He was but he is being sent to the Far East now. They are giving him a two week leave. The two of you can catch up. He is looking forward to spending some time with Susan here."

It was good to be back in the family home. The chestnut tree was like a reassuring friend. Every year it got bigger and bigger. Each year Dad would threaten to prune it but he never did. I liked that. The world might change but not the tree. Mum waved a hand upstairs as she hurried to the kitchen where the aromatic smell of rabbit stew drifted along the hall, "Susan, you can use Mary's room. Tom, well, you know where you are."

"Right Mum!"

"Help yourself to a drink and then you can come and help do the veg!"

Mum was a great believer in everyone helping. I did not mind. The kitchen range was a warm and comfortable place to be. Growing up there, the four of us would all be in the kitchen, helping out. It was where we learned about the world as Mum and Dad prepared our meals with us.

I dumped my Bergen and greatcoat on my bed. I slipped out of my battledress. I was tempted to change into civvies and then thought better of it. I would change for dinner. I poured myself a whisky. It was just a blend. I would wait until Dad arrived to start on the single malts. He had a fine collection. As I sipped the first whisky in a while, I reflected that this was the first drink of the New Year. I lifted the glass and said, just to myself, " Cheers lads, here's to you, Bert, Reg, Harry, Jack, Jimmy, John, Ken and Alan. You are gone but not forgotten." Somehow toasting the men who had died in the last five years made me feel better. It was as though they were still here.

Mum handed me the peeler, "You are on spuds."

"Mash?"

"Of course!" She suddenly looked worried, "Susan is not funny about rabbit, is she? I mean I…"

"She is fine, Mum. She is not a fussy eater. The rabbit will be fine. Where are they from?"

"Old Ron, down the road, shot them. He always has a few and as soon as I knew you were coming home I thought of him. The meat ration is so small and…"

"I would rather have rabbit."

"When you have done those open a bottle of the Burgundy will you. It needs to breathe."

"Do we still have the Chateau Bouzeron?"

"There are half a dozen bottles left. Your Dad likes it and it goes well with the stew."

Susan appeared. She had reapplied the lipstick I had kissed off and she was beaming, "Well, what can I do?"

"Carrots. We had a good crop this year. They might not even need peeling."

Susan was a hard-working girl and she donned the apron Mum offered and took the peeler. We chatted away as we prepared dinner. Mum had a good kitchen. When they had bought the house the kitchen had been a priority. It had had to be big enough to accommodate a small table so that we could eat there. I knew that tonight, we would be eating in the dining room. Mum knew when to make a meal into a special occasion. She even put candles out. This would be special for the four of us had not eaten together before. Either Dad or I were always away.

Mum was looking at her watch when we heard the key in the door. "It's me, I'm home!"

Susan and I did not need telling. We moved aside so that Mum could greet Dad. We knew that they needed the space. While they hugged in the hall Susan spread a hand around the room, "I like your house. We need one as nice as this."

I laughed, "On a Major's salary?"

"I have savings. Haven't you?"

"Of course but we have to decide first, where we are going to live."

"That depends on you, Tom."

"Me?"

"What do you intend to do after the war?"

I saw the concern on her face. I shook my head, "That is a good question. I haven't given it much thought. Chaps who look beyond the next mission make mistakes. I suppose we can live anywhere. How about that? You find somewhere you want to live and then I will think about after the war."

"After the war?" Dad had entered with one arm around Mum. He put his hand out for me to shake.

"Yes, Dad, Susan and I are trying to work out where to live when this is all over."

Mum shook her head, "You are both silly! You can live with us until you know what you want to do. We didn't buy this as soon as the war was over. We lived in a rented house. It was nice but I was glad when we bought our own."

"How on earth did you afford such a grand house?"

Mum and Dad looked at each other. Mum smiled, "The simple fact is that we couldn't, Susan. The mortgage would have crippled us but, luckily, Bill here was left money."

I nodded, "I had forgotten St. John Browne."

Susan asked, "St. John Browne?"

Mum said, "We will save that for dinner. It is all ready. Bill, go and wash up. Tom has already opened the wine."

Mum was like a whirlwind at times and the table was laden with food before we knew it. It was a wonderful meal not least because just a week ago I had been in the Ardennes fighting the S.S. and German paratroopers. I appreciated such moments. We told Susan the story of the benefactor who had briefly met Dad and left him a sizeable amount of money. We told her of the house in France. What we did not talk about was the war. Nor did we talk about when our leaves would end. For one night we were just a family enjoying good food, good wine and the best of company. Life did not get any better than that. Such moments, in wartime, were precious.

Chapter 1

As with every leave, it ended all too soon. Susan managed to come down at the weekend and we made the most of the brief time we had together. Once I went back to the war then Susan would know what I was doing. At Headquarters, she was privy to the signals and messages concerning Combined Operations. In the field, it was a comfort. I knew, from our conversations together that it both helped and worried her to know where I was and what I was doing behind the enemy lines.

I spent time with Dad. When we were away from Mum then we spoke of the war. We went to the village pub, largely empty now, where his familiar pipe filled the air with the rich smell of his tobacco and then we spoke of the war. He knew of the battles I had been involved in even if he did not know the details. I filled him in. He told me about his posting. He had been promoted to Air Commodore. With the Middle East now free from the Axis he was being sent to do the same in India and Burma. I was just grateful that he was not putting his life on the line any more. He was now an organizer. He had spent his life, since the age of sixteen, serving his country.

"Tom, I know you are good at your job. Everyone I speak to tells me so. Even Winston knows of you. But you need to pull back a little. There are others who can do what you do." Dad had first met Winston Churchill in 1919. They were not friends, the prime Minister was too lofty for that, but he and Dad got on well.

I shook my head, "Sorry, Dad, but that isn't true. My team have skills that I have not seen anywhere else. I have seen and fought alongside brave men: the Loyal Lancashires, the Free French, the Canadians, the American Rangers and Cavalry but none could do what we do. We have language skills as well as skills in sabotage and, let us be honest, in killing the enemy. If they sent less experienced men in then they would die. We lose less than most." I knew that Dad did not want to hear what I was saying but it was true. "The war in Europe will be over by the end of the year. We are at the Rhine already. When Germany is defeated then my war will be over."

"You are not staying on as I did?"

"I don't think so. I am a wartime soldier Dad. You were a pilot. I am a Commando. They need me in wartime."

"You are well thought of you know."

"That is good to hear but I don't want to sit behind a desk and just plan. That isn't who I am."

I thought of our conversations as I sat on the train, heading back to London. I looked out of the window and saw the scars of the war. Britain had been punished for defying the odds and taking on Germany alone. We had been in a dark place but now there was light at the end of the tunnel. We were nearly at the end. I had to be strong. I had to believe that I would survive. I had so much to live for. Susan and I would be married the moment the war was over. We would live with Mum and Dad until we had decided what we would do with the rest of our lives and where we would do it.

The letter which had summoned me back early from my leave had ordered me to London and not Falmouth. That meant I would get to see Susan again even if I could not be with her. The worrying part was that such a visit normally resulted in going behind the German lines again. The despatch rider had also brought me information about my team. I had recommended many of the men for promotions. Whitehall was still controlled by generals who had last fought in 1918. Things moved slowly there. Polly had been promoted to Lieutenant, Gordy to Sergeant Major, Bill Hay was now a sergeant. Roger Beaumont was promoted to Lance Sergeant.as were John Hewitt and Scouse Fletcher. In my eyes, the others all deserved promotion but I was pleased with the decisions which had been made.

I now had a section of twenty men. Half of them I knew and we had fought together for almost four years. The other ten were new. Lieutenant Poulson and Sergeant Hay were busy training them at our old camp in Falmouth. I knew that I would not have long enough with them. I would have to rely on Polly and my sergeants to bring me up to speed with their skills and attributes.

I would not be staying at my club. My father's old servant, Bates, ran a genteel hotel in London. We had arranged for a room there. I dropped my bag in the lobby before proceeding to Whitehall. John was not here but I was expected and the concierge assured me that my clothes would be hung in my wardrobe by the time I returned. Knowing Bates as I did I knew that would be a certainty. He was the most organized man I had ever met. His hotel would be no different.

I had some time before the meeting, which was scheduled for three o'clock, and so I went to my tailors in Saville Row to order a new uniform. It was one for the mess and for special occasions. My old battle dress would suffice for the battles we would face in Germany.

When I arrived at Whitehall I was disappointed not to be going up to our offices where I would have been able to see Susan. Instead, I was taken to a conference room. The disappointment was slightly offset by the presence of Captain Hugo Ferguson. He, too, had become embroiled in the Ardennes. He beamed when he saw me.

"I was delighted when I found out that we were to serve together again, sir."

"Me too Hugo. Any idea what it is about?"

He looked around and said, sotto voce, "Germany this time. You were especially asked for." He straightened my tie. "And the PM is here! Winnie is interested in this one!"

Inwardly I groaned. Whenever Winston Churchill was involved then the pressure increased. The presence of Hugo meant that I did not have to flash my papers as often as I usually had to. Once we reached the doors of the conference room, However, there were two MPs there. I guessed we would have to wait.

Hugo shrugged apologetically, "With the PM in there then it is security, security, security!"

I nodded, "Of course if I was here to kill the Prime Minister then I am not certain that two MP's would stop me."

I saw the Sergeant colouring and he began to rise up and down on his toes.

Hugo said, "The Major is just having a joke, Sergeant Haynes."

"It doesn't do to joke like that, sir! Even if he is a Commando with the V.C."

I smiled, "Let us just say, Sergeant Haynes, that I do not wait well!"

The door opened and a major from the General Staff stood there, "Ah we heard voices, come in Major, come in Captain."

There was a fog of smoke in the room. There were two tables. One had coffee, mugs, jugs and cups upon it and the other had just four people seated around it. Winston Churchill's *'Romeo y Julieta'* cigar provided the most smoke but the American colonel next to him was doing his best too. They looked like they were making a smokescreen. At the end of the table was an easel. It was empty. There were manila folders in the middle of the table.

Churchill looked up, "Young Harsker. You are the image of your father. He was about your age when I first met him in 1919. I can see, from your record, that you are a chip off the block." He nodded to a seat, "I have read of your recent exploits. Quite remarkable." He turned to the American, "I will leave the briefing to you, Colonel." He stood and nodded to me, "When all this is over we must have a chat. You have had a good war. I would like to hear what you did from your lips rather than others." Then he swept out of the room with the major from the General Staff, leaving me with Hugo, the American Colonel and an English Major of Intelligence.

The Colonel said, "Introductions first: I am Colonel Flynn. I am from Ike's staff. This is Major Mowett, Intelligence and Captain Ferguson you know. Help yourself to a coffee, Major. You will need all your wits about you today!"

"Sir." I went to the coffee pot. I saw that there were mugs and cups. I poured myself a mug of black coffee and returned to the table.

The Colonel chuckled as I came back, "Good. I like a man who knows how to drink coffee. Now, you will be wondering why we are here. It is quite simple. We have a spy at headquarters. Or rather, we have two spies. One in your Combined Operations set and one in ours, at SHAEF. That is why we are meeting here. This little group, your Prime Minister and General Eisenhower are the only ones in the loop."

I drank some of the coffee and the Colonel puffed on his cigar as I took that in.

Major Mowett took a map from the table and went to the easel where he pinned it up. He reminded me of an older version of Hugo. He was slightly built and, when he began to speak I noticed a slight twitch over one eye. "If you open the folder in front of you, Major, you will see a picture of a V-2 rocket. The V-2 is the terror weapon the Germans have unleashed on London and other cities like Paris and Antwerp. They are impossible to stop. There is a cutaway drawing of one such rocket. They are complicated beasts but damned well made. They are made in underground factories. The bunkers are in Austria and Germany. The main one is close to a concentration camp at Mittelbau-Dora. However, there is a chink of light. Thanks to Operation Crossbow and the bombing of the Germans factories they have had to spread the manufacture of the parts out. The vital parts are the four graphite fins. They are internal. They are in the jet stream. To put it simply, the rocket cannot be directed without the graphite vanes."

I finished my coffee. "Then bomb the factory where they are made."

"We tried that. They are underground inside a mountain. As you can appreciate, the factory and the men making these fins are small in number. We know the town where they are being made and we have a good idea of the building but the bombing doesn't work. We have tried."

The Colonel put the stub of his dead cigar in the ashtray, "So we sent in teams. First, we used the underground. They were captured and shot. So we sent some Rangers in." He smiled, "They are based on you guys. We figured they would get the job done. That was when we discovered the spy. They were caught too. The end result was we handed it over to Combined Operations. They sent some Commandos in."

Hugo said, "It would have been you, sir, but you and I were in the Ardennes. They sent in Captain Gregson." I looked up. He had been a lieutenant when I had served with him. "When they were caught and shot then we knew there was a spy in our headquarters." He waved a hand around the room, "This building. Other missions were compromised too."

I nodded, "Hence all the MPs."

The Colonel said, "Captain would you?"

"Sir."

Hugo got up and left the room. The Colonel continued, "We are sending you and your team in. The difference will be that not even your Major Foster will know where you are."

"Toppy can't be the spy!"

"That may be true. I know the Major and he seems a decent chap but we don't know. Everyone is under suspicion. We are creating a small section to support you. There will be just three of them. Captain Ferguson, a sergeant and a sergeant WAAF. The sergeant is on his way down to London now. We are billeting him here with the MPs."

"What about the spies?"

"We have spy catchers infiltrating the offices. The Sergeant WAAF was not in the office when the last mission was compromised and so she is being moved out. Her replacement is a spy catcher. We will get our little mole but you have to get in to Germany and destroy the factory making these graphite vanes."

The door opened. Hugo stood aside and I saw that the Sergeant WAAF was Susan!

The Major said, "I understand that Sergeant Tancraville is your fiancée. That is another reason for her choice."

"But she will be in danger! If there are spies then they may try to harm her!"

Major Mowett shook his head, "The sergeant assigned to the section will be the bodyguard for both the captain and Sergeant Tancraville."

"He will have to be damned good!"

"Oh, he will be. He is a Commando."

"With respect, sir, there are Commandos and there are Commandos."

Hugo smiled, "How about one of your men? The Sergeant is Joe Wilkinson. His wound means he can no longer go on active service. Would he do?"

I subsided. Joe was as good as they came. I was still not happy, but I was less anxious. Susan caught my eye and smiled, "It will be fine, sir. I can do this."

The Major said, "Now you will return to your unit. You tell them nothing about the spy, for obvious reason. You will be flown to Aachen. The plan is to drop you and nine of your men behind the Rhine. The factory is in a town called Hechingen in the Swabian Jura mountains. We are aware that it is winter. We believe that will aid you when you return back from Hechingen to the American lines."

The Colonel had lit another cigar, "In early March, General Patton will be launching a major offensive in the south and Field Marshall Montgomery one in the north. If you can destroy this factory then our offensive should mean that they can't produce more of these graphite vanes. A couple of those rockets could cause devastation to our forces; especially if they were at a bottleneck like a bridge. We believe that between now and the offensive they could build almost a thousand of these rockets. You and your team will stop them from building them."

"And how do we get out, sir?"

For the first time, I saw the doubt on the faces of the Colonel and the Major. Hugo said, quietly, "You and your lads will have to make your way through seventy-five miles of German-held territory to get to Strasbourg."

It was a daunting prospect but I had options. "I get to pick my own team, sir?"

"Yes, although you will take your whole section to Germany with you."

Colonel Flynn nodded, "The Major is right. You will need your whole team over there. When this mission is over there is another one. We will leave the briefing for that one until you have returned from Germany. Until we catch these rats yours is the only clandestine group we dare to send behind enemy lines. If we catch them soon then you and your men will be stood down. If not then after Hechingen you will be sent to take out another of their component factories. They have them all over Germany and Austria."

At that, my heart sank. Seventy-five miles through enemy-held territory was one thing but Austria was deep in the heart of the Third Reich. I would cross that bridge when I came to it. "Right sir. Then we had better get down to the planning."

The meeting went on until after seven. There were many details to be ironed out. Susan and Hugo would be in charge of communications and support. Joe would just be the muscle. They had thought it through well. They had a newly built office in a part of the building which had been storerooms. With just one way in and one way out, it would be secure. An assassin would have to negotiate a whole building which was teeming with MPs and then get past Joe. My former sergeant and Hugo would escort Susan to her barracks where they had increased the security. Then Hugo and Joe would return to their barracks in the actual headquarters building.

"So, Major Harsker, all your equipment is waiting for you, along with your men at R.A.F. Hendon. You leave tomorrow morning at 0600 hundred hours. After you land at Aachen you will be taken by lorry to a recently captured airfield some thirty miles from Strasbourg. Your aeroplane will drop you tomorrow night. You will have to familiarise yourself with the details between now and then."

I nodded, "So we hit the ground running."

The Colonel said, "That is another reason why you were chosen Major Harsker. You seem to hit the ground running so fast that the Krauts can't catch you. Let's hope it works again eh? There is a car waiting for you outside. The driver knows nothing so bear that in mind. He will drive you to Hendon." He shook my hand. "Good luck, son."

Major Mowett smiled, for the first time, "I am certain you will succeed this time. You were our first choice when Captain Gregson was sent in."

"But he was betrayed!"

"Major, you are one of the few Commandos to have been captured by the Germans and escaped. You have a charmed life. You are like a cat. You seem to have nine lives."

"Yes, Major Mowett but I am using them up damned quickly. What about Sergeant Tancraville? Who will escort her home tonight?"

The Colonel said, "We rather thought you might. You have a car, don't' you?"

Hugo escorted us to the car. The driver, Corporal Harris was waiting patiently for us. "Don't worry about Susan, Tom. You know I will look after her."

I nodded and shook his hand, "And luckily it is Joe who will be watching over both of you."

Once in the back of the car I gave the driver the address of John's hotel. "I will have to pick up my gear. Poor Bates will have made everything just right and I am leaving."

Oblivious to the driver Susan took my head in her hands and kissed me hard. Then she said, "At least this way I will know where you are, won't I?"

John was waiting at the desk when we arrived, "Good to see you, sir. Will you want a room for the young lady too?"

"Sorry John. A change in orders. I have a car waiting outside. I am here to pick up my gear."

He looked at Susan and shook his head, "No, sir, that won't do. Albert, go upstairs and pack for Major Harsker then take his bags to his car and give the driver a sandwich and a cup of tea."

"Yes, Mr Bates."

John put his arms around the two of us and propelled us towards the dining room. "If you are going off again into the wild blue yonder then the least I can do, as your father's former batman, is to give you a decent meal. We have a chicken casserole on the menu tonight. My treat!"

It was a delightful surprise and we both made the most of it. We tiptoed around the mission and stayed to safer subjects like Mum, Dad, the house and, inevitably, the wedding once the war was over. I did not mind for it meant I could defer having to think about the operation. I would need a clear head for that and talking about a wedding was just enough of a distraction.

It was nine o'clock by the time we finished. As John escorted us to the car he said to Susan, "Now you know where I am. Do not be a stranger. You are always more than welcome here. Tom here is as close to family as I have now. And you, my dear, are a delight. It would make an old man very happy if you came now and then for afternoon tea."

She kissed him on the cheek, "I should like that."

Once in the car, I said, "Everything all right Corporal?"

"Too right, sir. A nice brew and a bacon sarnie! Drive you anytime, sir."

When we reached Susan's barracks, just before curfew, I was reassured by the four squaddies who were there. In the old days, it had been just two men. The kiss and the hug were all too brief and then Corporal Harris whisked me away and I turned my thoughts to Germany and which men I would burden with a mission that could go horribly wrong very quickly.

By the time we had reached the airfield, I had my team assembled in my head. I would have to take some of the new men. The file Hugo had prepared had given me the information on each of the new men. They had been selected because they had shown skills which raised them above other Commandos; language skills, explosives, hand to hand combat. Each of them would fit in well with my team. They would fit in well on paper. The reality of operating behind enemy lines meant that we could not know how they would be under fire. Ours was an unforgiving world.

Harris took my Bergen and gear from the boot. "You take care, sir." He pointed to the Dakota waiting on the runway. "I think your next taxi is ready too, sir. Good luck."

"Thanks, Corporal."

I strode towards the hangar beyond the transport aeroplane. I saw the familiar figure of Sergeant Major Barker having a cigarette. As I neared him he stubbed out his cigarette and shouted, "Ten shun! Commanding Officer!"

I smiled. This was for the new men. Gordy and I had worked together too long for such formality. I tapped his new uniform. "Congratulations, Gordy. Long overdue."

"Thank you, sir, Lieutenant Poulson told me that you recommended me."

"No more than you deserve." The new uniforms marked the replacements. I said, quietly, "What are they like?"

"Good lads in the main but we will have to see what they are like Jerry side eh sir?"

I looked around and saw that we had the hangar to ourselves. Polly had organised mattresses. This would be our accommodation for the night. "Best shut the hangar door and move to the middle. I have to brief you before we get on the bus." We moved towards the centre of the empty hangar. I saw around the equipment we would be taking. I would get to that after I had introduced myself to the men and discovered a little about them. "Right lads I am Major Harsker. Normally we would have time to get to know one another but we are hitting the ground running. We leave tomorrow at 0600 and our mission begins tomorrow night. Starting on my right give me your name and where you are from."

The first Commando was a big man, "Private George McLean, sir, from Newcastle!" The short *e* and long *a* told me that he was a Geordie.

"Private Reg Richardson, sir, from Durham, sir. I was a miner." He had a similar accent to McLean although physically he was Different. He was much shorter. They had the look of a comedy double act.

"Private Samuel White, sir, from Norwich." He looked too neat and tidy to be a Commando. Then I remembered that he had been a teacher in a private school and he spoke four languages.

The next Commando looked squat and broad. He had a mop of black hair and angry looking eyes, "Private Ralph Betts, sir, from Ebbw Vale. I am a Welshman, sir!"

"Rugby player, Betts?"

He beamed, "Yes sir, hooker!"

"Private Martin Fisher, Manchester sir." Fisher looked too young to be enlisted. He had a real babyface.

"Private Wally Bond, sir, from Halifax." His Yorkshire accent was so thick you could almost cut it with a knife.

"Private Gerard Pickles, sir, Ged. St. Helens."

I looked at Gordy and Hewitt. "We met a couple of lads from your neck of the woods when we were in the Ardennes. They were in the East Lancashires. They like their pies."

He grinned, "Aye sir, they would be Pimblett's!"

"Private Eric Scott, sir from Cockermouth."

"Good walking country Scott."

He nodded, "God's own country, sir."

"Private Thomas Foster, sir, Haltwhistle."

"Hadrian's Wall, right?"

"Yes sir. We can see it from me mam's back garden, like."

"Private Stephen Ashcroft, sir, Falmouth."

"I recognise the face. Have we seen you there?"

"Yes sir. Dad has the Three Fiddles in the town. It was why I joined up. I used to see you come in of a night when you were training. I know Reg Dean."

"Well, we will all get to know each other but first, the mission. Nine of you will be dropped with me seventy miles behind the enemy lines. We have to blow up a factory and then make our way back. The rest of you will be getting ready for a longer operation. We will be heading for Austria." I pointed to the gear. "It is winter over there and they have snow. I am guessing we have snowsuits in the bags. Three of us have used them before. They are handy. When I call out your name then gather around me and I will go through the mission. If anything happens to me then one of you takes over. The rest can pack the gear on the Dakota."

This would be the hard part. I knew that I would be disappointing more than half of them. "Lieutenant Poulson, you will be my number two. Sergeant Hay, my number three." I looked at Gordy. "Sergeant Major I need you to help organise the next mission. We will be four hundred miles behind enemy lines for that one."

"Sir."

"If you go and find the Flight Sergeant, we can get the Dakota loaded."

He looked disappointed but he was an old soldier and he saluted, "Sir."

"Give him a hand, Hewitt."

"Sir."

I knew the two of them needed more time to recover from the Battle of the Bulge.

"Lance Sergeant Fletcher, you will be on the radio."

"Great sir!"

"Lance Sergeant Beaumont, explosives."

"Sir."

"Corporal Emerson, I have a feeling we may require your skills with motors."

"Right sir."

I turned to Peter Davis. He had been badly wounded on D-Day. "Peter, are you up to this?"

"Yes sir. I am raring to go. Do I need the Mauser?"

I nodded, "And if we have one, one with a silencer."

"We do sir. Quarter Master Grant found one for us."

I turned to the new men, "You new lads, Scott, White and Foster. You will make up the rest of the team. Which languages do you have White?"

"French, German, Italian and Hungarian sir." He smiled, "Mother was Hungarian."

"That might come in handy. The rest of you give the Sergeant Major a hand. My team front and centre."

I gathered them around me and told them the details of the mission. "Now we have a rough idea of where the factory is situated. By rough idea I mean we know to within a hundred yards. The trick will not be blowing it up. I have no doubt that Beaumont can manage that. The hard part will be escaping afterwards. Lieutenant Poulson, you will have Emerson, White, Scott and Foster with you. Your job will be twofold: firstly, to get us transport out of there and secondly`, to watch our backs while we do the business."

Beaumont said, "It is underground then sir?"

"It is."

"Then I am assuming that they bring these fins up and load them on to a vehicle of some kind to take them to their assembly plant. We don't have far to look for vehicles and it will keep us all closer together."

"Good thinking. I can see the promotion was justified." I handed them a piece of paper and a pencil. "Here is the map. Make your own copy. If anything happens to me then you lads will have to get out by yourself." They began to copy my map. We had found this the most effective way of doing it. By copying the map it, somehow, made it easier to remember. "And one more thing. This is important. You have all seen what a V-2 can do. We have a chance to stop them. If they don't have the fins then they can't fly!"

Chapter 2

The pilot waited until I had sent my men off to check their equipment. "Flight Lieutenant Ryan. I will be your bus driver for this op."

I saluted him, "Pleased to meet you, Tom Harsker."

"Is your father...?"

I nodded, "Yes, he is."

"Then we will treat you with kid gloves."

I laughed, "We are Commandos; we bounce."

"That is good to hear. We will be your bus over to France and then we will drop you over Germany. Our orders are to wait for you. You have a second mission coming up?"

"We may have. What will the flight time be?"

"It is just over four hundred miles, sir. By the time we get upstairs and tootle along then I think three to four hours. Depends on the winds. Then after we get some shuteye we take you up again at 2300. That will just be a short hop. Forty-five minutes or so."

"Will the snow bother you?"

"Not in the air and we have been told that they are keeping the runway clear. There are lots of Dakotas coming in with supplies."

"This mission is top secret. Tell no one where we are going. When we take off from France you don't tell them our target. Nor do you tell them when you get back."

"Really sir?" I nodded. "It is serious then?"

"If I told you who was at my briefing then you would know how serious. Impress on your crew too. Loose lips and all that."

"Sir."

"Right then I will get my head down. Let me know when you want us to load our gear. You are the boss."

Lieutenant Poulson came over, "Beaumont has the explosives and timers sorted out and Fletcher has the radio. It looks to be a fairly powerful one."

I nodded, "This is important. I will tell you more when we get to France. Did you bring the German ordnance and uniforms?"

"Yes, sir but will we be able to carry them?"

"We will take the field caps. With the white snowsuits, we should be able to blend in. I am going to take my Colt and the rest will be German weapons. We picked up ammo in the Ardennes. I want the team splitting up so that there is a German speaker with each group of men. You have Private White with you. I will have Fletcher and Beaumont. Divide the others up between you and Bill. We have never been this far behind enemy lines since Africa."

He nodded, "And we lost more men there than any other operation. Point taken, sir. How long will we be behind the lines? I am thinking of supplies."

"Better take supplies for five days. If it is longer than that then we will have to forage."

"I will go and get them sorted."

I waved Fletcher over, "You have the call signs and times?"

"Yes sir."

"Remember the times are English time. I want your watch set to that time. It is important."

"Yes sir and thanks for the promotion. The extra money will come in handy. I am walking out with a girl. When this lot is over I will be getting married."

"You Fletcher? I had you down as the kind of chap who plays the field."

"I did, sir, but I know a winner when I see one!"

I had done all that I could and so I lay down on one of the mattresses and pulled a blanket over me. I was asleep almost instantly. After this, I would be sleeping with one eye half-open!

"Sir, it's time."

As I opened my eyes I heard the buzz of conversation and the smell of fried bacon. Gordy stood there with a plate full of bacon sandwiches and a mug of tea. He grinned, "Now that I am a sergeant major I thought I should have a crack at the tea."

"Cheers."

I sipped the hot sweet concoction. "Perfect. Reg Deane would be proud!" I took a bite from my sandwich. They had dipped the bread in the bacon fat so that it dribbled down my chin. I knew we would be on rations after this and I made the most of it. "Everything loaded? Remember we need everything for two missions." I took another two sandwiches from the pile.

"Yes sir. Barring the kitchen sink, I think we are sorted." He handed the plate to Fletcher who was hovering nearby. "So I plan the next mission, sir?"

I wiped my hands on the napkin Gordy held out for me and picked up a manila folder. "For your eyes only, Gordy. This is the target and my outlines for what we need to do. You and the lads need to familiarise yourself with the terrain. We are about as far east as we can get. This is top secret. A couple of other missions have come to grief. It was either spies or careless talk. Let's eliminate the chance of that."

"What about when we are over there, sir? Won't we be asked questions?"

"I have a letter here." I took it from the manila envelope. "It gives us the highest authority. They have given us an old hangar. The Luftwaffe used this field before they fled. Make it like a fort. We cook for ourselves and you will organize the sentries. It will be good for the new chaps. The rigour should put them on a war footing."

"Right sir."

Having finished the food and the tea I said, "Right, Sarn't Major, get them on board eh?"

"Shake a leg you horrible lot! Time is wasting. Get aboard! Chop, chop!"

I picked up my Bergen and my greatcoat. I had an MP 34 with me. I had plenty of ammunition and it was a reliable weapon. I had picked it up in the Ardennes. I liked the Tommy gun but .45 ammunition would be harder to come by on the other side of the Rhine. As the last of the men disappeared through the hangar door I had a quick check around. There was no paperwork left. Apart from the cups and the metal plates from the canteen, there was no sign that we had been there. I stepped out into the sleet, snow and rain. I consoled myself, as I pulled up my collar, that it would be worse in the Swabian Jura. Gordy and Flight Sergeant Wilson waited at the small ladder. I stepped inside and they followed.

A C-47 could accommodate twenty-eight men. Although we only had twenty we had plenty of supplies. It would be somewhat cosy for the three-hour flight. As I moved down to the seat Sergeant Poulson had reserved for me I checked that the Dakota had been fitted with a rail for the parachutes. It was small details like that which invited disaster. It had one and, from the look of it, it had been well maintained. I took my seat and fitted the lap restraint. When we had travelled on the Sunderland we had been able to talk while in the air. The C-47 was noisy. Talk would be almost impossible.

When the door closed the interior became almost black. The pilot switched on the red light which made the interior look strangely hellish and then I heard the two huge Pratt and Whitney engines as they roared into life. The old hands closed their eyes but the newer ones looked around nervously. They had probably only been on a parachuting course and never been on an actual mission. They were going to war and the first time was always hard.

I didn't sleep. Instead, I took out the maps and aerial photographs of the site. The R.A.F. had tried to bomb it but the conclusion was that it would be counterproductive. There was too great a risk of civilian casualties with little chance of destroying the underground complex. I also read the sketchy reports of the previous failed missions. The resistance had found the factory and they had been dropped the supplies to do the job. When they were all caught so easily it should have made the planners warier. The second and third ones had done as we were going to do. They had dropped in and then hiked from the west. Once again they had been stopped before they could even reach their target. Our orders were to emulate them. I had already decided to override those orders. We would come in from the east.

I had seen a forest to the east and farmland to the east of our target. That was why the planners had chosen the west of the site. The west had fewer trees and less danger of an accident. Landing with a forest nearby was dangerous. The farms and clearings were small but, by making a lower jump, I thought we could land there and hike the mile or two west to Hechingen. The danger was the trees. If the winds were too high we were inviting disaster. I knew my old hands. They could cope but the three new ones? When we landed at the field, north of Strasbourg, I would have to interrogate them.

The flight was very bumpy. I knew how to fly and I sympathised with the pilot. I saw a couple of the new men looking a little green around the gills but they managed to hang on to their bacon sandwiches. After three hours the Flight Sergeant came through. "Flight Lieutenant Ryan says we are landing in ten minutes." He grinned, "I would brace yourselves if I were you. This could be a bit bumpy. They have had a recent snowfall and they haven't cleared it."

That made me annoyed. I knew, from Hugo, that the station commander had been expressly told how vital our mission was. If anything happened to the Dakota it would jeopardise our ability to carry out the mission. I turned to the new men. "Keep your feet up when we land. If the undercarriage goes you could end up with a broken leg."

The Flight Sergeant was right about the bumpy landing. We rose up and then came down heavily. Fortunately, nothing cracked or sheared and our next bump was gentler and we began to roll and slide down the runway. When we had taxied and come to a halt the Flight Lieutenant came from the cockpit, "Sorry about that. We will check the bus before we get our head down." He looked down the interior of the fuselage. "No one upchucked! Good. This is our billet!" He pointed out of the door that the Flight Sergeant had just opened, "That is your hangar. The one directly in front of you. I am afraid the roof looks like it needs a repair or two. I was told that it was sound. Sorry about this."

I stood, "Not your fault, Flight Lieutenant. We will sort it out. Right lads, get the gear out as quick as you can. The crew need their shut-eye."

I put on my greatcoat. Slipping the all-important letter into my pocket, I stepped out. The Flight Lieutenant had done well. There were snowy squalls. The side winds would have made landing tricky not to say dangerous. Polly and I went into the hangar. Ten per cent of the roof had gone. It meant that there was a pile of snow in one corner and a gale was blowing through the hole. It was not good enough. "Lieutenant, get the lads clearing the snow. Find somewhere dry for the men and the supplies. Then see if Gordy can find something to repair the roof with."

"Sir."

I strode out and headed for the control tower. I guessed that would be where I would find the station commander. As I crossed to the buildings and Nissen huts I saw that there were just transports on the field. They were mainly Dakotas. There were neither fighters nor bombers. There were sandbagged anti-aircraft positions and the gate and perimeter were guarded by R.A.F. Regiment personnel. That was good. My men and our equipment would be safe. The Corporal on duty saluted.

"Where will I find the station commander, Corporal?"

"He is in the officer's mess sir. The third Nissen hut on the left." He smiled, "It says 'Officer's Mess' on it, sir."

"And what is the name of the Station Commander, Corporal?"

"Squadron Leader Andrews, sir."

"Thank you."

As I entered the mess I was almost deafened by the noise coming from within. It sounded like a party and yet it was still the middle of the afternoon. I stood in the doorway and looked. Drinks were flowing and food was being served. I wondered who was actually working on the airfield. An older looking Flight Lieutenant came up to me, "Can I help you, sir?"

"I am looking for Squadron Leader Andrews."

He pointed to a round looking officer with a bright red nose and a handlebar moustache. "There he is. I'll take you to him."

The squadron leader had just told a joke and the four young pilot officers around him went into paroxysms of laughter. I suspected the drink made it funnier.

"Sir, there is an officer to see you."

He looked around at me, "Ah the Commando chap. Your quarters alright?"

He sniggered as he said it. It was confirmation that this was a deliberate act and not an oversight.

"Squadron Leader Andrews, my mission is of the utmost importance. I am afraid that they won't do. I need you to have some of your men help to repair the roof. And not only that. We need the runway clearing. We have a mission tonight, in case you had forgotten."

He burst out laughing, "There is more snow forecast. You will have to put your mission off for a day. The weather will be better tomorrow. We have better things to do than repair hangars just for a bunch of Commandos. I thought you chaps were supposed to be tough. Well, tough it out!"

I was in great danger of losing my temper but I knew that nothing would be gained by doing so. "Squadron Leader, I must insist."

"Insist all you like. It is not happening."

I had not wanted to do this but I took the letter out and opened it, "Perhaps this will change your mind." I did not give it to him, I just showed it to him and the two officers who were closest to him.

The older Flight Lieutenant said, "Good God, that is the Prime Minister's signature."

Squadron Leader Andrews became more serious, "Who the hell are you?"

"Major Tom Harsker, 1st Special Service Brigade."

The older officer snapped to attention and said, "Aren't you Group Captain Harsker's son?"

"Yes I am but he is now Air Commodore." I took the letter from the squadron leader and put it back in its envelope before putting it in my greatcoat. "So, Squadron Leader, I would appreciate you having your men begin repairing it now. I would hate to have to radio London and tell them that I was not getting the cooperation I expected."

As I walked out I was aware that the cacophony of noise had now become the silence of a church. I had dealt with men like Andrews before now but it was a distraction that I could do without.

When I reached our temporary home I saw that my men had worked wonders. The snow had been cleared from inside and the supplies safely stored. I said as I entered, "The R.A.F. are sending men to sort out the mess. Get the radio set up, Fletcher. Make contact with London and tell them we are here. Ask them if there are any changes we should know about."

As he started to unpack the radio he said, "You are an optimist aren't you sir?" He looked at his watch. In Whitehall, they will be nipping out for a lunchtime pint!"

I smiled, "I think not, Scouse." He nodded and carried on with unpacking and setting up the radio. I knew that it would take time. "Lieutenant Poulson we had better get the chutes and snow gear out. Lieutenant Ryan will not want to hang around. As soon as they are awake I want us to be ready to go."

"Sir."

I went to my gear. Gordy had laid it out for me already. We would not be able to use our rubber-soled shoes. We would have to wear boots. Mine were there. I took off my tunic with the medals. I would not need that. I took everything out of my Bergen and began to pack it. The first things I packed were the least essential items: socks, underwear and the like. I packed the battle jerkin with spare ammunition and grenades. Then I put the rest of the grenades and ammunition in the side pockets of the Bergen. I put in the food and water we would need as well as the camouflage netting, compass, wire clippers, toggle-rope and sap. We also had a lightweight blanket. This would be the first time we had used it in such extreme conditions. If it did not work we would be in trouble. Then I checked my two pistols and MP 34.

That done I shouted Lance Sergeant Hewitt over, "Foster is the other medic. Just make sure he is up to speed eh?"

Lowering his voice Hewitt said, "Sir, do you mind me asking why you aren't taking me?"

"Gordy will be the only N.C.O. here if I take you, John, and besides, you and Gordy did your bit in the Ardennes. I shall need you both in Austria."

Mollified, he nodded, "Thanks, sir. I understand now. I will make sure Foster has everything he needs and I will give him some tips too."

Fletcher shouted, "Hey up, sir. I got Headquarters! Good machine this!"

I went over to him, "What did they say?"

"It was a Judy sir, er, a girl like, you know, a WAAF? She sounded dead posh."

"Just get on with it Fletcher."

"Right sir. Anyroad up she said as how nothing had changed. The target was still the factory and she wished us good luck."

I nodded, "That is a relief. Hopefully, we can get in and out and do this job quickly."

Fletcher said, "Do we take the radio with us, sir?"

"No, Fletcher. We leave it here. You need to brief Bond. He is your replacement. If this goes wrong then he will be in touch with London and Sergeant Major Barker will be in command. We are all replaceable!"

The normally ebullient Fletcher had had the wind taken from his sails. "Right sir. This is proper serious then, eh sir?"

"Serious indeed."

A Warrant Officer appeared with twenty men, "Major Harsker?"

I stood and saluted, "Yes Warrant Officer?"

"Warrant Officer Peters, sir. We are here to fix the roof, sir."

"Thank you."

He shouted, "Right you lot, get on with it. These are proper soldiers!" His men raced off with tarpaulin and ropes, ladders, hammers and wood. The Warrant Officer came up to me, "Sorry about this mess, sir. I think the Squadron Leader mustn't have known the state of the roof. He has been a busy man. We will get it sorted. You'll be snug as a bug in a rug!"

"Thank you Warrant Officer."

"Oh, by the way, sir, I served in Ramelah, just before the war. There was an officer there, Squadron Leader Hobson. He was with your dad in Somaliland in nineteen twenty or so. He spoke very highly of him." He nodded to the medals on my tunic. "And I can see that you are a chip off the old block. We'll watch out for you, sir. You are like family."

It was always the Warrant Officers and NCOs who were the heart of any unit whether army, navy or air force. Warrant Officer Peters had been loyal to his commanding officer. As I fastened up my Bergen I reflected that the service was, indeed, one big family. There were connections all over.

Soon the far end of the hangar was a hive of activity. Flight Lieutenant Ryan came in with maps. He was smoking a cigarette and held a cup of tea in his hand, "There is a hole in the weather sir."

"I was told that tomorrow was going to be fine."

He shook his head, "No sir. Another storm front coming in. If we go in the next hour then the winds will be at their slowest. They pick up after that."

I glanced out of the hangar door, which was ajar. It was snowing. "We are good to go any time you like, Flight Lieutenant."

"It will be dusk in an hour. Jerry doesn't have as many fighters as he used to but they can still make a mess of my bus."

"Right. We'll be ready." I turned and shouted, "Sergeant Major Barker get the men."

"Number One Section, front and centre."

As they gathered around me I said, "Those of you who are on the mission get your gear on the Dakota. We are off. Remember, especially you new chaps, nothing personal with you. Our identity disks are the only thing we take. No papers, no letters, no good luck charms, football pools or diaries. Nothing." There were handshakes from those who were friends. I saw a couple of letters changing hands. It was not words, it was smiles, nods and the grip of a comrade you might never see again. When they had gone I said, "Warrant Officer Peters seems like a good sort. You should be fine. Private Bond, I want you to raise London every day at about 1000 hours. Is your watch on London time?"

"Yes sir, Lance Sergeant Fletcher told me."

"Good. There will be little to report but it is a good habit to get into."

"Sergeant Major, see if you can get a vehicle and find the front line." I handed him the letter. "Show this to whichever senior officer you can find and warn him that we might be coming back hot. Don't lose the letter."

"Sir. Have you any idea which road back you will be taking?"

"I shook my head. It may well be the river. Sorry that it is so vague, Gordy, but you know how it is."

"Yes sir. Don't worry. You can rely on me and since the Ardennes, I think I know the Yank mind a little better."

"It may be French here, I am not certain which sector is controlled by which army. I think that the French have the sector closest to Strasbourg. That is where we will head at any rate. General Patton is the one in charge."

Gordy nodded, firmly, "Then I shall find him!"

"Well, I shall see you chaps in a few days then."

They saluted.

I knew that Gordy would do his best. I donned my snowsuit and put my beret on my head. Gordy helped me into my parachute. My German field cap was in my battle dress pocket. I stepped out into a scene from a Christmas card with snow gently falling. The light was fading in the west and we would be heading into the blackness of the east. We were going back to war.

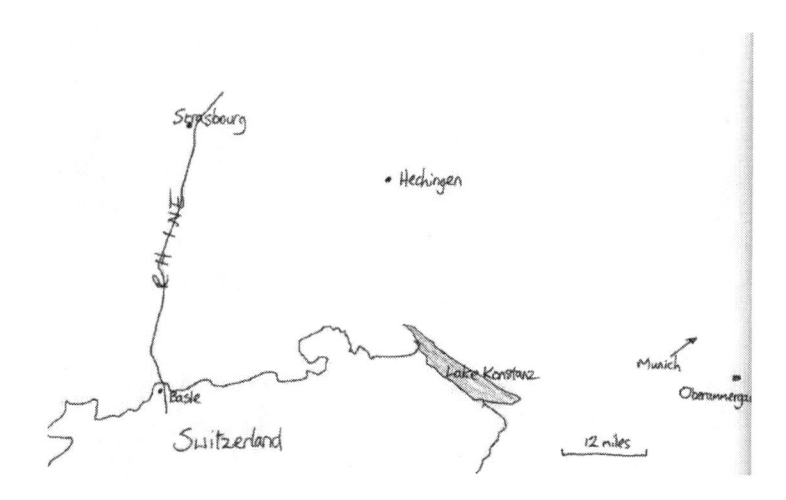

Chapter 3

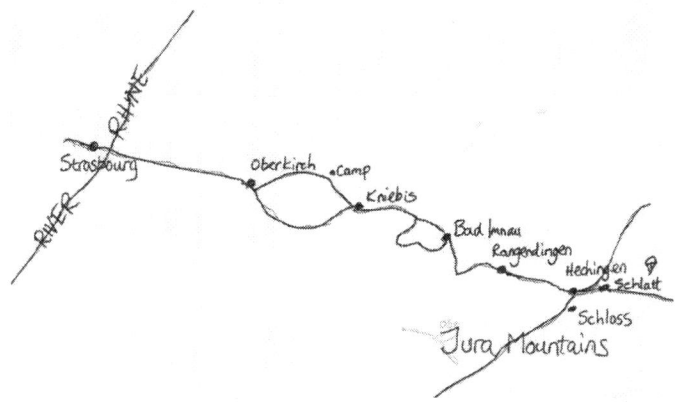

My team were all waiting for me. There was more room than before. They were seated on both sides. My older hands had automatically sat so that we were balanced. Flight Sergeant Harris closed the door after I had sat down and we were plunged into a red-tinged world. He would be in charge now until we left the aeroplane. I nodded to Sergeant Hay, "Bill, you are tail-end Charlie."

He knew what I meant by the nod. He would be following the new boys. If he had to he would give them a little push. There was a moment or two before the engines would start. "Remember, if we get separated then head for the village of Schlatt. From there we only have half a mile or so to go to get to the factory."

Lieutenant Poulson asked, "And the factory is hidden? Disguised, sir?"

"From what the resistance told London they are using a bakery as a cover for it. There are a yard and a gate through which lorries enter and leave. The bakery still functions so there will be civilians there but there has to be an entrance to the underground factory. The smoke from the bakery disguises the smoke from the factory. It is a clever deception. The bakery staff will have nothing to do with the fin making factory. But you will need to disable them. This is the heart of Germany. The majority of the people you meet will be loyal Germans. These aren't the Dutch and Belgians who will be sympathetic to us. They will shout for help."

Fletcher asked, "So we shoot civilians then sir?"

I shook my head, "We are Commandos. We disable them! Job number one will be to secure the bakery workers then find vehicles to get out."

Just then the engines were fired up and any further conversation would be useless. My eyes were accustomed to the red light now and I took out the map that the others had copied. Unlike theirs, mine had all the details on. What I was worried about was Hohenzollern castle. It was just three miles away and intelligence suspected that the Germans were using it as a command centre for the surrounding countryside. It was atop a mountain and surrounded by forest but there would be elite troops there. When the alarm was raised we would have to avoid the south.

We did not seem to have been in the air very long when Flight Sergeant Harris came out from the cockpit. He pointed to the rail. I nodded and we all stood and started to hook up our static lines. As soon as we had we all checked the next man's parachute and had our own checked. We had all packed our own parachutes. If anyone had a Roman Candle then it was their own fault. Once they were checked we shuffled down to the door with our guns attached to the bottom of the parachute bag. A few moments later Flight Sergeant Harris came down. He plugged his headphones into a socket next to the hatch and then opened it. The sudden rush of ice-cold air and snow was like a slap in the face. He beckoned me forward and I stood with my hands braced on the two sides of the opening. Beneath me was blackness. British night-time bombing raids meant that the Germans had a blackout as effective as the one we had in England. It was a black hole flecked with driving snow below us. The snow was still falling and showed no sign of abating. It had come earlier than the forecasters had predicted. That would help a little. Anything which kept people indoors and us hidden was a friend.

The Flight Sergeant was listening to the words of the pilot. I kept my eyes on him. I watched his eyes. I saw them flicker. I was already stepping out into nothing when he tapped my shoulder. The air took me towards the tailfin but I would not hit it. I looked down at my feet. I kept them tight together and waited for the jerk which would release my parachute. As soon as it did I looked up. We all did. You wanted to see that white shape blossoming above you. When it cracked open the downward acceleration slowed. I had had the pilot fly lower than he normally did. I was relying on the skill of my men. A lower drop meant that it was less likely that we would be spread out too far. I put my hands on the cords and began to turn. I saw a patch of clear white. That indicated a clearing. As I came down I saw to the west, the tiny hamlet of Schlatt. The light winds and the skill of the pilot meant that we would be landing just half a mile from our rendezvous point

The ground seemed to race up towards me. I braced myself and, as I landed, let my bent knees absorb the impact. The snow helped and I was able to land standing. It was a perfect landing. My instructors at Ringway would have been proud of me. I released my parachute and unclipped my gun. I took my knife from my boot and quickly cut the parachute cords. They were always handy. Lieutenant Poulson and Lance Sergeant Beaumont landed almost at the same time as I did. With the precious cords stowed in my smock pocket, I rolled the parachute and jammed it into the bag. I scrabbled a hole in the snow and buried it. It would be found but by the time it was, we would, hopefully, be heading west.

More shapes landed. I counted them. There were two missing. It was Scott and Hay. They were the last two out. We would not wait for them. Every man knew that if he became isolated then he was on his own. I checked that every chute had been buried and, with my MP 34 in my hands I waved my men forward.

It helps, in the Commandos, to have a good sense of direction. I had marked the position of the hamlet as we had landed and I headed down through the trees. It soon became obvious that I was following some sort of trail. I could see where branches had been lopped off from the forest through which we passed. I also smelled smoke. We were heading for houses. It was early evening here in Germany. With luck everyone would be indoors, in the warm, enjoying the rationed food. They would all have little to eat and that would make the meal something of a highlight. Germany was struggling for food. Much of their potato production now went to make aeroplane fuel. I guessed that those living in the Swabian Jura would hunt and have slightly better fare than in the cities but the principle was still the same. The evening meal was when you would be indoors.

The trees began to thin and I held up my hand. I did not look behind me. They would all stop and keep watch. I edged forward. I peered from behind the bole of a huge tree and saw the seven houses that made up Schlatt. There was a road running east to west. That would be the quickest and safest way into Hechingen. All that we had to do was cross the track and join the road on the far side of the hamlet. I waved Polly forward and I stepped out from the trees and made way across the darkened houses. The footprints in the snow from the daytime activities were already almost covered by the falling snow.

I was halfway across the clearing when I heard a door creak open. I dropped to my knees. A shaft of light showed a woman come out with a bag. She went around to the side of the house and deposited it, noisily, in a bin. I waited until the door closed and then I moved. As I was about to enter the woods on the other side there was a slight movement and a shadow. My MP 34 was up in an instant. A hand appeared and then a face. It was Bill Hay. He pointed to Scott. I saw that he had his left arm strapped to his body. We had an injury. I gestured for Hay and Scott to join us at the back.

After thirty or so yards I dropped down to the road and, after scanning left and right to make sure it was empty, I stepped on to the road. It had been cleared for there was just a thin covering of snow. It would get worse for the snow was falling faster and, since we had landed, the wind speed had increased. The storm front Flight Lieutenant Ryan had spoken of was arriving a little earlier than expected. After we had run a mile I could see, in the distance, the shadow of buildings that was Hechingen. I held my hand up so that I could check for danger. I heard a familiar noise in the distance. It was the sound of people. Hechingen was a town and activities were going on all the time. The town would not be empty. We would have to ghost in and rely on our white camouflage.

I waved us forward. The aerial photographs had shown us that the bakery was slightly away from the centre on a higher piece of ground to the south-west, on the road to the castle. As soon as we came to the first road on the left I took it. The houses to our right were dark but I could hear, as we passed the windows, the buzz of conversation from within. I knew that it would be nerve-wracking for the new men. We were walking through a town in enemy country. I had used the white snowsuits before. In the blizzard through which we trudged, they made us almost invisible.

It was the smell of baking bread which told us precisely where the bakery was. It would not be large. When I had spent holidays in our cottage in France I had often gone to the boulangerie. The tiny one in the village could still produce almost five hundred loaves a day. I guessed there would be no more than six bakers. They would not be the problem. It would be the soldiers guarding the underground factory who we would have to contain. We turned a corner and I saw the bakery. It stood alone. I saw that there had been buildings nearby. The R.A.F. must have destroyed them. I had not been able to tell that from the aerial photographs.

I slung my MP 34 around my neck and, taking my Colt from my holster fitted the silencer and then cocked it. Davis already had the silencer fitted to the Mauser. Now was the time for us to split up. Polly led his section to the bakery proper and I raised my hand to take my saboteurs around to the rear of the building and the factory. I was aware that Lieutenant Poulson had a wounded man with me. I hoped that he and Fred would be experienced enough to compensate. Davis came ahead, with me, at the front.

There was a high wall running around the building. When we reached the corner, I stopped and peered around. There was a sentry there. He was forty feet away. It was a risky shot with my Colt but Davis would be able to hit him with the Mauser. I pointed and made the kill sign. I levelled my pistol in the unlikely event that Davis missed. There was a pop and the sentry fell. To my horror, there was a second sentry on the other side of him. As Davis worked the bolt I aimed at the German's chest and fired. He fell back. We were on our feet in an instant and running to the two men. The widening pool of red in the white snow told us that they were dead. Fletcher and Hay quickly took the grenades and ammunition from the dead men.

Davis and I peered through the gates. There were fresh tyre tracks and I saw, in the yard, a German truck. It was not a military one and the snow melting on its bonnet told me that it was still warm. We ran to shelter behind it. I saw the glow, on the far side, of a cigarette. There was a German sentry having a sly cigarette. It would be his last. I tapped Davis on the shoulder. He slipped under the truck as the rest of my men ran to us. The pop of his gun was followed by the sound of a body slumping to the ground.

We ran around the truck and reached the door. Fletcher moved the body out of the way and I tried the handle. It was open. Before I could go in there was a flash of light from behind us. We all turned and levelled our guns. It was Emerson. He held up his hands. I nodded and pointed to the truck. We had our escape vehicle.

I held the handle of the door with my left hand and my gun in the right. I turned the handle and pushed slowly. From the interior, I could hear the hum of machinery. There was a dim red light; it was a safelight. I opened the door more confidently. They had a light lock system. The red light would not alert night time bombers and there would be another door at the bottom which led to the factory. I waved Bill Hay next to me. He also had a silenced Colt. Davis became tail-end Charlie. I went down the concrete steps. This was not an old stair. The treads were made of concrete and looked new. It had been built for the factory.

As I descended the hum of motors became more obvious. I hoped that it would mask any noise which we might make opening the door. I recalled that slave labour was being used in the factory and that meant German guards. I reached the door and put my hand on the handle. Bill Hay held his pistol in the two handed grip. He was ready to leap in ahead of me. I tried the handle and it turned. I pushed and the door opened a fraction. Light flooded from the crack and the noise from inside became louder; much louder. I pushed the door open and Bill leapt inside. I followed. There was a double pop and then the sound of a Mauser firing. It sounded ridiculously loud. Bill had gone right and I turned left. An S.S. Lieutenant was drawing his gun. I fired at his chest. He was five feet away and a .45 shell makes a huge hole at that range. Fletcher had followed us and his Colt, without the silencer, barked loudly.

I saw some emaciated figures. They looked terrified. "Get down! We will not hurt you!" I guessed that they spoke German.

A rifle cracked and a bullet gouged a lump of concrete from the wall. Peter Davis seemed to be aiming at me with his Mauser. There was a pop and, when I turned, I saw an S.S. soldier slumped on the ground.

Beaumont closed the door and began to unpack his explosives and timers. I ran around the machines to look for more Germans. There were none left alive. The six of them had been shot in the short firefight. "Anyone hurt?"

There was a chorus of 'No sir." From my team.

Leaving Hay, Fletcher and Beaumont to set the charges I said, "Search the bodies for any papers and the like." Then I turned, "All the workers come here. I wish to speak with you."

There were thirty of them. I had not expected as many. We were lucky that none had been hit by flying bullets. It was testimony to the skill of my men that what we aimed at, we hit. I said, "Do you all speak German?"

One older man said, "Yes but we are Poles. What will happen to us?"

It was sad but they would probably all be recaptured. "We are going to blow the factory up. Then we will leave. Upstairs is a bakery." I switched to English. "Davis, take these to the bakery. If there are any coats there then give them to them and let them take as much bread as they want. Have White tell them to get as far away as they can. The Swiss border is just forty or so miles away. They might make it."

"Sir."

I turned back to the man, "Davis will take you to the bakery. I am sorry we cannot do more for you."

He smiled, "We were doomed to die and you have given us a slight hope. If one of us survives then that is a victory. I was resigned to die here. Thank you!"

Davis led them away.

I saw that one of the Germans had a packet of cigarettes which had fallen from his tunic. I picked them up. "How long, Beaumont?"

"Almost done, sir. As soon as you are all out I will set a charge by the door. It looks like there is just one way in and one way out. Those poor sods must have had to lug everything up and down those stairs."

"Can we destroy this facility?"

"Oh yes, sir. There are plenty of weak points down here and when we bring down the door it will take them months to clear it. Eventually, they could get it going again but they will never use these machines again. That is for certain. I am using fifteen-minute fuses in here. That means we will have ten minutes once I am out."

"Right, the rest of you leave Beaumont to it and get up to the lorry."

I followed Fletcher and Hay. When we stepped into the yard the wind, snow and sleet hit me. It was a shock to be in the cold again. I saw that Lieutenant Poulson had the bakery workers lined up. There were just six of them. The engine of the German truck was running and Emerson stuck his head out of the cab. "Half a tank, sir. Should get us home."

"Right. Stick your German field cap on." I saw that Sam White was talking to the Poles in the bakery. "As soon as Beaumont gets here, tell the bakers to go and the Poles too. We will have ten minutes to get as far to the west as we can."

Lieutenant Poulson said, "Right sir. Cutting it fine."

I shrugged, "Beaumont knows what he is doing." I threw the packet of German cigarettes to Freddie. "Here, these might come in handy. Have you got an escape route worked out?"

Emerson nodded, "Yes sir. Head north-west through Rangendingen. There are lots of small roads along the route, sir. If Jerry comes after us we can slip down one."

I looked at my watch. It was after midnight. We had seventy miles to the front line. The easiest part would be the first part. The closer we came to the front line the more troops we would have to face. I saw that Foster and Scott had a couple of baskets of bread they had liberated. They were in the back of the lorry. Davis had managed to take two MP 34 guns from the dead Germans and he had one in the cab and one in the back.

I looked up as the Poles came out. I saw that some of them had managed to take old coats from the bakery and they all had loaves in their hand. They ran past us through the open gate, "Thank you, English! Long live the King!" The Poles were a defiant lot. I had met Polish pilots. If anyone could survive a forty-mile hike through a German winter then it was the Poles. The thick forests would hide them. The Germans would be more intent on catching us rather than chasing slave labour.

David handed me some papers. "Here sir. The papers from the S.S. in the factory." He took one out. "This is the one belonging to the S.S. Officer."

"Thanks, Davis." I examined it. He was Hauptmann Franz Dietrich. I put it in the pocket of the snowsuit.

Beaumont appeared. I turned to the bakers, "Run. We are going to blow this up and you do not want to be here then!"

They needed no further warning and they ran.

Bill Hay shouted, "Right everyone in the back. Major Harsker and Freddie will be in the front!" He handed me two loaves. They were made with rye wheat. "Here y'are sir. For you and Emerson. They are still hot. I guess the town will go hungry tomorrow!"

I waited until Beaumont reached the truck before I clambered aboard. "Take it steady through the town and then when this lot goes up give it all she has got."

As we drove through the gates and two dead Germans he said, "That won't be very fast sir. This bugger is slow as. God alone knows what they are using for petrol!"

As we descended the hill, towards the town, we had an inkling of what the journey would be like. The roads were slick with recently fallen snow and it took all of Emerson's skills with the clutch, brake and steering wheel to keep us on the road. A crash into a building would be a disaster. We had reached the square in the middle of the town when, in the side mirrors, I saw a huge flash and then, a heartbeat later heard the explosion. It seemed like the whole building rose and then fell. I heard, from the back, Lieutenant Poulson say, "Well done, Beaumont!"

We were starting to climb up the other side of the valley when I saw lights on the road from the south. They were some way away and, through the driving snow hard to estimate how far away they were. I guessed that had come from the castle. That was three miles from the bakery. They would get to the bakery first and then chase us. I had no doubt that the bakers would be ready to tell the soldiers where we were. That meant we had, at most, a fifteen-minute lead. The Germans' vehicles would begin to catch us. We would have to turn and fight them at some point. The trick would be to find the best place to do that.

I handed a loaf to Emerson. He picked it up and bit a chunk out of it, "Be nice this sir with butter and me mam's strawberry jam!"

"I nodded as I tore off a piece to eat it. "Yes indeed, or a nice cheddar with a pickled onion." The flour was not the best but it was hot food and it was unexpected. What was it Colley Cibber had said, *'Stolen sweets taste best'*? He was right.

We were not moving fast, at all. The road twisted and turned, rose and fell. Road maintenance was not a priority in the Third Reich and there were potholes as big as baths! Emerson said, "Sorry about this, sir. I daren't risk going any faster sir. I don't want to turn her over."

"You are doing fine, Freddie." As I looked out of the cab I saw that the snow had slowed and was no longer a blizzard. It was stopping. Soon it would no longer cover our tracks and when daylight came they would find us.

"Something ahead, sir."

I took off my beret and put my field cap on. "Heads up! Something ahead. If you have to speak then use German." I saw a light slowly swinging across the road. It was a roadblock. There were two German motorcycle combinations. I took out the Hauptmann's papers. I held them in my left hand and took out the silenced Colt which I kept hidden. "Slow down, Emerson and smile. Look casual. Be ready to put your foot down."

"Jawohl!"

I almost laughed at his accent. Emerson had not taken well to the language lessons. He could understand more German than he used to but when he spoke you knew he was English. I wound the window down and leaned my head out. The wind was still icy even though most of the snow had stopped. I saw that there were four men at the roadblock some sixty yards from us. It was a sergeant and three others. They had one MP 34 and the rest were holding rifles. The sergeant appeared to have a holstered weapon. I risked speaking to the others as Emerson brought us to a slow and dignified halt. "Four men in the road. I will try to bluff our way out."

Freddie stopped us and took a cigarette out from the packet I had given him. He had a German lighter from an earlier raid and he lit the cigarette. The familiar smell would allay the German's suspicions. I decided to play the arrogant S.S. officer. The four Germans were just line infantry.

"What is it? We are on important business!"

He saluted, "Sorry sir! But there has been an attack by British paratroopers. Have you papers?" He shone his torch in my face.

"Get the torch from my face! Here!" As I handed them over I felt the truck move slightly. Someone had got off. I slowly raised the Colt until it was just below the window.

"I am Hauptmann Dietrich and I work at the Uranverein facility in Hechingen. It is vital I deliver the case I have in the back."

I saw him frown and then he looked up at me, "You are not..."

He got no further for my Colt was pointing between his eyes, "Sergeant, do not make me shoot you. Tell your men to lay down their weapons."

I saw him about to argue and then saw Hay, White and Lieutenant Poulson rise behind his three men. Guns were pressed into their backs and Sam White said, "Do not move, gentlemen or we shall shoot you! Now drop your guns!"

The guns were dropped.

"Fletcher, get around here with Foster. Clear this roadblock. Lieutenant, get the prisoners on board. Take off their boots!"

Suddenly Freddie jumped out of the cab and ran to the motorcycles. He removed the two cans of petrol from the back and held them triumphantly. "This might be better petrol, sir."

"Well don't fill it now. Let's get out of here!"

After he had placed them in the back he climbed back into the cab and threw out the cigarette. "I like a fag sir but these are horrible!"

We now had a problem. We had turned off the main road a couple of times in an attempt to lose our pursuers but now we had told them where we were. Nor did I want to take the four Germans back with us.

We had to ditch them. I had grabbed the sergeant's torch and now I used it to examine my map.

"Take the next left!"

"Bloody hellfire, sir!" The next turn was almost upon us and Emerson threw the truck over so fast that we almost toppled over. The back wheels skidded along the road acting like a snowplough. "Drive down this road for one mile or so." It was a smaller road than the one we had left. I saw tracks in the snow where someone had taken a wrong turn and then turned around.

"They will see where we skidded sir."

"I know!" I shouted so that the others could hear me. "Blindfold the prisoners and tie their hands behind their backs. Use the parachute cord."

I heard Lieutenant Poulson shout, "Sir!"

"Next left! Slowly this time and then stop." I had seen on the map that there was a road which headed up through the forest. It was a narrow road. When Emerson stopped we were at the bottom of a slope. "Drive halfway up the hill and then stop and turn off the engine. You are going to have to reverse down the hill without an engine."

"Righto, sir."

When he stopped I jumped out. "Get them out."

The Germans were helped out. I pointed up the road and gestured for the others to walk behind them.

I said, loudly, "Walk up the road. We have run out of petrol." We walked them until we reached a slight turn. We were about four hundred yards from the truck. "Stop. Wait here!" I turned the sergeant around and around. The others caught on and did the same with the other three. I had my men spread them out.

"What is going on? My feet are freezing!"

"Better you have frozen feet than you are dead."

I signalled for my men to go back down the road. I walked backwards. They nodded and did the same. When we reached the truck I waved them back on board.

"Right Emerson. Slowly roll it down the hill and when you come to that part where someone else turned around in the road follow their tracks. Drive slowly and then take the first left."

I was aware that I was losing time to our pursuers but I hoped that this little detour would have them hunting in the wrong place. Emerson managed to get us to the turnoff and we headed down another narrow road through the trees. This time the sides of the truck knocked the snow from the trees and disguised our tracks. After half a mile we rejoined the road. We were less than a thousand yards from where I had left the skid mark.

"Now drive steadily and, if we are not followed take the turn off to the right after Kniebis. We are going to hold up until tomorrow night."

Chapter 4

Kniebis was just coming to life as we drove through. I waved at the only person I saw. They stared back at me. Half a mile from the village and just as the first grey appeared in the eastern sky, I had Emerson turn off and head down a small track. We stopped forty yards in. I told the men to climb from the back and, using a couple of branches, we covered our tracks. "Freddie, drive on a little further. We will catch up." We swept our tracks until we came to a turn in the trail. There it was so narrow that we would cover our own tracks with the snow we would knock from the trees above us. I was not certain a truck had ever been down the road. There appeared to be too many branches still intact. I used the map to find somewhere well hidden. The hills to the north towered over us. There were no roads there. As we stopped Emerson said, "The engine was overheating. She could do with a rest."

There was a German dixie in the cab. I handed it to him. "Fill this with water and stick it on the engine. We might as well use that extra heat. It will make a brew!"

He beamed, "Cracking idea sir."

"Right lads. We will lie up here for the day. Put on your German field caps. Foster, have you seen to Scott's arm?"

He climbed down, "Yes sir. He broke the forearm. I have given him a couple of painkillers."

Private Scott shook his head, "I can't believe it, sir! First mission and I smack my arm off a bloody great branch! There's no piggin' justice!"

"Never mind, Scott, it didn't cause any bother."

"Can we smoke, sir?"

"Yes, Emerson but no fires."

The smokers lit up. Private Scott asked, "What was that with the prisoners, sir? Why didn't we just shoot them?"

Polly shook his head, "We don't kill unless we have to."

I nodded, "Besides I used them to our advantage. I had Emerson skid so that they couldn't miss where we turned off. When I saw that turning place it seemed perfect. By making them disorientated they would spend longer freeing themselves and making the tracks hard to spot. I have no doubt that they will free themselves and escape. They will either go down the hill to the nearest house, it was more than a mile away, or, more likely, the Germans following us would find them. They would lead them back up the hill. As we have neither heard nor seen them then I am guessing we lost them. They will have an aeroplane up when it is daylight and they will search the road. There are plenty of turnoffs along this road."

Bill Hay asked, "Aren't you worried that someone will come down the road, sir?"

"That is possible but as there are no other tracks I am not particularly bothered and Emerson has the bonnet up so it would look like we have broken down. Lieutenant Poulson. I want a rota. Everyone apart from Scott pairs up and has a two-hour duty. The rest can sleep."

"But sir I can watch."

"Scott, you have been on painkillers! You sleep!"

"Sir."

"Freddie is making a brew. Make sure you all have a cup. I want no one suffering from the hypothermia."

Scott asked, "Hypo what sir?"

Bill Hay shook his head, "The bleeding cold! Did you not pay any attention to the lectures when you were training?"

"I couldn't concentrate, Sarge. It was too bloody cold!"

For some reason that made my men all laugh uncontrollably.

Freddie brought me my tea, "The engine was still hot sir so I put another dixie on. It will take longer but it should still boil. I have filled up the tank from the two petrol cans, sir. There is a drop left in each one. I filled our tank."

"We might need them yet. Make sure the lids are on tightly."

"Sir. Bombs?"

I nodded, "You never know when we might need them." As I sipped the tea and ate the biscuits from my ration I studied the map. This road trailed around the mountains. There were a couple of roads leading off it. I guessed that they were summer roads. Then we would come to Oberkirch. It was just fifteen miles from the river and the closer we came to the river the more likely we would be to run into Germans. I knew that there were no bridges over the Rhine; either the Germans or our bombers had knocked them out. That meant we needed a boat. As I studied the map I saw what looked like a cut and some docks. The rivers were used by the Germans like the railways were at home. Even if they were the big

Rhine barges they might have a dinghy on board. It was a possibility. My plan was to get to the river and then work out how to get across.

That done and the tea finished, I curled up in a ball and went to sleep. Billy Hay woke me up at noon. I had asked for that shift. "Anything?"

"A spotter plane was up but it seemed to be going over the road. Lieutenant Poulson had us rig the netting over the lorry."

I should have thought of that. "How is Scott?"

"Not so much in pain as feeling embarrassed."

I shrugged, "It happens. Landing at night in a forest? I am surprised we didn't have more injuries."

"So, how do we get over the river, sir?"

"I spotted a dock on the river. When I looked at the aerial photographs back in the hangar I saw some barges and small boats. I thought to dump and booby trap the lorry and then cross the river by boat. It is the only way I can see. It will be too icy to swim and the Rhine is a bit wide."

"Then we just have the problem of getting ashore without our own side shooting at us!"

"Let's get across the river first."

I woke them all up at dusk. No more snow had fallen and the clear skies bespoke ice. Emerson was happy enough with the lorry and we boarded it again. With just fifteen miles to go, we did not need to rush. I had various routes in mind but I thought we would try the Oberkirch one first. It was harder going than I had thought. The lorry got stuck a couple of times. The snow had frozen and the back end fishtailed around too much. It took us almost two and a half hours to reach the main road.

I had Fred wait in the trees and I went to check for traffic. There was none and I waved him out, clambering up into the cab as he slid and slipped his way on to the road. The going was much easier. There had obviously been traffic heading up to the front. As we approached the outskirts of Oberkirch I realised that we would have to find a better route. There was a roadblock. I was not certain it was just for us. There was a line of pedestrians as well as vehicles. They were checking the papers of women and children as well as men.

"Fred, take the first road on the right."

As he did so he said, "But sir, they might have another roadblock on this road."

"They might but there won't be as many people." I banged on the cab wall behind me. "Get your weapons ready. We might have to fight our way through."

"Sir!"

I took out a German grenade from my Bergen and my Colt with the silencer. If we made a noise then the last twelve or thirteen miles would be more than a little interesting. We had little choice in our route as the road did not cross another. We followed it around through small houses and the occasional shop. We did not look out of place. We were a German truck and no one took any notice of us. I began to think that we would get out of the town with no trouble when the road veered left and there was a three-man patrol. Beyond them, I could see the main street. Another road looked to run parallel to it. If we could get passed the patrol then we could turn right and head out of town.

"German patrol! We will try to bluff them again."

Even as we approached I saw the three of them cock and raise their weapons. They knew who we were!

"Freddie, hard down!" The petrol from the motorcycles appeared to have a beneficial effect on the truck for we actually accelerated. The Germans opened fire. I leaned out of the cab and fired three shots. I hit one of them. I smashed the porcelain cap on the grenade and primed it. As Freddie drove over the body of the man I had killed I dropped it.

"Take the road on the right!"

The windscreen had borne the brunt of their bullets but, luckily the Germans had been below us and they had finished up in the cab roof. I heard my men firing. I lifted up my foot to kick out the windscreen. It was worse than useless in its present condition. And then the grenade went off. If the Germans hadn't heard the bullets then they would most certainly have heard the grenade.

I holstered my Colt and took out the MP 34. The time for subtlety was gone. If we came across anyone else then we had to hit them and hit them hard. "Anyone hurt?"

"No sir. You alright?"

"Yes Lieutenant but we are not safe yet."

If there were roadblocks on one side of the town then there would be others on the other two. Our best hope was to head into the last vestiges of the Black Forest. We would have to get as far in as we could and then use our feet to get to the river. It was then I realised that we were now on the edge of the forest. There would be more farmland than trees soon.

"Sir, Germans. They are setting up across the road."

"Drive at them!"

With no windscreen, I was able to fire directly ahead. I leaned the MP 34 on the dashboard. It helped to keep it level. The Germans were setting up an MG 42. That could do serious damage to us. Its shells were more than capable of penetrating the radiator and that would be a disaster. I aimed slightly below the gun and fired. Our rapid approach and the tendency of the MP 34 to pull up meant that some bullets bounced off the tarmac to hit them and my bullets tore into the gun and gunner. I finished the magazine and reloaded as Freddie smashed the lorry through the bodies, over the gun and into two men who felt certain we were going to stop. I took in that they were Volkssturm, they were the German rescrvists; old soldiers and young soldiers. They had regular training but they were not line troops. We had a chance. Behind me, I heard my men firing as we raced away from the town.

We had to risk the main road again. We would make better time. "Sir, Jerry is following. There are two Kubelwagens."

"Beaumont," I shouted, "there are two empty petrol cans. Make them into a bomb of some kind. Slow them up. I want to get off the road as soon as I can. We want to do it out of anyone's sight!"

I heard his voice, "Right sir."

I heard the guns from my men behind as they fired at the two vehicles pursuing us. I saw, in the one remaining side mirror that one of the Kubelwagens had spun around. Its dim lights disappeared. Behind I saw two more sets of dim lights pursuing us.

Freddie almost turned us over as he threw the lorry onto the main road. I saw two vehicles coming the other way but they probably thought we were just a crazy driver. Then I saw that the road ahead was clear. According to the map, there was a road which turned off the main road. It looked to be a narrow track which ran parallel to the main road. I wanted us to take that one. We would use the smaller back roads to get to the river. My plan to get to the dock area had gone. We now just needed to get to the river.

I heard Lieutenant Poulson shout, "Bomb ready sir."

I knew the side road was less than half a mile ahead. It was now or never. "Throw it." I turned to Emerson. "We need another right turn. Up ahead. It is only narrow so be careful."

"Right sir. It will be slippery sir."

"I know. Do your best."

Suddenly the sky behind was lit up by Beaumont's bomb. I heard screeching. Then there was a second fireball. Just at that moment, Emerson threw us from the road. There was a house on the corner of the road and we scraped the wall which ran alongside it. I think the wall helped to keep us upright.

"Turn out your lights and slow down."

"Sir." We were pitched into what appeared to be total blackness. "Bloody hellfire!" Emerson slowed so much we almost stopped but I could see more clearly and, from the other side of the trees which were to our left I heard the sound of engines as the Germans headed north.

By my reckoning, we were six miles from the river. The problem was that there were now Germans following us and we had to get through their front lines. We were Commandos. If anyone had a chance then it was us. It seemed to take an age to get down the narrow road. The truck appeared to be going slower and slower. There were trees on both sides. Three miles after we had lost the Germans Emerson said, "Well that's buggered it, sir."

"What is the problem, Freddie?"

"One of those bullets must have hit the fuel tank. She has been making a funny noise for the last few hundred yards and ..." the engine stopped. "That's it, sir. She's dead." He patted the dashboard almost affectionately.

"Right lads, everybody out. It is Shank's pony from now on."

I kept the German torch and map in my hand as well as the MP 34. Everything else I put in the Bergen. Once out of the cab I said, "Beaumont, well done for the bomb. Tell me when we get home how you did it. For now, I want this truck booby-trapping."

"Sir."

Lieutenant Poulson said, "What now, sir?"

"We are less than three miles from the river and, I am guessing their front line. This road twists and turns but eventually it rejoins the main road about four hundred yards from the river. We will head down here." I looked up at the sky. Clouds had appeared. "A little snow would help. You and Hay bring up the rear. Put the new boys in the middle and I will lead with Beaumont and Fletcher."

"Sir."

As soon as Beaumont said, "Done sir." I pumped my arm and led the men down the road. The truck had done well. It had saved us over sixty miles of walking. As we headed down the road I saw that it was virgin snow. Nothing had come down it. That was not surprising, Germany was short of fuel these days and the main road would be easier to navigate. I decided to pick up the pace. I began to run. The snow absorbed the sound of our boots. Normally the sound of our running feet would have carried but there was just a soft crunch underfoot. I was anxious to get to the river as soon as possible.

Our road had moved further east from the main road and the sounds from it were more muffled. When I heard the sound of a vehicle I stopped. It was on the road, behind the trees. I did not want to risk the torch and the map. As far as I could recall the road was six hundred yards away. The vehicle noise did not recede. They had stopped. Suddenly the sky behind the trees was lit as a flare was sent up. At the same time a mile and half down the road there was the sound of exploding German grenades. They had found the truck. Commandos survive because they make deductions and then decisions based on those deductions. The Germans would put two and two together. The men on the road to our left would head for us. The ones behind would be coming down the road with vengeance for their dead in their mind. We had to use stealth. We would have to creep through the trees and hope they went all the way to the river.

I turned, "I want those with silenced guns at the front. We are going through the trees. Those at the back have grenades ready. No noise. Watch for my signals."

"Sir!"

I slung my MP 34 and took out the Colt. I slipped a fresh magazine in. Poulson, Hay and Beaumont joined me. In a line, four abreast we headed through the woods. I knew without looking that Emerson, Davis and Fletcher were at the back. They were old hands and our three virgins were tucked safely away in the middle. It was easier to navigate the wood than I expected. The trees were widely spaced. There was evidence of copsing. This was managed woodland.

I could now hear the sounds of pursuit. The Germans knew where we were. These might only be Volkssturm but they would have enough guns to make life hard for us. They were driving us towards their regular troops waiting at the river. I had no doubt that they would have alerted them. Ahead I saw that the sky was becoming lighter. It was not dawn, for we were heading north, it was the woods ending and that meant the river.

I held up my hand. I took out a strip of parachute cord and held it up. My old hands nodded. They knew it meant lay booby traps. I made the sign to keep watch to the three new men. I took out two German grenades. Davis had done well to collect twelve. I made a booby trap between two trees. I then put four Mills bombs in my snowsuit pockets. It did not take long to set the traps. Davis had good ears and he waved to signal the arrival of the Germans. I led my men towards the river. We went more slowly. It was nerve-wracking for we could now hear our pursuers. They were not as disciplined as regulars and they were talking. Some were even shouting.

As I peered ahead I saw that the trees were not only thinner there were also shadows which suggested vehicles and defences. I had no idea what they were but caution was required. I held up my hand and then pointed to the three with guns. We moved forward using every bit of cover that we could. It soon became clear that we had stumbled upon a strongpoint. The river was on the other side. That had been the lighter sky we had seen.

I edged us closer. The smell of the cigarette told me that it was a sentry ahead of me and that was confirmed by the glowing butt. I heard a phut as Bill Hay shot him. As his body hit the snow I heard, to my right, "What is it, Hans?"

Another phut from Lieutenant Poulson silenced him. I scanned ahead. I could not see any more sentries. We began to move forward. I could see a bunker. There were sandbags and corrugated metal for a roof. I could hear voices within. It was a gun emplacement. I pointed to Hay and Beaumont to watch the entrance and then I headed one way while Poulson went the other. There was barbed wire in front of the post and I saw, twenty yards upriver a second. But I did see the river. There was hope ahead.

Just then there was an explosion in the woods behind us and then a second. The booby traps had been triggered. Two figures rose before me. I just reacted and fired four shots. The two Germans fell. One of them dropped back into the river making a splash. I heard German voices behind me but then they were silenced. I took a grenade and hurled it high into the air towards the second machine-gun. I ducked and, as the grenade exploded I heard cries.

Fletcher led the rest of my men through the woods to the emplacement and the river. I could hear more explosions as the Volkssturm triggered more booby traps. From the allies side of the river, I saw the flash of rifles as they reacted to our firefight. It was all going horribly wrong.

Suddenly Beaumont appeared, "Sir!"

I ran to him, "What is it?"

"Sir there is a table here. It will float. If we sent two men across the river they might have some boats eh sir? Worth a try."

"Good man. Get it in the water. Lieutenant Poulson, Sergeant Hay." They both appeared, "Lieutenant, turn the MG 42 around and make a perimeter. You take charge of the southern end. Bill get White and Scott. I want the three of you to paddle a table across the river. I think they are French who are there. White's French is perfect. See if they have boats and if not then bring back the table!"

He grinned, "Right sir. Don't take this the wrong way sir, but you are as mad as a bag full of frogs!"

"Aren't we all!"

I turned and unslung my MP 34. I saw that we now had a defensive line. I leaned the gun on the sandbags. "Fletcher, you and Davis watch the north side of the line. Foster, you will be with me and Beaumont."

Fletcher sounded worried, "Sir. Are we going to have to swim sir?"

"I hope not. The river will be bloody cold and it is very wide." Just then I saw a muzzle flash from the woods. I fired a short burst and was rewarded by a cry. "Here they come. Beaumont!"

"It's in the water, sir. I am just making two paddles and a rudder."

"Good lad." Beaumont was the brightest of my men. I had not thought of a rudder. The Rhine would be flowing quickly. Our three men would end up well to the northeast of us.

Beaumont threw himself next to me. "She is launched, sir!"

When the MG 42 began to chatter then all conversation was impossible. We just had to hang on. I took a Mills bomb from my pocket, pulled the pin and hurled it high, "Grenade!"

It struck a tree which slowed it down so that it exploded in the air. The casing showered the advancing Germans. It would make them fall back. Just then I heard firing from behind me and voices shouting in French. Then there was more firing. Did our allies think this was a German trick?

Fletcher shouted, "Sir, A little help!"

"Beaumont, you and Foster hold here." I crawled down to where Fletcher and Davis had used two dead Germans as a barricade. I could see shadows advancing. They were spread out from the river to the woods. "On my count rise, give them a burst and then we each throw a grenade."

"Sir!"

"Sir!"

We ducked down and bullets shredded the two dead Germans. I took out a grenade and laid it where I could grab it. "One two, three." I raised my head and, firing from left to right emptied my magazine. Davis fired his Colt and Fletcher his Thompson. Then I took the pin from the grenade and hurled it. I ducked. The three grenades went off simultaneously and we heard moans from before us. I reloaded. "They will be back!"

I wondered how long it would take for Hay to get across the river and, more importantly, how long to get back! I heard the MG 42. That was our best weapon. I also heard Beaumont encouraging Foster. This was his first action and it was a true baptism of fire.

"Here they come again, sir!"

Just then the sky became day as a flare was fired from the other side of the river. Mortar shells began to drop amongst the Germans who were suddenly illuminated. We opened fire too. Then machine-guns added to the fire. Hay had reached the other side. Would the boats reach us before the Germans killed or captured us?

A voice from the river shouted, "Here sir!"

I looked down and saw a grinning Sam White. He was with French Commandos and they had three rubber boats. "Good lad! Everybody, throw one grenade and then back to me. We have boats."

I threw a grenade and emptied my magazine. Davis and Fletcher did the same and scurried down to the boats. I heard the others as they were ordered back by Lieutenant Poulson. I counted them as they came by. Foster, Emerson, Beaumont and, Finally, Poulson.

Fletcher shouted, "Come on sir. We are all in!"

I ran back and threw myself next to Fletcher. He handed me a paddle and we began to stroke as fast as we could. I heard explosions from the emplacement. I guessed that Beaumont had left booby traps. The flare had died down plunging the river into darkness. The French soldiers knew where we were going. As we reached the other side a

French Captain with blacked-out face stepped up to me. "Captain Harsker! It is good to see you!"

"And you Lieutenant Lemay!!

"It is now Captain thanks to you and the breakout to Paris. Come, let us get away from here."

I turned to Sam White, "Well done, Same. Where are Scott and Sergeant Hay?"

His face clouded over. "Sergeant Hay was wounded sir and Eric is dead."

Captain Lemay said, "I am sorry my friend. An overzealous soldier did not believe that you were British. He fired before we could stop him."

I had thought we had escaped without losses. I had been wrong. I would not have sent Scott back but for his broken arm. Who would have thought that a tiny accident like that could end in death? Any sweetness of success was taken away by the sourness of Scott's death.

Chapter 5

Captain Lemay led us to a mess tent where they were serving coffee and croissants! It was the French army! He said, "You have arrived just as the breakfast was being prepared. Good timing my friend."

"Pure luck."

"Your Sergeant Barker, sorry Sergeant Major Barker, he visited all the units along the river and told us that Commandos would be returning from a raid. The soldier who fired was nervous. Once again I am sorry."

"Accident of war but it was Private Scott's first mission. He had potential."

We chatted for a while about what we had both done since the drive on Paris. I then asked, "My sergeant, could I see him?"

"Of course. He is in the sickbay. He was lucky. It was a flesh wound. The man who died stopped the bullet which hit Sergeant Hay."

Bill was as upset about the death as I was. "It was a shame, sir. Mind you but for Scott, I would be dead. He was struggling with the rudder Beaumont had made and we were sinking. If he had kept control of the table it would have been me or White who copped it."

I looked at his shoulder. "Will that keep you out of things?"

He shook his head, "Nah, sir. I have had worse shaving. It will ache for a bit and I will have to keep a clean dressing but I should be apples! Any other injuries sir?"

"We were lucky. The French mortars and machine-guns deterred them. And sir, the doc says I can come with you." He gave me a grin. "I told him that we had a doctor in the field."

"A doctor?"

"Yes sir, John Hewitt!"

The lorries to take us back to the field arrived just after dawn. We loaded Eric Scott's body. We would bury him ourselves. I had a letter to write as soon as we got back.

We saw a great deal of work on the roads as we headed back. It slowed us down. This was France and the French were keen to repair the damage done to their country. We also saw troops arriving in great numbers. There was bridging equipment too. It would not be long before they crossed the Rhine. Captain Lemay had telephoned the airfield so that, as we arrived, Gordy and the rest of the section were waiting for us.

They would not know about Scott but I knew that Barker and Hewitt, as old hands would be counting us off the lorry.

White and Foster carried the body of their fellow recruit. Barker shook his head as he watched the body being carried indoors, "Shame. He seemed a nice lad. First mission too. It is not right, sir." Then he looked up at me and became business-like. "Job done, sir?"

"Job done. Of course, the proof of the pudding will be if the number of rockets diminishes." I turned, "Fletcher, you had better tell Bond to get in touch with London and report that the mission was a success and…"

"If it is all the same to you, sir, I will do it. It will be nice to hear that WAAF again."

I nodded. I did not want to burst his bubble just yet. "How has it been here, Gordy?"

"Better sir, Warrant Officer Peters is a good bloke. We get on and he has helped us to get ship shape and Bristol fashion. The station commander? A bit of a…"

"Gordy!"

"Sorry sir, but I thought the ones like him were either behind a desk or promoted so that they couldn't cause any more trouble. Anyway, sir, the hole in the roof is fixed and we have running water. We managed to use a couple of oil drums to make our own fire pit. There is plenty of firewood and we cook on an open fire. Cosy little billet here." He glanced at Foster and White who had returned for their Bergens. "The young lads do alright?"

Lieutenant Poulson had wandered over, having made sure that everything had been taken from the lorries. He answered Gordy, "They were terrific, Sergeant Major. The new lads acquitted themselves well. Bill Hay said that Sam White was as cool as a cucumber under fire. He didn't panic when the French started shooting. He just kept telling them that it was Commandos coming in. Even though he was covered in Scott's blood he still had the presence of mind to paddle and to tell the French who we were. And Tommy Foster did well to splint Scott's arm."

Gordy nodded, "And when do we go over for the next op then sir?"

I pointed to Fletcher who was with Wally Bond setting up the radio, "That depends what London says."

Lance Sergeant Hewitt brought me over a mug of tea, "Here you are, sir."

"Thanks, John."

"It is easier being in the field than stuck here sir. We were just wondering what was happening to you. I felt so helpless, you know what I mean?"

"I think I do."

Fletcher came over, leaving Bond to shut down the radio. "London were dead pleased, sir. It seems they knew that we had done something. The Germans were going doolally tap. Our lads picked up the radio traffic. The WAAF said as how they were going to monitor the number of rockets."

"Thanks, Fletcher."

"I don't think I have any chance with that WAAF sir. I tried all my best lines and she was just asking how the officers were. Some WAAFs are like that though. Taken in by pips on the shoulder."

"Quite. How long do we wait until we know?"

"She said it could take a week. I have to get in touch at the same time every day."

I waved over Lieutenant Poulson, "We have been stood down for a few days. Have the men keep up their German lessons. Use Private White. He was a teacher. He should be able to make a better stab at it than Bill or me."

"Right sir."

"And see if Fletcher and Beaumont can scrounge some more ammo for the German guns."

After I had found pen and paper I went to the table we used for our meals. I had a letter to write to Eric Scott's next of kin. I took out the manila file with their details. His mum was a widow. His dad had been a fisherman who worked part-time with the coastal forces. He had been lost when a German Kondor had bombed them. Having lost her only child, Scott's mum would be left alone. This would be a hard letter.

I was struggling with the letter when Tom Foster came over, "Sir."

"Yes, Foster?"

"Is that the letter to Eric's mam?" I nodded. "We both joined up on the same day and we were mates. He was a good lad. He wanted to join the Commandos to get back at Jerry for killing his dad. He was made up to be picked to go with you. He took it as a badge of honour. We all did. He wrote a letter to his mam before we left." He held it up. " I haven't had a chance to post it yet. He told her how he was going on a mission with someone who had won a V.C. He wanted to be like you, sir. A lot of us do."

"This isn't helping, Tom. I feel bad enough that a man was lost on our first mission without thinking it was my fault!"

"No sir, sorry, sir. When we were coming back we talked in the back of the lorry. We both knew that the war we thought we were going to fight wasn't the war we read about in the papers. Those Poles sir; they were little more than skeletons. If they were a dog or a horse you would have put them down. You did all you could for them. Those Jerries who stopped us, you didn't kill them. You could have done but you didn't. And I know that when you sent him across the river first it was to save his life. Eric knew that. It was just bad luck. What I am trying to say, sir and not very well, is that, if that was me lying there dead then I wouldn't regret joining up or serving in the Commandos. I don't want to die but I know that sometimes you have to stand up for what is right. We have stopped some of those rockets, perhaps all of them. They weren't dropping them on Cockermouth or Haltwhistle. It doesn't matter. They were dropping them on our country and our folk!"

I nodded, "Thanks, Tom. That helps. When we bury him would you say a few words over him? I will say my bit but you knew him better than the others."

"It would be an honour, sir."

I did find it easier to write the rest of the letter. That done I summoned Sergeant Major Barker. "Gordy, we need to bury Scott. Find out from Warrant Officer Peters what the procedure is. Thankfully we haven't had to do this too often have we?"

"No sir. Will do. And sir?"

"Yes, Gordy?"

"Get your head down! You look all in. Lieutenant Poulson and I will handle things."

I nodded. I think writing letters of condolence was the hardest thing I did. It seemed to drain me. When we had been fleeing through Germany I had had no time to think and I just reacted. This was harder. I went to my mattress and lay down. I was asleep before my head touched the ground.

We buried Eric Scott at midnight. It was not planned, it just happened that way. There was a cemetery at the airfield. There were French and Germans buried there already. Eric would be the first Englishman. Warrant Officer Peters attended and brought a bugler from the station band. Tom made a poignant speech and 'last post' was played over the grave. It was touching and, somehow, brought us all together.

Eric's death had bonded the new with the old; the veterans with the rookies.

It took four days for the message to reach us but we had made a difference. Reports from Germany said that their production of rockets had fallen dramatically. The fall of rockets had slowed until now it was a trickle. Fletcher was beaming. "That WAAF sounded dead proud of us sir! Anyroad up there is some bloke coming to brief us next week. A Major Sam Politho from the O.S.S."

Lieutenant Poulson said, "Sir, wasn't he with the Rangers at Amalfi and Salerno? The one who helped to get us those bazookas?"

I nodded, "I remember him. I wonder what the O.S.S. is? This means we have more time to prepare and Hay has more time to get fit."

I wrote two letters. One was to Mum and the other to Susan. My letters would now have to be censored. Lieutenant Poulson, as adjutant would do the section's and I would do his. I did not mind but I could not be as personal as I might like. Susan would understand. When we had had our last dinner at Bates' hotel I had told her of the new arrangement. I finished and I was on my way to give them to him when I saw Sam White. He was the least Commando like of my men but he was as tough as they came. During our hand to hand practice he had surprised Private Maclean, the biggest Commando we had, by beating him three times out of three.

"White, I just wanted to say that I appreciate the lessons you are giving the men."

"I am delighted, sir. They are more receptive to them than my students were. They see a real purpose in being able to speak another language. I find it refreshing that an officer should think of this."

"You don't have a very high opinion of officers then?"

"It is not that, sir. The ones who trained us were all right but they seemed bigger on brawn than brain. That came as a shock. I thought Commandos had to think on their feet."

"They do. I suspect that now that we have so many Commandoes they are trying to get them as fit as they can."

"Anyway sir, I like the way you run the section!"

I gave him a wry smile, "Thank you, White. I will sleep easier knowing that."

He realised that he had made a gaffe. I think he said what he had done for genuine reasons even if it came out as patronising. He blushed and said, "Sorry sir." He scurried off.

I gave the letters to Lieutenant Poulson, "Sir if we are going to be here for some time do you think we ought to divide it up; you know officers, non-coms and the like?"

I laughed, "Is this because you are an officer now Polly?"

"No sir, it doesn't bother me, it was you I was thinking of. I mean you have nowhere private to go! It doesn't seem right."

"That is not a problem besides we all have somewhere we can go to be private; even in a crowded room." I tapped my head, "In here. No this is fine although I am a little concerned that the Americans are coming to brief us." I hesitated. Then I realised that I ought to confide in Lieutenant Poulson. After all, no one had sworn me to secrecy. They had just said to keep it on a need to know basis and the Lieutenant needed to know. "There is a spy in our headquarters. Two other attempts were made to do what we did. The fact that we succeeded means that they were right."

"But Fletcher has been on the radio to Headquarters!"

"Not quite. Hugo Ferguson is there along with Joe Wilkinson. Until the spy is caught they are our handlers."

He grinned, "Sounds exciting!"

"Lieutenant!"

"No sir, I mean, I am shocked and all that but it is something that we achieved what others didn't."

I burst his balloon, "Captain Gregson and his Commandos were all shot."

He sat down, "Good God sir. You must think me…"

"You weren't to know. Now you can see why I am worried about this American Major. It suggests that we are going in, again, to replace someone who was killed. We were lucky. You and I know that. We won't be able to repeat our escape act a second time. We will have to think of a new way to escape."

"And if we are deeper in Germany then that will be harder."

"Exactly. Keep what I told you to yourself and make sure the men are on their toes."

"Of course sir and thanks for confiding in me."

The American Major arrived alone and that was unusual. He drove himself and carried a briefcase chained to his wrist. I recognised him immediately. He grinned when he saw my insignia. "You were promoted too. Knew it would happen. There are a lot of our guys think you should have had an American medal too."

"We both know that winning medals is either luck or politics. Come in to our humble abode." He followed me in and I led him into the cavernous hangar. "So what is the O.S.S.?"

A bit like your S.O.E. Wild Bill Donovan runs it. I got the job after working with Colonel Darby."

"How is the Colonel?"

"He is in Italy. Had he been closer, then we would have had him take on this mission." As he entered he rolled his eyes, "Not particularly cosy is it?"

"Functional is the word. And I am afraid that if we want privacy then we have to send the men out."

He nodded, "I'm afraid I do."

"That is not a problem. I cupped my hands and shouted, "Lieutenant Poulson and Sergeant Barker. Take the men on a fifteen-mile run. Pop and see Captain Lemay and then come back!"

Gordy grinned as though it was the most reasonable request in the world. "Righto, sir. Come on my lovely lads, running gear!"

As they started to change Major Politho said, "I thought they would just hang around in the mess. It is minus two out there."

"We don't waste an opportunity like this. It will do them good."

Lieutenant Poulson saluted, "See you later sir! We'll try and pick up something decent to eat. We are fed up of rations."

The Major shouted, "Hold up there Lieutenant. There are twenty steaks in the back of my jeep. A little bribe for the major here."

"That will make the lads shift. We could break the Olympic record today!"

After they had gone I said, "Very generous of you."

Smiling he said, "We like meat and if we can share it with you guys then so much the better. Besides, you are going to earn it. You are going up against the S.S. He took out a photograph of a German S.S. General.

"This is S.S. Obergruppenführer Hans Kammler. He is a Civil Engineer who has risen up through the party. He has been given the V-2 programme and Hitler has given him control over some parts of the Luftwaffe."

I looked at his face. He seemed innocuous enough but I had met enough of the S.S. to know that they were ruthless. I began to fear the worst.

"He is, at the moment, at Oberammergau. It is in Austria." He took out some aerial photographs of the area. There were two red circles. "They have huge factories deep in the mountains. This is one." He pointed to the larger of the two circles. I saw that it was close to a castle marked as Schloss Linderhof. "It is where they are assembling their rockets. Thanks to you their production has slowed up. In fact, they may even have stopped. However, they are developing, in those mountains, a weapon which makes poison gas seem like a kiddie toy. I don't know all the technical details but let us just say that a warhead on a V-2 rocket could destroy Paris or London. It is that powerful. You have done what we asked. But they now have a weapon they can use with the remaining rockets. We don't know how far they are as yet but the closer we get to Berlin the more likely they will try to use it. The project is called **'Uranverein'**."

"I saw that in the factory in Hechingen!"

He nodded, "It is something to do with uranium. You don't need to know how it works what you do need is to stop them working on it."

"This will be heavily guarded. If there is an S.S. general running it then he will be well protected."

"He is but we have identified a weakness. Because of the bombing by the R.A.F. and U.S.A.A.F. they have had to build the barracks for Kammler, his scientists and his guards under the mountain too." He pointed to the second, smaller circle to the east of Schloss Linderhof. "The uranium means that it is well away from the place they are manufacturing it. They have an underground barracks. One of the scientists there fled to Switzerland. It is only seventy miles away. That is how we know so much about it. We would have sent a Mosquito to blow it up. They have the accuracy we need but it is just too far away and we can't guarantee that they will succeed. We want you and your team to drop into Austria and blow up the entrance to their barracks. We want you to bury then alive."

Chapter 6

"Come on Major, you know we are not killers! There will be innocent people in there."

He shook his head, "I am sorry, Tom, this has to be done. It is extremely unlikely that there will be innocent men in the barracks. The barracks is there to protect the elite. These are the hardcore Nazis. The scientists who were not fled before the war. If they had stayed there then God alone knows what might have happened. They would have had this weapon years ago. They are desperate. Apart from the scientists, the senior S.S. officers live there."

I looked at the map. "So the barracks is near to Linderhof?"

"It is. They have an S.S. garrison. They provide the sentries and security. You will have to eliminate the sentries and gain entry to the barracks. We believe that the facilities are extensive. They have their own power plant. They have the ability to stay in there for years."

"So when you say bury them alive that does not mean killing them. They could survive."

"Some will but the only way in and out is through elevators." He smiled, "You guys call them lifts. There are three of them. We want you to send explosives down them to blow them up at the bottom and then blow up the entrance."

"How did you find all of this out?"

"I told you a defector came a week or so ago and another two of the scientists escaped six weeks ago. They made their way to Switzerland. It took three weeks to get them to England and another two weeks to debrief them. When the third one reached Switzerland we debriefed him there. He told us that they are close to finishing this weapon. It has to be done now. You are over here. Johnny on the spot so to speak. We still have our spy in SHAEF. Until we find them then we can't use our guys. You are it."

"How do we get in?"

"C-47."

"And out?"

He looked down at his shoes, "That is trickier. You are seventy-odd miles from the Swiss border. Your men have the skills to climb mountains. This is the Tyrol. There are many hiking paths and trails. We want you to walk out."

"Walk seventy-odd miles through hostile territory in the heart of the most fanatical Nazis?"

He said nothing.

I looked at the map again and the report on the Uranverein. He was right. If the Nazis used this weapon then London could be wiped out. Susan and Mum would be gone in a flash; quite literally. "I can see how we get in and I can see how we destroy the barracks but I am sorry, there is no way that I could get my whole section out alive. I would be lucky to get two or three out."

"I don't like this any more than you." He took out an envelope. He handed it to me and I opened it and read it. It was from Winston Churchill. Without specifying my mission it ordered me to obey the orders.

"It seems I have no choice. Our fate is sealed."

"If anyone can succeed Tom. It is you. Now I have a list here of the equipment available to you."

I held up my hand. "I understand the secrecy and why this is for my eyes only but the planning has to involve my men. Lance Sergeant Beaumont knows more about explosives than anyone else. They have a right to hear this part."

"You are right but Uranverein is not open for discussion nor the defection of the scientists. Just tell them that they are going to stop the V-2 menace for good."

I did not like it but I had no choice. I nodded and our fate was sealed. The men arrived back and I shouted, "Have a quick wash and then join us. We have our mission."

The men hurried to comply. The men were eager to hear what the major had to say. That was in their nature. These were not lazy men. They were Commandos and, like me, they relished the action. However, I had a bad feeling about this particular mission.

While they were getting ready I examined the map again. "Where is the drop zone? This looks to be a mountainous country. Trees and rocks make for bad landings."

He pointed to a village north of Oberammergau. "This is the widest and flattest area. Your pilot would approach from the north. There is a flat area which has no houses between Oberammergau and

Unterammergau. The Austrians have an airfield there so we know you will be able to land safely."

I took a piece of paper and, using the edge and the scale, marked out the distance. "That is ten miles to the target, here near Linderhof. It would mean either going through the town or over the mountains."

He nodded as though that was a reasonable assumption. "There are trails. Before the war, it was a popular area for skiing."

"And you may not have noticed, Major, it is still winter. At this time of year, the snow is highly unstable. There could be avalanches."

He frowned. "I have to say the boys back in the office did not have long to plan this."

"Please tell me that this wasn't planned at SHAEF."

He shook his head, "Washington."

"Then you weren't there at the planning?"

"I am a field officer. A courier brought this to London and I came directly here. This is hot off the press."

My men began to drift over. They said nothing but pulled the metal and canvas chairs we used closer. "So if we find kinks and flaws then we can iron them out?"

"Within reason."

I laughed, "Have you forgotten how we operate, Major? Once we are over there we think on our feet. When we are all here we will see if we can improve on this plan from a bunch of chaps sat in an office thousands of miles away from the target. I have no doubt that they are clever but I am guessing that they have never been to the Tyrol. I have and believe me this will be no picnic. The odds on us getting to the target are slim and getting out slimmer still."

I stopped and waited for the last of my men. When there were all gathered I nodded to the Major, "We have orders for our next mission." I held up the map, "We are flying to Austria. We will parachute and land between Oberammergau and Unterammergau and then hike eight to ten miles through the snow-covered mountains. Here," I had circled the entrance, "is an underground barracks. Inside are S.S. They are working on the V-2 rocket."

Fletcher said, "Sir, didn't we just bomb one factory? Why this one?"

I nodded, "You are right, Lance Sergeant, However, they could begin to manufacture the graphite fins here at Linderhof. This is deep in the heart of the Third Reich. It will be a long time until we manage to get there. Our job is to take the entrance to this underground barracks. Once inside we blow up the lifts and the entrance. The complex is underground."

Lieutenant Poulson said, quietly, "We are going to bury them in their mountain."

I nodded and let that sink in.

Bill Hay said, "The best way to deal with the S.S. in my view."

"They have two machine-gun posts outside the entrance. There is a barbed-wire fence around the front of the complex. In the entrance, they have a guard of between eight and twelve men depending upon the time of day. There is accommodation for a hundred men in the underground bunker. They have built this into the side of a mountain. That way they only have one entrance to guard. The mountainside above the entrance has no paths. That, however, is their weakness. One entrance and exit gives us a target."

I let them take that in.

"The factory which produces engines for Messerschmitts and for the V-2 is another half mile along the road. Just the other side of Schloss Linderhof. That is where the S.S. will be during the day. We hit them at night."

The Major lit a cigarette and cocked an eye as I allowed the men to come up with any questions. They were experienced enough to spot flaws in plans. The newer ones would not say anything but I had enough faith in my veterans to know that they were looking at the task and assessing it.

Lieutenant Poulson said, "If we have to hit it at night and go in at night then it means we will have to lie up during the day."

Gordy said, "That looks easy enough. It is winter. There will be no bugger on the mountain. It is only posh tourists who like to ski who would be there. We make a camp."

Davis said, "Actually sir, that might help. Instead of having to cut through the wire we could abseil and climb down. The guards wouldn't be looking behind them, would they?"

I nodded. I had already come up with that as the best way to attack but I wanted them to come up with the bones of the plan themselves.

"Is the door going to be locked sir?"

"I doubt it, Freddie. The sentries in the machine-gun posts will need to get drinks, have a leak and the like."

"So, we need two teams, sir. One to take out the machine-guns and one to take the entrance."

"Right, Lieutenant."

"And the rest of the men will be underground, sleeping?"

"We assume so. They buried the quarters in the mountain so that they could not be bombed."

Beaumont coughed and we all looked at him. "You want them burying so that they can't get out?"

"Yes, Beaumont. Be under no illusions. We are going in as killers this time. I have told the Major here that I am not happy about it but we have orders."

My Lance Sergeant smiled, "Oh I don't mind burying S.S. They are bastards, sir. I was just thinking about how best to do it."

"The chaps who planned this suggested bombs in the lifts and bombs in the entrance."

"Ah, now I can see why they picked us, sir. That is going to involve perfect timing. We will have to send down the lifts with timed bombs at exactly the same time. Then we will have to blow the entrance as the lifts reach the bottom. Leaving us with the problem of how we get out without being blown up."

He was our expert. "Can we do that?"

"Oh yes, sir but we will have to shift. We will not have much time once they start to go off."

"Another thing, we take our rubber-soled shoes. We need boots to hike through the mountains but the descent down the cliff and the actual attack need silence."

"Yes sir."

"Sir?"

"Yes, Hewitt?"

"When this goes up the sound will be heard. There must be a garrison at the factory where they make the engines. They will be after us straight away. How do we get out?"

"That is the best question so far!" I held up the map and moved my finger from the factory to Switzerland. "We climb these mountains and walk the eighty miles to safety."

"Sir, I can see another problem."

"Yes, Lieutenant?"

"The photographs show a river and a bridge. That is going to be our escape route isn't it?"

"Yes, we have to get across the Linder."

"I can't see very well from the photograph but there look to be guards and guns. What about them? They will hear the firing and the explosions. I am guessing they will try to stop us. I can see us climbing the mountains and disappearing. We are Commandos but we have to get to them first." He jabbed a finger at the Ettaler Forest. It was just half a mile south of the Schloss Linderhof and marked the beginning of the mountains. "We have to get there and I reckon that they will have soldiers in Schloss Linderhof. They may not be S.S. but Jerry would not leave a nice house like that empty. We are going to have to fight our way to the mountains."

For the first time, I saw the doubt on some of their faces. Then Fletcher said, "Sir, how do the blokes get from the factory to their barracks? I can't see Jerry walking it."

Major Politho said, "They have cars and trucks. There is a lorry park cut into the mountain."

Fletcher grinned, "Then we get Freddie to steal a couple and we drive. We have done that before."

"This might be harder, Fletcher."

"For us sir? It is just another challenge."

Gordy Barker nodded, "From what the lads said, Freddie knows how to drive on snow. All we have to do is to get across the bridge and drive as close to this forest as we can get. I would back these lads against any Germans in a footrace!"

I nodded. I had already had another plan in my mind but I would not say it yet. So long as the spy at SHAEF was loose then I had to keep something secret, even from those who sent us.

"Right we spend the afternoon planning. We can enjoy the Major's steaks and then I will need to find Flight Lieutenant Ryan." I turned to the Major. "I take it we go as soon as the explosives arrive?"

"That should be tomorrow."

"Then we go tomorrow night."

I left the Major to answer as many questions and then spent an hour with Flight Lieutenant Ryan. I took the aerial photographs with me and briefed him in the cockpit. "Can we go tomorrow?"

"Depends upon the weather. We have been cooling our heels since our last mission so the bus is maintained and good to go."

"Would it be possible for a low drop. Say a thousand feet?"

He looked at the map, "If we have a north to south run in then yes but I will have to give it all she has to get over the mountains. Isn't that a little low for your chaps to drop, sir?"

"We have more men this time and I don't want us spread all the way to the forest and back."

He asked, "This small airfield here, they don't have fighters do they?"

I smiled, "No." I examined the aerial photograph. "It looks to be a Junkers."

I had more questions to ask him and it was an hour before I felt left. I was slightly more confident than I had been before I had spoken with the pilot. I was slowly eliminating problems.

The major was impressed with our oil drum cookers. "They are like the barbeques we have at home."

Lieutenant Poulson had managed to pick up a few bottles of the local red wine and the men enjoyed themselves. I recognised that we were in for a few hard days. My men knew what they would face too. They filled up, after the steak with bread. They might be living off their reserves if we had to climb and hike through more than fifty miles of unforgiving mountains in the middle of winter. It would be a real test of our endurance. I was not convinced that the plan to steal vehicles would work. It was an option but the German guards on the Swiss border kept their eyes on the roads from Germany! Too many POWs had tried to escape that way. It would be more tightly guarded than the front line.

The Major, even though he had been promoted, was still a Ranger and he did not mind the Spartan conditions of the hangar. The next morning we began to organize ourselves. I had Fletcher radio London and tell them when we were leaving. The men then emptied their Bergens in preparation for the arrival of our equipment. We would need a great deal of explosive. Beaumont could not carry it all and we would have to share the burden. They were the priority and so we kept our bags empty.

Major Politho was interested in the way we prepared, "So you let your guys take what they want?"

I nodded, "The specialists like Hewitt and Bond have to take what they need but as far as weapons the men pick what they are comfortable with. I normally take my Mauser sniper rifle. I won't need it. We have Davis. I will take my Colt, my Luger and my MP 34."

"Not the Thompson?"

"Ammo is in short supply. We have four men with Thompsons and they have plenty of ammunition. The other older hands all have German weapons. On this trip, we have the luxury of a grenade launcher. That will be with Foster and White. McLean and Richardson have a Bren and the rest have Lee Enfields and Colts. We take plenty of Mills bombs and we still have six German grenades from our last mission. We waste nothing. When we get rid of their sentries then we will have more. All of us have saps and daggers. We have wire cutters and compasses. A couple of the lads have knuckle dusters and we take the spare parachute cord. Very handy. The only difference for this mission is that we will not be taking as much camouflage netting. We will take our chutes and improvise."

"You have a good bunch of guys here, Tom. I just wish there was a better way to get out."

"We have the same distance to travel as we did from Hechingen. My worry is that we have used up all of our luck."

The American truck with the explosives arrived not long before noon. The drivers were exhausted as they had driven non-stop from Antwerp. I had wondered why they had not flown them in and discovered why when Flight Lieutenant Ryan arrived to say that the mission had had to be scratched. "Low cloud sir. The weather is set like that for forty-eight hours. It should clear the night after but…"

"But you can't guarantee it. I know. Thanks."

The Major said, "I have to head back to London."

"That's all right, Sam. We know what we are doing. We will just make sure everything is packed and prepared eh?" I held out my hand. "Thanks, anyway. Hopefully, we will get together when all of this is over."

After he left, Beaumont carefully checked all of the explosives, timers and fuses. He then divided the weight equally amongst the Bergens. He had a wonderful memory and he would know exactly what was in which bag. Some would have timers and some explosives. Once that was done then we all loaded our Bergens. We distributed the four ropes we would be taking so that we all had the same weight of bag. After that was completed I gathered them together and told them how we would get in and get out. I saw them nodding. They trusted me. It was a great responsibility.

"I am not certain when we will be leaving, just be ready and keep this in the hangar. We are going too far behind the lines to have our mission compromised because someone opened their mouth."

I waved Lance Sergeant Fletcher over, "What did London say?"

"The WAAF sounded worried. It's weird, sir, normally the voice on the radio sounds interested and concerned but this one, well sir, she seems to have a personal interest."

"It may be that she is sitting next to Captain Ferguson. He has known us since 1941. Perhaps it is his personal interest."

He seemed convinced, "Oh aye, sir that'll be it. She asked if we would transmit every day until we leave. London is keen to follow our progress."

I bet they would. Hugo, Joe and Susan would have been apprised of the original plan. It amounted to little more than a suicide mission. They would be worried and there would be no one in whom they could confide. Even Major Foster would be a suspect.

The bad weather began overnight and continued the next day. It was not snow. It was sleet mixed with rain but the low cloud was the danger. We were all ready to go on the mission and this hiatus did not help any of us. All around Strasbourg we saw the signs of the March offensive. The Dakotas were augmented by Mitchell bombers. We heard the constant rumble of tanks as they headed to the Rhine. It made it harder for us. We knew we had a job to do. For me, it was even more acute. Unlike my men, I knew that the Germans were closer to producing a weapon which would be both terrifying and devastating if it was ever employed. As much as I hated the thought of killing so many men I knew that it would make the world a safer place. I would keep it from my men. Nothing would be gained by revealing it to them.

Two nights later we were able to go. I had made good use of my time. I had spent hours in the cockpit of the Dakota with Flight Lieutenant Ryan. I needed to get into our pilot's head. Dropping at a thousand feet was risky. I had already decided that I would be the last man out. Lieutenant Poulson could lead.

After our last session, the day before we left as it turned out, Flight Lieutenant Ryan, Jack, said, "You could have been a pilot sir. I mean your dad is a pilot and a great one. Talking to you in here I know that you know aeroplanes. Why the Commandos?"

"I did not want to spend the war being compared to Dad. He is a great pilot but everyone would have expected me to be as good. It wasn't fair on him either. That was why I joined the Loyal Lancashires as a private. I wanted to see what Tom Harsker could do. The world already knew what Bill Harsker had achieved. Besides, when the war is over then I can fly again. And I will fly in peacetime. I won't be worried about a Jerry on my tail like I was the last time."

"You have flown in the war, sir?"

I nodded, "We stole an aeroplane in France when we were trapped there once. I have taken an aeroplane up a couple of times since then. One advantage of having an old man who is an Air Commodore is that I know a lot of squadron commanders who will let me take a trainer up. I have kept my hand in."

Chapter 7

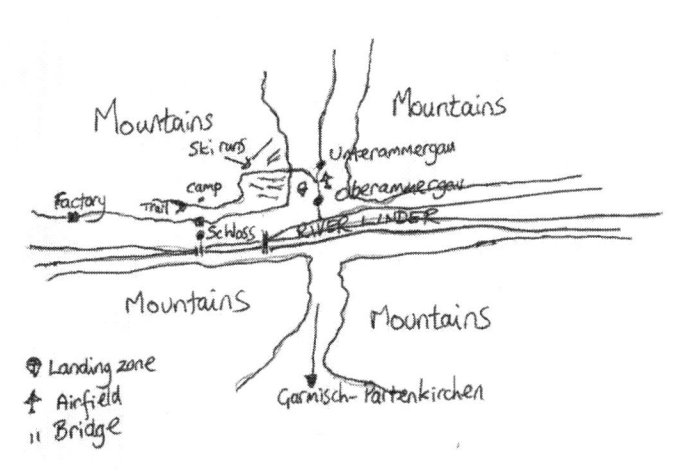

When the door shut and we sat beneath the red light the mission was all too clear. We were off. There was nothing more to do. Bill Hay was as fit as he was ever going to be. We had made our last contact with London and Hugo and Susan knew that we had left our base. They would either hear from us when we returned or wait for the brown telegram; missing in action. There appeared, to me, to be the two options.

We had a longer flight this time and Jack had to climb higher and quicker. There were German night fighters between us and the target. We felt it in the cabin. The ones who had not flown on the first mission looked nervous. Eric Scott had died. The new men looked at each other nervously. I was proud of the way that Samuel and Thomas went out of their way to put the new boys at their ease. They had been with us and knew that we were a band of brothers. They joked and bantered even though the interior was very noisy with the sound of the two engines. This time Flight Sergeant Harris had brought a couple of Thermos flasks filled with soup. As I drank the mug he proffered I realised that there was a tot of rum in it. I gave him a sideways glance and he shrugged and grinned. Flight Lieutenant Ryan knew the enormity of our task. The rum-infused soup helped. I had to regard this as any other mission. The distances and the size of the task were irrelevant. We just did what we always did - our job. At the end of the day that was all that we could do and yet I knew that the war was nearly over.

When we had driven from Hechingen I had seen the old men and boys who were facing us. There were still S.S. They were tough elite units. The Germans had their Panthers and King Tigers, their Me 262 and their V-2 but the men who would fight us on the ground were not the same ones who had chased us through Belgium in 1940. Their bones lay in Kursk and Normandy, Italy and Libya. They had been good soldiers. The ones we now faced were pale shadows. I could understand why we had been given this mission. We were not killing the poor Hans or Fritz. We were killing those who would carry on with the war until the world itself had been devastated. I had to be ruthless. It was not something I admired in others but for my future wife and any children we might have, it had to be done.

Although the weather had improved it was still marginal. We were going to drop at one thousand feet above Oberammergau. The cloud ceiling was barely a thousand feet above us! Flight Sergeant Harris collected the mugs and when he took mine held up ten digits. I nodded and stood. It was time to prepare. I was the last man and so just Sam White checked my parachute. When I had done his, I tapped him on the shoulder and we stood. We shuffled forward. We had to be as close to each other as possible. Once we started we would have to jump quickly as to avoid fouling the chute of the next man.

It was some time since I had been at the back and it was disconcerting. I was normally the one looking into the void. I felt the rush of air from the front and the I hurried after White as we ran down the cabin and hurled ourselves out of the door into the black night. This time there was no snow obscuring our view and I saw the parachutes mushrooming in a line. Our approach meant that I would be the closest to Oberammergau. I did not think that we would be seen but Oberammergau was a bigger place than Hechingen had been. They had an annual passion play which had attracted people from all over the world before the war. We would be avoiding the village by heading into the mountains as soon as we could. There was just a narrow window where we would be at risk. As the ground swung below me I saw the airfield. It was tiny with just one Junkers Ju 52 sitting forlornly on the runway. There were no fighters. That was a blessing.

Dropping so low meant that we reached the ground much quicker. I was helped by White and Foster who both hit the ground before I did. I saw them roll and prepared myself. I was ready and I flexed my knees and landed on my feet. I gathered my parachute. There was no wind. We would need the parachute for camouflage and so I jammed it back into the bag. When we camped I would take the cords. I hung the parachute and bag around my neck and cocked my MP 34. If I had to use it then it was all up but we had to be ready. I pumped my arm and White and Foster joined me. I pointed to the ground and then I ran towards the distant woods.

The place we had landed was called Pulvermoos. The snow-covered it but if it had been England I would have called it moorland. It was undulating and featureless. There were no bushes and no trees. It had been a perfect landing sight. I saw the forest just four hundred yards away. Halfway there I stopped and did a three-sixty turn. The only things moving were my men. I ran back, using my footprints in the snow to guide me. When I reached them I saw Lieutenant Poulson had gathered them all together. I pointed to Gordy and Billy Hay and made the sign for them to watch the rear then I turned and followed my own footsteps. This was not crisp snow. It was soggy snow into which we sank. When daylight came, unless there was another snowfall, then we would have left a clear marker for the Germans. That Junkers Ju 52 had no snow on it. The runway only had a thin covering. They kept it clear for a reason. They were using it. Even if they were just flying locally they would still see the tracks. We would have to disguise them once we reached the mountains.

As we neared the forest and mountain I saw where the ski runs were. They had cut trees to give them a good run. I doubted that anyone had done much skiing in the area for some years but it took time for trees to grow back. They were useful to us, however, for I knew that we had to keep to the south of them.

The energy-sapping soggy snow was an obstacle for which I had not planned. It would be a test of our stamina. When the ground flattened out I held my hand up. There were trails through the trees. I had seen them on the aerial photographs. I looked up at the ski runs. When my eyes came back down I saw the hut which I had also seen on the photograph. It helped me to locate our position. I headed south and paralleled the edge of the forest. I saw the gap in the trees and headed into it. I would be happier when we were hidden by the trees. Although we had seen no one we had been exposed. Once in the forest, I put the safety on my gun. Walking through icy trails was a risk with a cocked gun.

The trail headed towards the south-east and the first hundred yards was a hard slog uphill. It flattened and, after half a mile, met another trail coming from Oberammergau and then turned to head due west. It was then that it climbed. Our experiences on our first raid in the snow had taught us that we could use the snow-covered branches to initiate a miniature snowstorm. The wet snow on the branches was ready to fall. Gordy and Bill began to use the butts of their guns to knock snow behind them as they trudged behind my line of feet. It would not completely cover our prints but it would disguise them.

As we had discovered in Hechingen the snowsuits kept you warm as well as hidden. That meant that I soon began to sweat. The night was not cold; not for mid-February. Sweating was not good. The sweat could be an enemy when we stopped and the temperature fell. I paused when we met the trail from Oberammergau. I checked the trail. There were no fresh marks in the snow. I turned and we began the climb. This trail led to the top of the southern set of ski slopes. I guessed it had been made for the instructors and others who serviced the skiers. It was wider than the first trail. My men were stepping into my footprints but the gap between the trees meant that it would be harder for Hay and Barker to disguise our trail. They would have to improvise.

When we reached the top of the ski run we stopped. I drank some water. I was sweating and the last thing I needed was to dehydrate. I took out my binoculars and scanned the village of Oberammergau below us. It was black and it was silent. The Allies had made such gains of late that I knew every German town would have Volkssturm. There would be a garrison, albeit made up of part-timers who would respond to any enemy. When the factory and the mountain exploded they would know. Volkssturm might be the old and the young but they had guns and they could hurt us. I had to have a plan to deal with them. Even while we were still preparing to make our attack I was thinking of our escape. It was like a game of chess. You had to be two or three moves ahead. If you did not then you lost.

The main trail went due south but I had spied, on the photograph, a trail which went south and west. It was small. It suited us for two reasons: one, it was easier to disguise and two, it cut off a corner and saved us distance. I waved my arm and led them into the forest. It seemed oppressive after the wider trail through which we had hiked previously. We rejoined the main trail three quarters of a mile later and found ourselves exposed. The trail headed due west again. This was the bare side of the mountain. The huge trees were no longer there to hide us. We had over one and a half miles to walk without trees to mask our progress. We would be reliant on our snowsuits and the fact that no one would be watching the mountains at night.

    One advantage of the exposed nature was that, in places, there was no snow. The ground fell away alarmingly to our left. There was an urge to hurry and that would have been a mistake. I kept the same pace. I alternated glancing down to see the trail with looks ahead and below. Being point was never an easy job. When I saw the trees ahead I breathed a sigh of relief. Once we were in the trees we would be hidden for the last two miles. It was, however, a tortuous two miles. We had gained the height getting to the top of the ski run and that had been easy. This was a twisting trail which often disappeared into drifts of snow. No one had been down here since the last snow had fallen. It took us longer than I anticipated to negotiate. I checked my watch as we reached the part of the trail which ran along the side of the mountain. It was an hour until dawn. I wanted to be hunkered down before the Linder Valley came alive. Despite the forests and the mountains, this was no backwater.

    When a trail turned off our track and headed back and up the mountain I took it. We were less than half a mile from the place I had identified as a camp. The lower trail passed within two hundred feet of the cliff above the entrance to the complex. That was just too risky. The site I had chosen looked to be fifteen hundred feet away and better hidden by trees. When I estimated that we had covered the half a mile and found a slightly more open area I circled my arm and my men began to make camp. I dropped my Bergen and, taking my glasses I waved Davis to come with me.

    We plunged through the trees. Here there was no path. We took it carefully. When we reached the other trail I was pleased with my decision to use the upper one. There was no cover. We both dropped to the ground and crawled to the edge of the drop. Using my binoculars I saw the river and the bridge. A tiny red glow told me where the sentries were. They had a brazier for warmth. I moved the glasses back and saw that they kept the road clear of snow. The two emplacements could be clearly seen on either side of the barrier. What I could not see, for it was below us, was the entrance. But the road heading towards the mountain passed the Schloss Linderhof, told me we were in the right place. I turned and looked for somewhere to keep watch on the road. Behind us, about forty feet away was a single stunted tree, some rocks and a snowdrift. The ground behind was lower. We could use that. I pointed to it as I tapped Davis on the shoulder. He nodded. Then I looked around and identified where we could tie the four ropes. Satisfied we headed back to the camp.

Lieutenant Poulson and Sergeant Major Barker had organised our temporary accommodation. Parachutes were draped in the trees. The folds in the material created the perfect cover. If an aeroplane flew over he would see no movement beneath. Gordy had risked using one of the small stoves we had to make a brew. We were high enough for the smell to dissipate before anyone could detect us and we needed the hot drink. I gathered them around me as the snowy water began to heat up.

"There is a spot we can use to keep watch. I want an NCO or officer and one other on duty all day. There are enough of us to just have ninety minutes there. Any longer and we risk exposure. I will have the first duty with White. Get something to eat and then get your heads down. We have done the easy part and now we have the hard job." I saw the sky turning lighter in the east.

I took the mug of hot sweetened tea Ashcroft gave me and ate the biscuits from my rations. It was still dark but I could see light in the east. I wanted to be in position before dawn. As I ate I scanned the camp. Gordy had had the men clear the snow so that they could lie on drier ground. We had enough parachutes to use them on the ground as well as in the canopy above us. We both knew the dangers of lying on wet, cold ground. When I had finished I checked to see if Sam had finished. He had.

"Come on White. First stag!" Before we went I wiped some black charcoal down his face before doing the same on mine. It would break up the outline of our faces.

The first part was covered by the trees. I knew that the others would be following our footsteps when they came to relieve us. I chose a route which kept us hidden. We approached the rock from behind so that we would not be seen. We crawled the last ten feet and squatted between two rocks. I did not use glasses. We would not need them. We could see the road from the north and the bridge. I did not expect to be surprised but we needed as much information as we could get before we attacked. It was still dark but I saw the thin glow from the headlights of vehicles as they moved down the road. Before true dawn, I counted ten such vehicles. That was a warning for the next morning. We would be trying to escape down that road.

Sam shifted next to me. Without turning, for we had to be as still as possible I said, "Try not to move eh Sam? It is okay now but I want us to look like a pair of rocks when dawn comes. When we move we just lie back and roll slowly over. We disappear."

"Yes sir, sorry sir. There is so much to learn. Now I know what the kids I was teaching went through."

"We don't get many teachers in the Commandos nor do we get blokes as old as you. Twenty-five aren't you?"

"Twenty-six in November sir."

"So why the Commandos?"

"Reading the newspapers, sir. I just wanted to do my bit and when I read about how the Commandos were the ones who had to use their heads then it seemed right. I like chess and puzzles. I don't think I could have been a soldier who, well, just obeyed orders."

"Independent eh?"

He nodded, "Yes sir. I get it from my mum. I never knew my dad. He died in the last week of the Great War. Mum and dad married just a month earlier. She only found out she was expecting me after she got the telegram. She brought me up on her own. Luckily we had my Nan. Her husband, my granddad, he was killed on the Somme and the two of them brought me up. It wasn't easy. There was never much money. There were no men for me to copy. I just read about the men who fought in the Great War and then in the wars before. Rorke's Drift, Balaklava, Waterloo, Agincourt, Crecy, Poitiers."

"So why didn't you become a history teacher?"

"One of our neighbours was a little French woman. She had married a Tommy and come to live in England. He died of gas poison and she stayed on. She taught me French and I found it easy. After that, I just learned languages because I enjoyed them. I didn't have a degree. We couldn't afford university and it was easier to get a job teaching languages than history. I still love history though, sir."

"Your Nan died recently didn't she, Sam?"

"A year ago, how did you know?"

"Because you waited until then to join up. I bet your mum wasn't happy."

"No sir. Nan was ill for such a long time and I didn't want me to be the cause of her death. Mum was very tearful. She said I was leaving her alone and I had been her life."

"Perhaps she was right, Sam."

"What do you mean sir?"

"Look, this war is going to be over soon. Poor Scott died and he left his widowed mother alone. There are others, ones with bigger families who can fight right to the end."

"You have any brothers sir?"

"No, a sister."

"So it is all right for you to die because you have a sister but because I am an only child I should stay at home? I am sorry sir, but that is not right. If I have learned anything from history it is that our country became what it did because of ordinary chaps who did their bit. Not the generals and certainly not the politicians. Besides I don't intend getting killed."

I chuckled, "Then you have joined the wrong section."

"No sir. When we were being trained they talked about you. The sergeants said that you were lucky and you couldn't buy that. You are a legend, sir, I know Scottie got killed. That was bad luck. It could have been me. I was in the boat with him but it wasn't. And I will be careful sir. I want mum to have grandkids."

"You have a girl at home?"

"Yes sir. She was an English teacher at the school where I worked. I am engaged. She moved in with mum after I left to keep her company. They get on together. She didn't want me to join up either."

Our conversation was ended by a sudden flaring of the sky to the east. The sun burst through beneath the low clouds. It illuminated the bridge and the gate. I saw that there looked to be twelve men at the bridge and the same number at the gate. There looked to be about fifteen hundred feet between them. The Schloss was between them. I saw a Kubelwagen drive from somewhere beneath us. It was stopped at the gate and papers examined. They were taking no chances. When it reached the bridge it had to go through the same procedure. Then it headed west, presumably to the underground factory.

As dawn broke there was more movement. Trucks plied the road but the majority of the traffic was between the barracks, the factory and the castle. Bill Hay and Private McLean came to relieve us as a veritable convoy left the barracks.

"Sir."

I didn't turn when Bill called out, I just lay flat, rolled over and crawled back to the two of them. It was safe to stand in the lee of the rock. "It looks like the S.S. have gone to work. See if you can work out when they change the guard and count the vehicles on the road."

"Sir."

As we headed back I said to Private White, "Get your head down straightaway. A tired man makes mistakes. This mission is already on a knife-edge."

"Your plan is a good one, sir."

"Well thank you, White. Compliments are always welcome. Although there is one flaw in it isn't there?"

He grinned and suddenly looked much younger than his twenty-five years. "Oh yes, sir. If anything happens to you then we are up the creek without a paddle!"

I shook my head, "I despair. You are in charge of young minds and you are as mad as a fish!"

"We will survive sir. I can feel it."

Polly was still awake and, as White rolled up in his blanket I said, "There are twenty-four men for us to deal with. Twelve will be relatively easy. They are at the emplacement. It is the others who will cause the problem. The ones at the bridge."

He nodded, "Gordy and I have worked that one out. We use our two silenced Colts first and then rush them. We man the machine-guns while Freddie and Wally Bond go and find us a couple of vehicles. If we have had to open fire and make a noise then we will just hold them with their own machine-guns. It might be they just call for help and wait at the bridge. That will suit us, won't it sir? You won't be long with the charges. We will have double their numbers to attack them when you have finished with the demolitions."

"Well, there are no obstacles on the bridge. They don't have a barrier and they don't have wire. There are two MG 42 machine-guns at each end."

"And this time we have rifle grenades."

I nodded, "A shame we don't have Alan Crowe to use it."

"Give the new lads a chance sir. Alan had to learn."

"True but he learned at the camp in Falmouth. These pair are learning on the job and under fire. Anyway, I will get my head down. I want waking up by one, at the latest."

"Sir."

I drank some water and ate the last of my biscuits before I went to sleep. I had an internal clock. I had asked to be woken by one. I knew that I would wake myself up before then. As I came to I heard the unmistakable sound of aero engines. I was awake in an instant. Gordy was standing close by. "I was just going to wake you, sir. It's almost one."

"The aeroplane?"

"It is that Junkers sir. It flew west about half an hour after you got your head down sir and it is coming back now."

I nodded. "Hasn't gone far then?"

"My guess was the Rhine sir. The Lieutenant is on duty. I risked another hot brew, sir. Fletcher and Beaumont did a quick shufti down the track and there was no sign of anyone."

"As you say, Gordy, risky, but they must feel secure here. Hitler has his Eagle's Nest not far from here."

He handed me a cup of tea and he had used the hot water to make some porridge too. "The last lads who came back from sentry duty said they haven't changed the numbers of sentries. It looks like they do four hours at a stretch."

"That is handy. The same time for the bridge and the gate?"

"Yes sir but there is a problem. They come from the castle."

"It isn't really a castle, Gordy, just a posh house but that might be a problem. If they have a four-hour duty then it must be company strength. Perhaps a hundred and twenty men." I was already adjusting my plans. "The main entrance to the Schloss is close by the road and the bridge. There are trees and a wall between that and the emplacements. When you have eliminated the emplacements you need to have Foster and White target the entrance to the Schloss. It is a narrow road and grenades could do serious damage. When Freddie gets the vehicles then mount the MG 42 guns on them. We will batter our way across the bridge."

"Then I hope Emerson can find a couple of decent vehicles, sir. A tank would be nice!"

I laughed, "I can't see that but a good solid lorry would do."

Hewitt and McLean were relieved by Lieutenant Poulson and Private Foster and they came back to join us. "Any change, John?"

"No sir. It looks like they are doing four-hour shifts. I reckon there will be a change over at 1600 and another at 2000."

"That suits us. If we start to go down the cliff at 2100 then we will be in position by 2200."

Gordy said, "Isn't that a little early sir? They might still be up."

I shook my head. "They were heading to work at 0600. From the file I read on Kammler, he works very long hours and is known as a hard taskmaster. They will be in bed early. These are fanatical Nazis."

Lance Sergeant Beaumont woke and came over to me, "We had a look around, sir and saw no signs of the enemy."

"Good. Now the timing of these explosions, how are you going to work them?"

"I am guessing that the lifts will not go down empty. There will be some sort of weight sensor. I was going to use the dead Germans as triggers for the bombs."

"Dead Germans?"

He shook his head, "I am pretty certain that we will not be taking S.S. prisoners, sir. The weight of the Germans will trick the lift into descending. I will use the bodies to hide the explosives. When the lift doors open then the bombs will be detonated."

"And if they don't?"

"I will have a backup timer set to five minutes. But as we will already have exploded the bombs at the top the Germans will be rushing for the lifts in any case."

"I thought you were going to set them all off at exactly the same time?"

"I realised that was too risky. Sealing the top is more important than destroying the bottom. This way I can destroy the entrance too. The rocks here are stratified. I had a look when we went on our walk. It means if I put the charges in the right place then we can use the rocks' natural structure to seal it up forever."

"You are the expert, Beaumont, just so long as the job gets done."

"It will sir. If this Kammler is in the bunker then he won't be seen ever again! He will be buried under this mountain!"

As the afternoon went on we maintained our vigilance and prepared for the attack. The ropes were taken from the Bergens and moved to the observation point. We would not be abseiling down in the true sense of the word. The cliff was only sheer in a couple of places. The first part was sheer and then it cascaded down in a series of rocky steps. Each team would have two ropes. We already had the parachute cord and that would be used for booby traps and to secure any prisoners we might take.

It had already occurred to me that we might just capture one of these high ranking Germans. It was an unlikely scenario but we were prepared. Beaumont had redistributed the explosives, timers and fuses amongst my team. All of us changed into our rubber-soled shoes and put our boots in our Bergens. We had more room for the ropes were already out and soon the explosives would be put to good use.

The Lieutenant had the larger team by one man. They would have plenty of firepower. In addition to the two German guns, we assumed we would capture there were two Bren guns, the grenade launcher and four Thompsons. Even though the Germans would be sending up to a company against them I was confident that they could hold. What I was less certain of was the number and make-up of the German garrison at the factory. If they had any kind of armoured cars then we were in trouble. From the photographs, we had seen and from the intelligence gleaned by the O.S.S., we did not think there were soldiers in either Oberammergau or the small villages through which we would have to pass. There was a garrison at Garmisch-Partenkirchen. If we were going to Switzerland then we would have to deal with them first. That was many hours away. A commando did each job in order while anticipating problems he would have to deal with in the future.

At 2030 we began to break camp. Just as we had with the parachutes we each checked another man's pack. I had made sure that I had a fresh magazine in my Colt and two spares in my snowsuit pocket. My MP 34 was fully loaded and hung from my Bergen. It had been dark for some hours. As we moved to the departure point I saw dimmed lights as vehicles took advantage of the darkness to move down the road. We had seen no allied aeroplanes but the Germans would be wary of aerial attacks.

We attached one rope to the single tree and the rest to rocks. We used some of the parachutes to stop the ropes chafing on the rocks. By 2050 we were about ready. Gordy, Beaumont, Hewitt and Fletcher would be the last ones down. Lieutenant Poulson, Hay, Davis and myself would be the first. We all had a silenced Colt.

Nodding to the other three I wrapped the rope around my back and below my Bergen. My left hand held on to one end of the rope above my head while my right hand held the other end out. If I started to fall too fast then pulling it across my chest would stop me. I stepped out and lowered myself using my feet until my feet were at ninety degrees to the cliff. I began to walk down. I kept looking over my shoulder for obstacles. It was like trying to pat your head while rubbing your stomach. You had to remember to move your feet while letting the rope slide through your hands. The first fifty feet were the hardest for it was vertical. I could have risked bouncing out and letting the rope run through my hands. It was the fastest way down and the most spectacular but we had the time and we needed silence.

The rubber-soled shoes enabled me to feel the rougher rock which indicated that I was on rock which was less steep. Falling stones had been stopped by the gentler angle. I was able to walk backwards, just using the rope for support. I knew that the last fifty feet was a sheer cliff once more. The Germans had blasted it to make the lorry and vehicle park.

I saw the cliff and tightened the rope. I moved slowly as I neared the bottom. I wanted no sudden moves to alarm the sentries. We were well within the view of any sentries. The cloudy skies helped for there was no moon. I glanced to my left and saw the shadows, three hundred yards away, of the sentries. I could not see them and that meant they could not see us. However, I knew the men at the gate could if they turned around far enough see us.

My feet touched the ground and I gave three tugs on the rope to tell those above that I was clear. As I drew my Colt I saw the rope pulled up a little just to make sure that I had let go. I turned and moved along the rock face. The snow beneath my feet was virgin. Luckily it was soft. The crunch of ice could have spelt disaster. When I reached the vehicle park I stopped and waited. Peering in I saw that there were four Kubelwagens and three lorries. I touched the bonnet of the nearest one. It was warm and had been used, After they had secured the emplacements then Emerson would come and start the chosen vehicles. That was his department. He knew what to look for.

Davis tapped me on the shoulder as he joined me. He had his sniper rifle at the ready. He was our secret weapon. It seemed an age before Bond, Pickles and Betts joined me and even longer until Fletcher and Beaumont arrived. All assembled I tapped Lieutenant Poulson on the shoulder and he led his men off towards the gun emplacements. We had to reach the sentries at the door first. We hurried through the snow. When we were a hundred yards away Davis threw himself to the ground. He would shoot anyone who moved before we reached them.

There were just two sentries outside. Obligingly they were facing each other. The smell of tobacco told me that they were smoking. Bill

Hay and I walked towards them with levelled pistols. Behind me, someone stepped on a piece of ice. It broke. It was a tiny noise but one of the Germans turned. Bill and I fired at the same time. The two of them fell. When I reached their bodies I saw that one had two bullets in him. Davis had done his job. I looked towards the gun emplacements. I could see Poulson and his team crawling towards them. Their backs were towards my men. Every foot closer meant it was more likely that they would succeed. The two sentries might have spotted them had they been doing their job. As Bond and Betts slid their bodies away to remove grenades and guns I saw that they were Waffen S.S. The men inside would be good. Bill and I stood on either side of the door. Fletcher and Beaumont held the handles. We had gone from the known and now we were going into the unknown. We had surmised up to twelve men. When we opened the door we would find out.

Chapter 8

I nodded to Fletcher and Beaumont. They turned the handles and pushed the doors open. Bill and I leapt through the gap with guns levelled. There were two tables and Waffen S.S. soldiers were seated around the sides smoking and drinking coffee.

I had to make an instant decision. "Hands up and you will live!" My men's guns covered them. We had four automatic weapons. If we opened fire it would be a slaughterhouse.

None had a gun in their hands but they were within easy reach. These were Waffen S.S. How far did their dedication go? Just then, from outside, came a single shot. It was like a trigger. The men around the table grabbed for their guns. I was less than six feet from them and I could not miss. The Colt threw the sergeant backwards and the corporal next to him had his head blown off. The next two managed to get hold of their guns but I was faster and the last was thrown six feet from his chair by Davis' Mauser.

Outside I could hear the sound of an alarm. The men at the bridge had realised something was up. "Beaumont!"

One of the Germans was not dead and he managed to stand and throw himself at a red button on the wall. Even as Hay shot him a klaxon sounded. The Germans in the bunker would know that they had been compromised. They would be racing for the lifts. Bill Hay raised his gun and shot the klaxon. We heard another one from below our feet.

"On it, sir. Scouse, get the lifts, have all the doors opened. Betts, Bond and Pickles throw a body in each one and make sure the doors don't close."

While he and Bill Hay began to set their charges, Davis and I went around the huge hall to make sure that there were no more entrances. There were two cupboards. When we opened them we discovered that one was for German uniforms while the other was their armoury. Fletcher was helping to set charges. "You three come and get as many grenades as you can from here and then go with Davis and help Lieutenant Poulson."

Outside I heard machine-gun fire and the crump of grenades. It was difficult to know how it was going. We were using German weapons too.

"Sir!"

Beaumont had briefed Fletcher and Hay well. There were three lifts as the Major had said, Fletcher and Hay were setting the charges around the bodies while Beaumont was at the doorway. He was standing on a chair and packing explosives into a fissure above the lintel. "Need any help, Roger?"

"Yes sir. If you could pass me that plastic explosive." I picked it up and gave it to him. "Now the timer." I gave him the timer. He shouted, as he worked, "How is it coming you two?"

"Almost done!"

"Stick any spare German grenades in with them. When the doors open and the charges go off it will be like a giant shotgun. Jerry will be waiting for the lifts to escape the death trap. So long as they are up here they can't get out." He reached down. "Hand me that haversack, sir."

I picked it up and gave it to him. I saw that about three feet above his head was a hole in the rock. Obviously, it was natural and followed the stratum of the rock. Beaumont threw the haversack and it disappeared into the hole. He shouted, "Right lads, down with the lifts and get the hell out of here. I am using an eight-minute fuse."

I hoped that Emerson had the vehicles ready or we could be caught in the avalanche which I knew would ensure. Even as I picked up my MP 34 I heard the sound of vehicles. I looked out of the door and saw a Kubelwagen driven by John Hewitt followed by a lorry with a grinning Fred Emerson at the wheel. We had transport. How many of my men would board them? Beaumont pushed me in the back as he slammed the doors shut. "Come on sir! This is no time to hang around!"

We ran down the drive and followed the lorry and Kubelwagen. We had fifteen hundred feet to run and then a few hundred yards to the bridge. I saw the muzzle flash of bullets. A grenade was launched by my two new men and I heard the two MG 42 guns as they chattered death. I had no idea where the enemy were, save by the muzzle flashes. As we reached the lorry I saw bodies being carried aboard. We had lost men. Hewitt was dismantling one of the MG 42 machine-guns and fixing it to the Kubelwagen.

Lieutenant Poulson said as I neared him, "Pickles and Bond. They didn't duck fast enough. We got the bastards who did it though."

"Inquest later. Get everybody on board. We have four minutes before half of that mountain comes crashing down on us."

I jumped behind the wheel of the Kubelwagen. As Hewitt finished off loading the machine-gun Beaumont and Fletcher jumped in the back seats. I changed the magazine in my Colt. "Let's go!"

Hewitt stood and began firing the MG 42 as we hurtled down the track. I saw Fletcher holding onto Hewitt's webbing to keep him from falling out of the vehicle Beaumont had a bag of grenades. A German loomed up five yards from us and raised his gun. I fired at him with the Colt. Two of the bullets hit him. The drive was like a rollercoaster at the funfair. The road was slick and it twisted and turned. Beaumont hurled a stick grenade high in the air to our left. Ahead of us, I saw the bridge. There was still one machine-gun firing. White and Foster had done well. Their rifle grenade had been effective. Hewitt turned the gun and the bullets tore through the last of the defenders. I hit the gun and the defenders. Two bodies flew into the river while we crunched over others. The lorry crushing them beneath its tyres would make them unrecognisable. There were still Germans pouring from Schloss Linderhof and firing at the truck following us. We had taken them unawares but these were Waffen S.S. and they were fighters.

Beaumont said, "Floor it, sir! One minute to go!"

I threw the wheel to the left as we cleared the bridge and we skidded and fishtailed into the main road. It afforded me a good view of the mountain as the charges went off. There was a flash and then we heard the explosion. At first, I thought we had failed. There was a cloud of smoke and then nothing.

Scouse said, "What went wrong?"

Beaumont said, calmly, "Nothing. Watch."

There was a second, louder explosion and then an almighty crack that we heard almost a thousand yards away. More flames leapt out and more smoke and then I watched in amazement as the side of the mountain slid down. It was as though it was a film and in slow motion and then the fall of the rock wall began to gather pace. More rocks fell and I saw that, while the Schloss, was going to escape, the wall of stones and rocks was racing towards the river and us.

"Shit!"

What saved us was the river. The larger stones fell into the river although some of the smaller ones flew alarmingly close to our heads!

"Hewitt, reload. Well done Beaumont. Have you any explosives left?"

"A bit sir. The next bridge?"

I gestured behind me, "I am guessing they will be on our tails very quickly. There is a bridge at Graswang. If we can blow it they will have to go further downstream and we might just make it."

It was just two and a half miles to the bridge and as we approached I saw that there were no guards there. I screeched to a halt. "Beaumont, do your stuff, Fletcher, help him. Hewitt, keep the bridge covered."

As the German truck thundered over with bullet holes in the canvas sides Lieutenant Poulson shouted, "Fisher bought it and Davis has a bullet in the leg."

"Hewitt, go and see to him."

I took the binoculars from my Bergen. I could see, in the distance, the dim glow worms of German vehicles as they raced along the road. They were level with the bridge which meant we had about five minutes, no more. "How long, Beaumont?"

"Three or four minutes, sir."

"White, Foster, get on this machine-gun. Emerson, take the lorry down the road. I don't want any more men's lives risking."

Sam and Thomas jumped from the truck and manned the MG 42. They checked that it had a full belt and then peered down the sights. I knew that Beaumont was working as fast as he could but I saw the column of lights as they zoomed down the slippery and slick, ice-covered road. It was a race against time.

Beaumont and Fletcher scrambled up. "Time to go, sir! A two-minute fuse!"

"You two on the lorry."

"Sir!" The two of them passed me and ran to hurl themselves into the back of the German truck.

"Sam, give them a burst! Frighten them!"

"Sir!"

White fired two measured bursts. He did not have the luxury of tracer but, even so, he hit the leading vehicle. No damage was done but the driver became cautious. I put the Kubelwagen into gear and floored it. I was barely a hundred yards away when the bridge exploded. I saw pieces of wood and stone fly into the air. Some debris passed generously close to us and the wave of concussion hit us. The bridge was not totally destroyed but no vehicle would cross it. They would have to go further upstream. Lieutenant Poulson had now taken the lead. We raced through the village of Graswang. The inhabitants had come from their homes to see what the noise was. We left them unharmed. Just before Ettal, we would have to take a left turn and then we would have to negotiate Oberammergau. I did not want to hurt or injure civilians but we had to get through unscathed.

We had barely two miles to cover. The town should have been asleep but the side of a mountain cascading into the river tended to make a noise. People would be up. I trusted Emerson to keep his foot hard down. There were enough men in the truck to lay down a withering fire should they be attacked. I hoped that the people would just spectate and not try to stop us.

The town loomed up ahead. Before the war tourists had flocked here. If the Germans had not built their factory under the mountain then they might have survived the war without incident. Our dash through their town was their war. I saw that they had Volkssturm and they came out to fire at the lorry. "Sam, give them a burst. Try to frighten them!"

"Sir!" He opened fire and his bullets thudded into the ancient building behind which they sheltered. They took cover.

"Keep it up! Foster, take a German grenade and drop it behind us."

"Sir!"

The grenade would not hurt anyone but shrapnel flying through the air would worry an older soldier. As the MG 42 clicked on empty the grenade went off in the middle of the road. I heard metal smacking into stone walls and they stopped firing. The village was small and we were soon through and into the darkness. Once we had passed the outskirts and reached the Pulvermoos we pulled up next to Lieutenant Poulson.

I pointed to the airfield. "Freddie, ram the gate and we will follow. Lieutenant Poulson, take the personnel there prisoner and secure them. I will go directly to the Junkers."

"Sir!"

We followed them and Emerson did exactly as ordered. He ploughed through the gate. I heard a couple of shots and, as we passed through, I saw the two dead guards. As the lorry headed to the huts by the windsock I raced towards the Junkers. I had devised this plan back at our own airfield. At first, it had been a contingency plan. I had seen the airfield and the Ju 52 but I had had no idea if it was airworthy. As soon as we had seen it flying we knew we had a chance. I pulled up by the tail.

"Get the gear out of the Kubelwagen and into the cabin."

"Sir!"

I opened the door and clambered up. I made my way to the cockpit. Opening it I saw that I recognised the dials and controls. While I waited for my men I familiarised myself with them. It was as I was going through them that I realised fuel was low.

I went back into the cabin. "White go and find Emerson. Tell him to fetch the petrol bowser. We have to fill it up."

"Sir."

I pointed to a side panel and unclipped it, "Foster put the MG 42 here. We may be attacked on the way back."

"Sir."

Satisfied with what I had found I went outside and examined the exterior of the German transport. They had tethered her. That was not a surprise. It would be windy up here. I went around and untied them. By the time I had finished Emerson and White had returned with the petrol bowser. "Get her filled up Freddie."

"Right sir."

"How did it go inside?"

"We got them all but they managed to get a message off. Bill Hay caught enough of the transmission to know that they were in touch with Munich."

"That means they will send aeroplanes after us. As soon as the Lieutenant is here we will take off."

"They are just tying the ground crew and pilots up. There are only twelve men there. They gave us no bother."

"When you have filled it up, shift the bowser and booby trap it. Then get aboard and let me know. Sam, when Fletcher arrives, tell him I need him in the cockpit."

"Sir."

I went back to the pilot's seat. Foster had fixed the machine-gun to the mountings. Although intended for an MG 15, the fittings for the MG 42 were the same. I looked down the cabin. It was intended for eighteen men. It would be a tight squeeze. We would be taking our dead back with us. The fuel gauge was reassuringly full. I took the flying helmet and headset which were hanging behind the seat. I put on the helmet and hung the headset around my neck. Once we were in the air that would be the only way I could talk.

Emerson appeared in the doorway, "All done sir."

"Then let's see if they start." With typical German efficiency, the three engines were all logically labelled. I began with the port. It started and then the centre engine. That too started. The starboard turned over but would not fire. I tried again. It failed. I was not sure if it would take off fully laden with two engines.

Emerson said, "I'll go and have a shufti."

Our mechanical expert might be our only chance to get off the ground. The lorry arrived and disgorged the men. I saw from the side window that they brought the two dead Commandos aboard first. Fletcher made his way up to me. I pointed to the headset. He nodded and put it on. I donned my own. I made sure we were both plugged in and then said, "There is a radio. I want you to man it when we are in the air. Listen for German traffic."

"Sir."

"But when we take off you will be in the co-pilot's seat." I pointed to three levers. "When I push these you need to help me and when we start to rise I want you on the second joystick."

"Me sir?"

"You can do it." I gestured outside, "That is if Freddie can get the engine going."

Lieutenant Poulson put his head in the door, "All aboard apart from Emerson. There are lights approaching from the south sir."

"Get the men to be ready to fire from the windows. Foster has the MG set up. We will not give up without a fight."

Lieutenant Poulson grinned, "Of course not sir."

I saw Freddie appear in my eyeline. He put two thumbs up. I tried the starboard motor and the engine fired. Turning, I shouted, "Let me know when Freddie is aboard. Fletcher, buckle up. You are going to get a flying lesson." The Junkers had a fixed undercarriage and we would not need to retract it but it was slower than any German we might meet in the air. I checked the wind direction and moved the throttle so that we moved. The Germans had, obligingly kept the runway clear of snow.

As I lined us up for take-off Lieutenant Poulson shouted, "Sir, Jerry!"

"Right Fletcher, it is now or never. Hands with mine." We pushed the throttle and the three BMW engines began to power us across the grass. I heard the MG 42 begin to fire and then the Bren gun. I felt something hit the fuselage. The huge mountain ahead of us seemed even bigger as the nose slowly came up. We would have to bank to port as soon as I had gained enough altitude. "Hands on the stick, Fletcher. We turn to port, now!" We were still climbing but the mountain looked to be dragging us like a magnet. I had committed us. The guns had stopped firing. The enemy was no longer the Germans, it was the land itself. The three engines were powerful and inch by inch we climbed. As the rocky peak slid beneath my starboard wing I began to straighten her out. "Thanks, Fletcher, have a go on the radio now."

"Sir. I thought we were a goner then sir! That mountain was bloody close!"

"I know. The German pilots must have a technique of avoiding it. I am a little rusty. Sorry."

"Hey, sir I think it is great that you can fly! This is easier than heading south through the mountains!"

He turned on the radio. I could hear the static in my ears. He began to turn the dial. I heard German. I held my hand up and he left it there while I listened. They mentioned us. Night fighters were being scrambled. Munich was less than sixty miles away. I checked my heading. We were flying north-west on a course of 265. I had estimated it would take us an hour to reach the Rhine. German night fighters would be all over us before then. We had passed the mountain but I still climbed. I knew that if the Germans came after us I could gain a few more knots by diving. I also saw that up above us was thick cloud. We would be flying blind but that might hide us from Jerry. It took us seventeen minutes to gain 10000 feet.

As we climbed I shouted into the cabin, "Everyone all right?"

Lieutenant Poulson shouted back, "We have a few more ventilation holes but other than that we are tickety boo, sir!"

I heard Gordy shout, "And it could do with being a bit smoother sir!"

They were fine. "Anything Scouse?"

"When I was in Strasbourg I only tried the frequency for London. There won't be anybody there, sir. It is the middle of the night. Even the WAAF has to get some sleep!"

"Keep turning the dial until you hear English or French. We need to warn them that we are coming in. They use these as bombers. The French are likely to fire first and ask questions later."

"Right sir."

"You lads in the back keep your eyes peeled for fighters."

"All we can see, sir, is cloud."

"I know, we are hiding, but I will be coming out in about ten minutes to begin our descent to the Rhine. As soon as you see them call out and then fire everything you can at them."

I trusted the instruments and compass. That was all a pilot could do when flying in cloud. I knew that Dad would have flown this bus better than I was doing but I was doing the best that I could.

We had been flying for thirty-five minutes. I estimated that we were about eighty miles from the Rhine. As we descended our speed would increase slightly. The maximum speed of the Ju 52 was 165 miles per hour but that was at sea level. I did not want to risk missing our airfield. Flying around allied air space would be as dangerous as flying over German. We needed to be on the ground.

I pushed the stick forward. We began to descend. I did not make it a steep dive. I watched the altimeter to make sure that it was a gradual descent. Suddenly the cloud cover was gone. Ahead I could see nothing. Then, in my headphones I heard French being spoken, "Fletcher, stay on that frequency. Transmit and just say Mayday, British Commandos in a Ju 52 coming into land. Keep repeating it."

"Sir! Mayday, British Commandos in a Ju 52 coming into land. Mayday, British Commandos in a Ju 52 coming into land." It sounded like some sort of mantra. It was not the regulation radio procedure but as Scouse's French was not up to muster it would have to do.

"Sir, a fighter on the starboard beam. It looks like a Me 110. It is diving."

The twin-engined fighter had four machine-guns and would make mincemeat of us! I pushed the stick forward and began to steepen my dive. I heard Lieutenant Poulson shout, "Wait for my command!"

I shouted, "I am going to climb to meet him. It might put him off! Fletcher!"

"Sir!" He grabbed the second stick and I nodded.

I began to pull back, "Keep it steady. I don't want to stall!"

I saw the twin-engined fighter. They had been used briefly in 1940 when the Luftwaffe tried to bomb the northeast of England. The Hurricanes shot them down too easily and now they were relegated to night fighter duties. My manoeuvre took him by surprise. He fired a hopeful burst at where we had been before he turned into me. We were on a collision course.

Lieutenant Poulson's command to fire coincided with the Messerschmitt's volley. Nine automatic weapons all fired on a cone have a devastating effect. Even as the German's shells took out the starboard engine I saw the pilot's head almost explode as some of my men's bullets struck the cockpit.

"Keep climbing! He is coming straight at us." We were struggling as the starboard engine was dying. As soon as the Me 110 slipped beneath us and began its death spiral I said, "Level out." With the two of us working together we gradually settled. "Thanks."

We were labouring now. I knew that the Ju 52 could fly on two engines but I had never done so. It felt awkward and ungainly when, earlier, it had been a dream. I turned back to my heading and began my descent. Strasbourg was a big target. It was the only town of any size on the west bank of the Rhine. The field was to the northeast of it. I watched the altimeter spin down and prayed that there were no more fighters nearby.

Fletcher shouted, "There sir! I can see the Rhine!"

I saw that we were too far south. The shadowy buildings of Strasbourg lay to the north of us. I began to come around and gradually throttled back. I had no idea what the stall speed would be. The landing would, in all likelihood, be hard.

"Brace yourselves and get your feet off the floor. We are coming in hard. Link arms and put your head between your legs!"

I heard someone say, "And kiss your arse goodbye!"

Gordy shouted, "Emerson!"

"Sorry Sarn't Major!"

Guns were firing at us. They were allied guns. I could do nothing about that. I had to hope that they would miss us. There would be no lights on the runway and I could not see the windsock! Other than that, everything was fine! I kept descending over the town and then I spied the airfield. The squadron leader had kept the runways clear and for that I was grateful. There was, however, a line of Dakotas to the left of the runway. If I crashed into them that would be a disaster. I throttled back some more and the two engines began to hunt. I gave them a little more power and used the flaps to slow us down.

"Fletcher, keep your eye out of the window and tell me when I am about to land."

"Yes sir. You are doing great sir!"

I nodded and concentrated on keeping us straight with the aeroplane trying to pull us to port.

"Getting lower sir, almost there, nearly there!" I lifted the nose ever so slightly and Fletcher, shouted, "Down sir!"

We bumped. Dad would have shaken his head as we rose a couple of feet in the air. I throttled back some more and said, "When I tell you, push down on the brake!"

"Right sir. Which one is that?"

"Look at the one under my left foot and your pedal is the same one." As we bumped down I shouted, "Now!" We both pushed down. The runway had been cleared but it was still slick and we started to slide. We were in danger of hitting a Dakota and I use the rudder to swing us away from danger. We pirouetted alarmingly but slowly stopped. From behind me, I heard a cheer.

Private Betts shouted, "Just like the waltzers at Blackpool sir! Can we have another go?"

I switched off the engine and realised that I was sweating. Fletcher said, "Sir, on behalf of the lads, thanks! I know they call you lucky sir but you have some skills and that is no error."

As we opened the door we were greeted by Lee Enfields and Ercs in tin helmets. Warrant Officer Peters grinned when he saw me, "We had a message that some Commandos had captured a Jerry transport and were heading here. As soon as they said it was a Liverpool accent I knew who it was." He shook his head, "Squadron Leader Andrews didn't believe me. That is why we are tooled up sir. Welcome home."

"I am assuming you lads can park it!"

"Leave it with us, sir! I'll get some tea and sarnies sent over. You look like you deserve them." As the men began to disembark he saw the bodies and he stood to attention, "Ten shun!" All of his men presented arms as the dead Commandos were carried to the hangar. "Sorry about your lads, sir."

"I hope, Warrant Officer, that after this war people don't forget what lads like Bond, Fisher and Pickles did for their country. I know I never shall!"

Beyond the Rhine

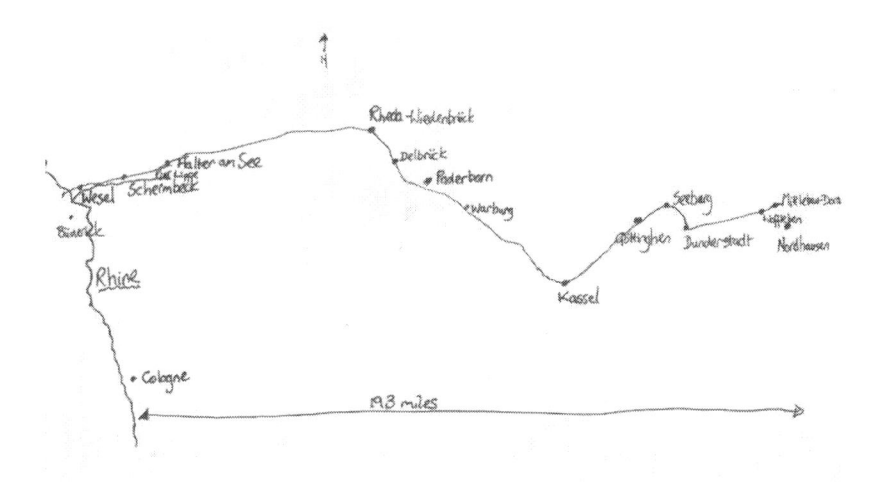

Chapter 9

We buried our men at dawn with grey clouds scudding overhead. Once again Warrant Officer Peters attended the funeral of the three men. I felt guilty. The ones who had perished were all new men. Four of my section had died and all of them were novices. What could I have done better? Perhaps I should have left them at the airfield until an easier mission came along. Then I realised that we did not have easier missions and we had needed every man we had and then some.

Lieutenant Poulson told me that Bond and Pickles had just been unlucky. They had both raised their heads at the wrong time. Their deaths had been instant. Fisher had also been unlucky. The bullets which had stitched a line along the truck had only wounded Davis but killed him. I had three more letters to write. These three were no easier than Scott's had been but at least I knew them slightly better and I could write with more authority. I felt drained at the end of it.

Fletcher radioed London. They already knew of our success because of the radio traffic they had picked up. They would send over an aeroplane to take photographs to confirm when the weather allowed. I knew we had succeeded. The mountain had fallen. Beaumont had excelled himself. I began to write my report and to recommend medals and promotions. They all deserved something.

Most of the men just wanted to sleep but I could not. I would be haunted by four young faces. Instead, I decided to go for a run. Many men would have thought me mad but my men knew why I did it. As I was getting changed Sam White asked, "Are you off for a run sir?"

"Yes, White. It clears the head."

Mind if I join you, sir?"

"You are more than welcome."

We ran from the airfield to Strasbourg. It was cold and fresh and that was what I needed. Neither of us spoke. It was companionable. We received strange looks from the sentries at the gate but they snapped to attention as we ran through the barrier. The looks from the French civilians were even stranger. I was used to it. Even in Falmouth, the locals could not get used to the Commandos who ran in all weathers. We were both in the same rhythm. It just seemed to happen. Commandos have an affinity for one another and that is translated into a rhythmic gait. I was certain it was akin to the warriors of old, like the Vikings, Romans and Spartans who had been able to keep in step even when fighting.

We reached the cathedral and ran around it. I stopped, "Everything all right sir?"

I nodded, "I am not a religious man, White, but something made me stop. I think I will go in and say a prayer. You can wait here if you wish."

"No sir. I would like to as well. My Nan used to make me say my prayers when I was little. I haven't done it since. I don't know why."

I knew that this Gothic edifice had been the tallest church in the world for a while. That seemed unimportant as we stepped into its gloomy interior. Mum had taken us to church but I had never been a regular churchgoer. They say that in war there is no such thing as an atheist. Certainly, as we knelt to pray I hoped that there was an afterlife and my four young Commandos were there. I was self-conscious and I spoke my prayer in my head. I prayed that the four of them were at peace and I asked forgiveness for not preventing their deaths. For some reason, and I still don't know why, I began to cry. The tears flowed down my cheeks. I didn't want to cry. I was a major in the Commandos! Perhaps it was all the men who had died before. There had been a lot. When my tears subsided I stood. White was waiting in the aisle. He had given me space.

Neither of us said a word as we ran back but the run and the church had a cathartic effect on me. I felt purged. I had needed to mourn. Dad had told me of men who had bottled things up inside. One had served with him in Somaliland. He had been a hero but after some of the men he had been training had died in an accident he had never been the same. He had taken his own life. That had upset Dad. He had wondered if he could have done more for poor Eric Hobson. I had wept and I had mourned. I would now put that behind me. That chapter had ended and I had a new page to write.

We walked from the gate. It was our cooling off. White said, "Thank you for letting me come with you, sir. It helped."

"Helped, White?"

"Understand sir."

I did not fully understand what he meant but I nodded anyway. "I think, White, that we will use the showers in the main block? I do not relish a cold one."

"No sir, highly overrated in my view."

We had not been using our rations what with our missions and the generous gift from the Americans. Warrant Officer Peters, who seemed to have taken on the role of a guardian angel, brought over fresh meat, freshly baked bread and some tinned vegetables. We couldn't have everything. He had also managed to get some tinned fruit for us. As Gordy said, as he gratefully accepted it, "It is like Christmas again."

One of the best things about being a Commando was that we generally ate together. It didn't happen as often in any other branch of the service. Dad never liked the change from Sergeants' Mess to Officers' Mess. We all mucked in together. It was pork chops that the Warrant Officer had brought and I joined Bill Hay at the oil drums to cook them. Gordy and Lieutenant Poulson had managed to get some milk and some rice. They were making rice pudding and arguing the merits of the preparation.

"Of course, sir, it can never be as good as my mum's. She did hers in the oven and it always had a lovely, crisp skin."

Lieutenant Poulson said, "I was never a skin man myself, Gordy."

"And that is the beauty of rice pudding sir. The ones who like skin take it off and the rest have it the way they like."

I turned the chops and said, "Mum used to put cream in ours and serve it with homemade strawberry jam."

Gordy sniffed, "Then you were posh, sir. The only time we got cream was if you managed to get to the top of the milk before the birds or someone else in the family!"

I smiled, Mum would be appalled to think that others thought us posh. But I now knew that we were. I had had a privileged upbringing. A second home in France and Dad's cars marked us as different. I don't think it made us snobs but it did make us act and sound different. "And she would grate some nutmeg too."

"Nutmeg!" There was scorn in Gordy's voice although I am not certain he even knew what nutmeg was.

Bill turned his chops, "Five minutes for the chops. How is the gravy coming, John?"

"It will be lovely. Perfect to mop up with the bread. I am glad that Fletcher managed to find those onions."

"Pinch more like!"

"Sergeant Major I am offended. Not everybody from Liverpool is a thief!"

"I don't think they are Scouse but you…"

"Veg is almost ready too, Sarge!"

"Right, Beaumont." Over my shoulder, I shouted, "Foster, White, get the tops off those wine bottles."

"To let them breathe sir?"

I laughed, "No so that we can drink it! This is as rough a wine as you can get!"

We had put the two tables together so that we could all sit around it. The bread was no longer warm but the bakers had used French-milled flour and it tasted wonderful. As well as the onions Fletcher had managed to buy some cheese. I would enjoy that with the last of the bread after the pudding. It was a convivial meal. We took advantage of the fact that no one had come up with another mission for us yet. They would, eventually, and then we would be behind the lines again living on our nerves and eating dehydrated food.

At the end of the meal, we stayed around the table. Most of the men smoked. They didn't smoke while we ate out of deference to the non-smokers but now that it was over it was as though they had another course to devour. We spoke of the end of the war and our plans and, inevitably, the four dead Commandos. They had no future but we did.

Private Betts took out his mouth organ and began to play. I had no idea why he chose the song he did but it seemed to fit in with the reflective mood. Fred Emerson took out his and joined in.

We'll meet again don't know where don't know when
But I know we'll meet again some sunny day
Keep smiling through just like you always do
Till the blue skies drive the dark clouds far away
So will you please say hello to the folks that I know
Tell 'em I won't be long
They'll be happy to know that as you saw me go
I was singin' this song
We'll meet again don't know where don't know when
But I know we'll meet again some sunny day
I know we'll meet again some sunny day

We sang it a couple of times. It was a sentimental song but that was our mood, sentimental.

The next morning Gordy had us all up at the crack of dawn. "Major Harsker put us to shame yesterday! He went for a run while we all slept. Today we all go. All right, Major?"

"Perfect, Sergeant Major, it will blow away the cobwebs."

When we were back and showered Fletcher made his daily contact with London. When he had finished he said, "Well, sir, it looks like the holiday is over. They are sending someone down tomorrow. They are coming by car and the WAAF said we should begin to pack up. It looks like we are finished here. A shame. I was just getting used to it!"

"Right. Okay, Sarn't Major. Better get things started. You know the way the brass works. We will have to leave here within minutes of whoever they send!"

"Righto, sir. Okay, my lovely lads. I want this place as clean as a new pin. We wouldn't want these Brylcreem boys to think we are a bunch of tinkers, do we?"

I put on my greatcoat. The snow had stopped but there was a wind which felt it had come all the way from the Urals! I went to the officers' mess where I knew I would find Flight Lieutenant Ryan. He stood to attention when I entered, "At ease. Just came to tell you that I think we have no further need of your taxiing services."

He nodded, "I know sir. The Squadron Leader told me that I was now assigned to the squadron here until further notice."

I nodded. Andrews could have let me know. It would have been just courtesy. The Squadron Leader had never once invited any of us to dine with them or even to come and see us in our quarters. I did not understand the man.

Ryan said, "Let me buy you a drink sir."

He looked eager. "Why not? Whisky, neat if they have it."

He waved over the steward and gave him the order. "You know sir, when you started to interrogate me about flying I thought it was some sort of test. You know, your old man being a high up and all that."

"No, nothing like that. When I looked at the aerial photograph and saw the transport plane I began to see an easier way out of Germany than climbing through seventy odd miles of mountain in the middle of winter."

The drinks came, "But sir, how did you manage without a co-pilot?"

"I didn't. I used my radio operator. Commandos are quick learners you know. Besides so long as we managed to take off then I guessed we could get some way closer to home. We knew the land between Hechingen and Strasbourg. Once I got her in the air we were halfway home."

"But you were attacked by a 110! I would have been shot down!"

"I had more than a dozen armed Commandos. The problem with aeroplanes attacking transports is that they think they are easy targets. We were like a Trojan horse. We did what we had done before. We threw up a wall of lead. And we were lucky. The Ju 52 is a solid aeroplane. I was impressed. Kept flying with one engine shot!"

We chatted for a while and he asked me about the German aeroplane. I had just finished my whisky when Squadron Leader Andrews came in. I was about to buy the Flight Lieutenant a drink when Andrews approached me, "I hope Major that you will leave the hangar in the state you found it! We don't want any army mess you know!"

"Ah, then should I have my men put a bloody big hole in the roof on one side then? I am certain we have some explosive left!"

Flight Lieutenant Ryan could not hide his grin. "Flight Lieutenant, I am sure you have better things to do!"

He stood and said, "Yes sir, sorry sir!"

I leaned forward and said, "You know Squadron Leader, you really are an arsehole!" He began to move his arm back. I laughed, "And you are as thick as two short planks! You are going to take a swing at a Commando! You would be flat on your back before it got halfway to me. Act your age and not your cap size." I shook my head and said, loudly, "I feel sorry for you chaps. You have a leader who is about as much use as a chocolate fireguard!" I saw smirks as I brushed past the white-faced Squadron Leader.

I put him from my mind as I began to organise myself. We were on ordinary rations again but we still made the most of our last night in Strasbourg. After the meal, Fletcher organized a card school. I saw that Sam White wisely stayed out of it. He sat with Hewitt, Hay and Polly. They were all interested in Sam's late decision to join up.

"You know you could have sat out the last few months. You could have joined a headquarters section and had a safe and cushy war. Why on earth you felt the need to join us head cases is beyond me, Sam."

He smiled at Hewitt, "One day I want to have kids of my own. I didn't want them to grow up and ask me what I did in the war and I said something like, oh I translated at the peace conference. When I am back at school and meeting parents at parents' evenings I want to be able to look the dads in the eyes. I want to know I did my bit. It is my country and I want to fight for it."

Bill said, "I admire that but four of the lads who came with you will never have kids. Perhaps it would have been better if they had stayed at home and been the great dads I know they would have been."

"Perhaps." I could see he was not convinced.

As I had expected Fletcher ended up the biggest winner from the card school. It galled Gordy for we both knew that Fletcher wasn't cheating but he knew how to win and Gordy could never figure out how.

We were all packed and ready to go by 0900 but there was no sign of our visitor. Warrant Officer Peters came to speak with us before we left. "We will miss you blokes. I know that we are doing something that needs to be done but transporting supplies doesn't match up to what you Commandos did. When the war is over I can go home and tell my kids about what you did. I mean we don't know the details but Flight Sergeant Harris told us where you were dropped." He shook his head. "You got back twice!"

"It is what we do, Warrant Officer and we are grateful to you and your lads for all that you have done."

"And as long as we are here sir, we will tend those graves."

"Thank you for that. I know they will be interred in a Commonwealth grave at the end of the war but it is good to know that someone will remember them."

"Here they are sir."

I turned around and saw a jeep and two lorries at the gate. Warrant Officer Peters saluted, "Cheerio sir."

I held out my hand, "Take care Warrant Officer."

My back was to the lorries and Lieutenant Poulson said, "Sir, it is Major Foster."

I turned and saw that Major Foster was the passenger in the jeep. I wondered what this said about the hunt for the spy.

"Better get the lorries loaded with the gear as soon as they reach us, Sergeant Major. The Lieutenant and I will go inside with the major and have a chat."

Toppy had a big grin on his face. He strode over to me and pumped my hand. "You cannot begin to know how much the Americans are singing your praises. Major Politho had the last mission down as a suicide job. I knew that you would get it done."

"You knew about it?" We entered the hangar which was marginally warmer than the outside.

"After the event so to speak. I was in Paris when he arrived. I was there to tell them that we had caught our spy and so, as you were in the air by then, he was able to tell me the rough details. I was with him when the news came through that you had not only succeeded, you had actually got out. By air!" He shook his head. "After all these years I should not be surprised but I am."

"A spy sir?" The Lieutenant was a good play actor.

We both looked at Lieutenant Poulson. Major Foster said, "Of course. You did not know. There is no harm now I suppose. After all, I was under suspicion."

"You sir?"

"Start at the beginning, Major."

We sat down and the Major lit a cigarette, "There was a spy in Combined Headquarters. Everyone was under suspicion apart from Sergeant Tancraville, the Major's fiancée. That was why we brought in Captain Ferguson and Sergeant Wilkinson." He looked at me and shook his head, "It was maddening. I knew it wasn't me but, like the other innocent people, I couldn't prove it. It wasn't as though we knew the moment the enemy had learned of the operations. They infiltrated a couple of spy catchers and they caught her."

"Her?"

"You won't believe who it was. It was Doris. You know the blonde with the red lips! Susan's friend."

"But she was, quite literally, the dumb blonde."

"And that is why the German spy used her. Remember how she was keen to be on the arm of an officer?" I nodded. Toppy had been the target of her amorous advances. "Well, this spy dressed up as a colonel and wined and dined her. He was a smooth-talking Irishman and he played the part of a colonel of intelligence. He was clever enough not to be seen near Whitehall. Poor Doris thought he was doing the same job as she was. He spoke of the operations she dealt with as though he was privy to them himself. She never questioned the fact that she never saw him near other intelligence officers. That is how they caught them both. Doris was proud of her new man. One of the spy catchers was a woman. She took Susan's desk and listened when Doris spoke of her love life. It didn't take long to realise who the spy was. They then had to prove it and catch him. They were both arrested when they were in bed together."

"What will happen to them?"

"Doris gave away secrets. Of course, she was duped but she will have to go to prison. At least she won't be shot. The Irishman will. He comes from Northern Ireland; he is IRA. So Susan is back on normal duties. She came out of this well. She has been given a section of her own to run. I am afraid she will no longer be your liaison." He stubbed out his cigarette. "Anyway, we are sending you and your team north. You will be working under Monty again. We are crossing the Rhine in the middle of March. You will be inserted before the push to secure a couple of major crossroads. The 6th Airborne will also be going in. Monty has Finally, learned to appreciate what you bring to a campaign. You two will come with me in the jeep. I can brief you on the way north. My driver will travel in the lorries."

"How long will it take?"

"Oh we will have to stop a couple of times but we should be there before midnight!"

The thought of driving in a jeep for eight hours did not fill me with joy!

Even though he had the canvas top up I wore my greatcoat and contemplated donning my snowsuit! We put the Bergens and weapons in the lorry and headed out of the gate to head north. "Where are we heading, sir?"

"Rheinberg, Lieutenant. It is more than two hundred and fifty miles north."

"Right, Major, what exactly do we have to do?"

He handed me a map. There were two circles. "There is a forested area just on the other side of the Rhine from Rheinberg. You are going to cross the river in boats and make your way through the forest to a place called Schermbeck. There is a crossroads there. It is where the road which crosses the canal and the Lippe meets the road heading east. When we begin to cross the river we expect the Germans first to use the crossroads to reinforce the front and second to try to hold us there. The forest is your sort of terrain. A small group of skilled men such as you lead, could hold the enemy up. You could disrupt their attempts to counterattack."

"That sounds a bit easy, Toppy. Looking at this map it is just ten miles from the river to the crossroads. We will have air superiority and from the Germans, we have seen so far the odds on them being a good unit are slim. What is the catch?"

He sighed and lit a cigarette, one handed, "The catch is, Tom, that you will then leapfrog ahead of the army and secure the other crossroads between there and their ultimate target."

"Berlin?"

"Probably."

I looked at the map. "That is over three hundred miles."

"I know."

"And the Russians are almost at Berlin now!"

"In which case, your job will be over sooner rather than later."

"This is ridiculous."

"You only have yourself to blame. You have been so successful that the brass think you can do anything. We learned, with Market Garden, that a few determined men behind the lines could achieve great things. You won't be alone. The 6th Airborne will be north of you doing exactly the same. They will be deeper in Germany and they will be dropped by parachute. We are also sending in Frankforce. Three hundred SAS with jeeps and the like will be even deeper in Germany doing just what you are going to do. You will both stop the Germans being able to consolidate. When Monty hits them he will use better armour than the Germans have. Their offensive in the Ardennes stripped the Germans of some of their best armour. However, they are still able to dig in at strategic crossroads and slow us up. We know that they still have the 655th Heavy Anti-Tank battalion. Thirty heavily armoured tank destroyers could slow us down. Patton and Monty are going to use speed this time. Once we are over the river we don't stop."

I looked at the map. It showed the river, the roads, the forest and the towns. What it didn't show were the defences. "When we crossed the Rhine at Strasbourg we came through the German defences. They had machine-guns and sentries. They will have the same close by Rheinberg, surely?"

"They do, but there are gaps. The plan is for you to slip over and through their lines undetected. This time you won't have to take explosives with you. You will travel lighter."

I was not convinced. It wasn't as though we could just slip into the forest. It was a good half a mile from the river. We had to get through open country or towns. That would be tricky.

I was silent for a while. I glanced out of the jeep. All along the road, it was a sea of olive. The Americans were building up their forces.

The Battle of the Bulge had been costly but the Americans had been able to replace the lost armour and men whereas the Germans had not.

"Look, Tom, this is not happening now or even in the next few days. You will have time to do a recce. We don't mind if you choose the place you will cross the river. The only thing that Monty wants is for you to be at the crossroads twenty-four hours before the offensive begins."

Behind me, Lieutenant Poulson asked, "Do you mind if I have a look at the maps sir?"

I handed them back to him, "Be my guest."

We drove in silence for a while. "Have you seen Susan then?"

"Briefly, before I left. Hugo and Wilkinson have been attached to Combined Ops for the duration. It was thought that your sergeant could provide extra security and Hugo has proved invaluable. He liaised with Major Politho. The Americans were impressed by him. It has made the communications smoother. Hugo is an affable chap."

"And their problem?" Polly did not know about the American spy.

"They still have it. I am afraid that the Germans will know that Patton and Monty are coming."

I shot him a look, "But not us?"

"Not you. To be fair there is such a build-up that they must know we are coming."

Lieutenant Poulson showed that he had been listening as well as studying the map. "He is right sir, it might just work. For the first time, we won't be alone. The SAS is just as good as we are and we know that the paras are too. And I have been looking at the map. If we cross the Rhine we can keep going up either the Lippe or the canal. They can't guard every inch of the banks can they sir? In fact, sir, we could get much closer to the forest that way."

"And, another thing Tom, Jerry released water to flood the area through which we have to cross. That means that the current is not as strong as it might normally be. The Lieutenant's plan might just work."

I was silent. I held my hand for the maps and the lieutenant handed them to me. I saw what Polly meant. It would take a couple of hours to paddle up the Lippe. I recognised that as a better option. There was more cover. It would take us closer to our target. The trick would be to avoid detection.

"Tom, we have just completed Operation Veritable and Operation Grenade. It took three weeks but we now have the Rhine under our guns. Monty is cautious, you know that. He has assembled so many big guns that he will clear the opposition from the banks of the Rhine. The Engineers assure Monty that they can get a pontoon bridge over the Rhine in under six hours. That is what you need to buy us; six hours. Stop reinforcements coming through the crossroads for six hours."

It sounded simple enough but I knew that it was not.

Chapter 10

The journey was a nightmare of clogged roads through the remnants of the German-engineered flood. We reached our new billet at eleven. Our new home was a large barn on the southern side of the town. As we discovered, the next morning, we were just a couple of hundred yards from a small lake, the Haferbruchsee. The farmhouse had been destroyed in the last offensive. We had eaten while on the road and we just collapsed into our blankets, grateful for a roof.

Major Foster left us the next morning. "The lorries and their drivers are yours until you leave for the river. Your dinghies will be here in the next twenty-four hours. I am taking the jeep to Antwerp. That is where I will be based. The operation will begin in two weeks' time. That should give you and your chaps time to familiarise yourself with the other shore and the boats." He pointed to the Haferbruchsee, "You can use the lake. There is an island in the middle."

I smiled, "This looks remarkably well planned, Toppy! It isn't like you to be so thoughtful!"

He shook his head, "Cheeky bugger! I think I preferred it when you had to yes sir, no sir to me!"

When he had left us I had Sergeant Major Barker organize our new accommodation. Lieutenant Poulson and I took the maps and one of the lorries. I needed to put my own eyes on the river. There was still a large area of the plain which was flooded and there were few tracks we could use. We were forced to use the main road and that inevitably took us close to the first of the jump-off areas. That meant roadblocks and questions. It took almost two hours to cover the twelve or so miles to the nearest point of the river. Büderich was just one and a half miles from the Lippe. I would have liked to have been closer but I could not find a road which would allow us to get near to the river. We left the lorry and walked across the boggy fields to the river bank.

As we neared the river we heard a Canadian voice shout, "I would keep your head down, sir. They have snipers across the river."

The machine-gun was well hidden. We ducked and made our way to the back of it. There was an eight-man section there.

"Thanks for the warning, sergeant. Do you mind if have a look-see from here."

"Be my guest sir but I will tell you what you will see. Nothing! Zip! Of course, that doesn't mean that the Krauts aren't there. They are. It took two men wounded to find that out."

I used the glasses to scan the woods opposite. The Canadian was almost right. The Germans were hard to see but when you knew what to look for then you recognised the signs. I saw at least two MG 42 machine-guns. I moved the glasses to look further north and I saw the mouth of the Lippe. I handed them to Lieutenant Poulson.

The Canadian saw my Commando flash. "Say were you the guys with us on the road to Antwerp?"

"Yes, Sergeant, I believe we were."

"You did good work. Are you guys going over there?"

I smiled, "You know I can't tell you that."

He nodded, "It is no secret that we are going to assault it though, sir. Monty is lining all of his ducks up again. He sure is cautious!"

"Perhaps that is a good thing. It will save lives."

"Sir, I just want this over with and then get back to Calgary! I have a life I put on hold. I am not like you, sir, I am no regular."

"Neither am I, sergeant, I joined up in 1940." Lieutenant Poulson handed me the glasses. "We'll be off. You take care sergeant and keep your head down."

"I will sir. I didn't come all the way from Normandy just to fall at the last hurdle!"

As we headed back to the lorry I said, "Well?"

"If it is night time then Jerry in those woods won't see us, sir. The current would do most of the work. I reckon it is about half a mile, may be a little more, to the mouth of the Lippe. We bring the boats in the afternoon and then carry them to the river after dark. It should only take an hour to get them from the lorry to the water."

As we neared the lorry I said, "We could cut that distance if we drove across the field."

"We might get stuck, sir."

I grinned, "Then when we get stuck we carry them. It isn't as though we will have to move the lorry is it?"

Once back at the barn I saw that the men had made it cosy. I couldn't see Fletcher, Emerson and Beaumont and the other lorry had gone. I looked accusingly at Sergeant Major Barker and he shrugged, "I have sent them foraging sir. I hope you don't mind!"

"Just so long as they aren't escorted by a couple of MPs when they return."

When they did come back it was with a couple of oil drums. We could cook again! They had also managed to buy some food to augment the rations which Major Foster had brought in the lorries. I went with Gordy and the lieutenant to examine the lake.

"It is a while since we have practised getting in and out of boats. We can't replicate doing it under fire but we can make sure it is as slick as possible We have time, over the next ten days to make certain the boats are well balanced and the crew of each boat know each other. I am thinking about three boats. One for each of us."

"Sounds good, sir and I don't think we need to worry about landing under fire."

"Why not lieutenant?"

"Because if it is under fire then the mission will have failed before we start. As far as I understand it we have to get ashore and inland without anyone being the wiser."

"You are right and that means burning our boats, quite literally, behind us. We will have to puncture and sink them."

Gordy coughed, "Isn't it about time you told the lads the mission sir? We have worked out we are going across the Rhine in boats but that is about it."

"You are right Gordy. After we have eaten I will brief the men. You keep me straight."

"Don't worry sir, you have had a lot on your plate lately. We understand."

Once back at the barn Lieutenant Poulson and I went through the maps and photographs. It was vital that we reached the crossroads without being seen. We needed the edge. I could imagine the shock if the Germans tried to reinforce their front and found themselves under fire. "I want a mortar. The rifle grenade is a good weapon but the mortar is more reliable."

"The major said we could have whatever we needed. Supplies are flooding in through Antwerp now."

"Then make sure we have ammo for the Thompsons. We didn't pick up any German stuff on the last raid."

Polly laughed, "I think we had a bit on our mind, sir!"

"I know. And it is a shame we can't use the snowsuits. They were the best cover we have had."

"At least we won't have to parachute in. We were lucky the last two times. It could have gone horribly wrong."

"I know."

By the time Gordy shouted, "Grub up!" The two of us had it clear in our own minds what we had to do.

After we had eaten we gathered around the table in the middle of the barn. "As you know we have a new mission. We are going to paddle up the Lippe river and then make our way through German lines to hold a crossroads. Our task is quite simple. We have to stop Jerry reinforcing the Rhine front for six hours. We will not be alone. The Paras and the SAS will also be out there doing the same. The R.A.F. will use their Typhoons and Mossies to strafe and bomb the roads but we all know that determined men can still get through such deterrents."

I saw them nodding. "We will be using three rubber dinghies. We take them in the lorries to the river and paddle down the Rhine and then up the Lippe. We have about two and a half miles to paddle and then another eight to run through the forest. We have one night to get there and then the offensive begins. Each boat will be a separate team. If we lose contact with one another we do not wait. We get to Schermbeck. Even if only one team makes it, then we hold."

Lance Sergeant Beaumont showed that he was a thinker, "We want to keep the crossroads intact sir?"

"We do, Lance Sergeant. We will need it for our amour. This is the start of the race to Berlin."

I let them take that in. Berlin meant the end of the European war. Lieutenant Poulson had said that he would stay in after the war but I was not sure if any of the others would.

"Anyway as soon as the boats come we practice all day and, when we have it right then we do it at night. Once we have mastered that we do it blindfold. We have been given the luxury of time to train. I do not intend to waste it."

The dinghies, all four of them, did not arrive until noon the next day. The engineers who delivered them were apologetic. "Not our fault sir. There were so many ships to be unloaded that these were pushed back."

"That is all right, sergeant. They are here now."

We manhandled the boats carefully. We had a spare but I did not want to risk a puncture. When they were taken from the lorries I saw that we could, if we had to, just take two of them. That would mean we would be a little overcrowded. We carried them to the lake and tethered them. I divided them into their teams.

"My team, Beaumont, Davis, White and Foster. Lieutenant Poulson's team, Fletcher, Hewitt, McLean and Betts. Betts and McLean, you have the Bren. Sergeant Major Barker's team, Hay, Emerson, Richardson and Ashcroft. Richardson and Ashcroft will take the mortar."

We had ensured that the rookies were spread out and the experience was too. I saw that Beaumont and Fletcher were unhappy at being split up. They would have to learn to live with it.

"You have one hour to work all the wrinkles out of your team. Find the best balance. In an hour we have a three-lap race around the island!" We had decided this was the best way to approach the mission. Make this part competitive. It would highlight any weaknesses in the teams and it was better to discover that here rather than on the Lippe under fire.

I took my team to our boat. I shouted, "I name this one Lucky Lady!" I saw that the others had been going to do the same.

The new boys look mystified. Davis said, "We had a German E-Boat. We used it for missions and we called her the Lucky Lady."

"Davis and Beaumont you take the front. White and Foster the rear. I will be the rudder. The key to this is a clean stroke delivered together. Right, let's try to get aboard without tipping it up. As I recall that is never easy."

As if to prove the point Big George MacLean was too eager and, as he stepped in, he slipped. He fell backwards and the boat slid across the water. He splashed spectacularly into the lake. Luckily Scouse had hold of the rope. "Typical Geordies! Always too much in a hurry!"

I smiled at my crew, "See!"

Beaumont and Davis climbed aboard together from the stern. Once seated Beaumont turned, "Right you lads, come in together."

Once they were in I took my paddle and stepped into the stern. I used the paddle to push us away from the bank.

Beaumont said, "How about a song sir to help with the rhythm?"

"What do you have in mind?"

"There can only be one sir, the Eton Boat Song."

"Of course. You start and we will all pick it up."

__Jolly boating weather,__
__And a hay harvest breeze,__
__Blade on the feather,__

Shade off the trees,
Swing, swing together,
With your bodies between your knees,
Swing, swing together,
With your bodies between your knees.
Rugby may be more clever,
Harrow may make more row,
But we'll row for ever,
Steady from stroke to bow,
And nothing in life shall sever,
The chain that is round us now,
And nothing in life shall sever,
The chain that is round us now.

Others will fill our places,
Dressed in the old light blue,
We'll recollect our races,
We'll to the flag be true,
And youth will be still in our faces,
When we cheer for an Eton crew,
And youth will be still in our faces,
When we cheer for an Eton crew.

Twenty years hence this weather,
May tempt us from office stools,
We may be slow on the feather,
And seem to the boys old fools,
But we'll still swing together,
And swear by the best of schools,
But we'll still swing together,
And swear by the best of schools.

It was easy to pick up and actually helped us. Beaumont had a fine voice. We didn't pick all the words up but that didn't matter. We did two circuits of the island and then I said, "Let's stop and see if we need any adjustment." We slid into the bank. I grabbed a branch to hold us there. "Are you all happy with your seat? If you want to swap then you can."

"No sir. It's fine."

"Where did you learn that song, Beaumont?"

"Eton of course sir. I did two terms there."

Davis said, "You went to Eton. I thought that was a posh school."

"It is." He sighed, "Father had a good business. He had, however, too much invested in the stock market. The Spanish Civil War saw him lose a packet. We weren't poor but the school had to go. I didn't mind but I had some good chums there. We had been at prep school together."

"Right, let's go again. Foster and White, if you turned the paddle after you take it out of the water it causes less drag and less splash. Keep it smooth. The song helps."

By the time the hour was up, they were all confident about their stroke. I had the boats beached and we stepped ashore. "Any problems?"

Poulson and Barker shook their heads. "No sir. It took a couple of laps to get the balance right but we are happy now."

"Good, then it is time for the race."

"What are the rules, sir?"

"Rules, Sarn't Major?"

"Yes sir, rules."

"I will count one, two, three, go and we run to the boat, launch them and then row around the island three times. We finish up here at the starting point."

"We can sail as close to the island as we like, sir?"

I smiled. My men were competitive. "Of course, Sarn't Major, of course, I should point out that there are underwater obstacles close to the island. If you puncture your vessel then you have to repair it!"

"Righto, sir."

"Any questions, lads?"

They chorused, "Sir, no sir!"

They were ready.

"One, two, three, go!"

Gordy wanted to win. He and his team were in their boat and on the water first. Lieutenant Poulson and my team were neck and neck in second. What I had done was to check the wind. It was from the east and was quite strong. I intended to use it.

Jolly boating weather,
And a hay harvest breeze,
Blade on the feather,
Shade off the trees,

Swing, swing together,
With your bodies between your knees.
Swing, swing together,
With your bodies between your knees.

We began to draw away from Lieutenant Poulson. I saw that our paddles went in as one. The other two teams were slightly off. It was not much but it meant we were faster. The song helped too. I saw white around the blade of Emerson and Ashcroft's paddles. In contrast, Billy Hay's was as smooth as my team's. We were catching Gordy. He had a length and clear water on us but I was not worried. When we reached the end of the first lap the clear water was down to two feet. He glanced over his shoulder. A sure sign that he was worried. I kept us directly behind him as we headed west. The wind was from behind and we took it from Gordy. Lucky Lady closed with the back of his dinghy. He exhorted his men to paddle harder. That was a mistake and they became more ragged. As we turned to head south I used my paddle to steer to the starboard of Gordy and we began to overtake the rear of their dinghy.

Gordy's team were paddling far harder than we were but they were not as smooth.

Jolly boating weather,
And a hay harvest breeze,
Blade on the feather,
Shade off the trees,
Swing, swing together,
With your bodies between your knees,
Swing, swing together,
With your bodies between your knees.

We drew level with Ashcroft and Richardson. They glanced over and Richardson missed his stroke. We began to overtake them. As we came around to the start position we were ahead. With one lap to go, I knew that we would win. My men were singing and that showed they were not out of breath. The last lap was a victory parade. I saw that Lieutenant Poulson was now catching Gordy. The two of them were desperate not to come last.

We pulled in and were out of the boat as the two crews paddled towards us. My men all cheered for one boat or the other. In the end, it was a dead heat but both crews looked wrecked.

Beaumont said, cheekily, "We could go again if you want a rematch!"

He received a murderous look from Gordy and Lieutenant Poulson just laughed and gasped, "That is all right Lance Sergeant. We know when we are beaten!"

The last few hours were spent in launching the dinghies and then paddling and landing at the island. Now that the men were comfortable with their paddling they were able to focus on making a good and safe landing. The two men at the bows watched for obstacles and the second two were able to use their paddles to control the approach. By the time the light had gone from the sky, we were all exhausted. We were fit men but we were using muscles we did not work as hard, normally. I had them carry the boats back to the barn. They were as valuable any weapon we might take.

That evening, after we had eaten, they shared their experiences. Sam and Tom approached me, "Sir, we have that song in our heads. We can't get rid of it."

"Good. When we row up the Lippe you will not be able to sing it you know."

"Yes sir, we know."

The next morning would be more of the same but I was giving them the afternoon off. I wanted to practice night launches and landings. In the end, it proved serendipitous for Major Foster arrived just after we had eaten lunch. I could see from his face, that he was troubled.

I turned to the men, "Have a couple of hours off. If you want to go into town for a beer then that is fine by me." I saw their faces light up, "Just a beer mind!" They all left the Lieutenant and me to get washed and changed. "Problem?"

"Patton has crossed the Rhine!"

"What? But it is not scheduled for another nine days!"

He shrugged, "Publicly he is saying that his men found the Ludendorff Railway Bridge at Remagen still standing. He is pouring men across."

"And privately?"

"Sam Politho reckons that he does not want to lose out to Monty. He intends to beat him to Berlin."

"Does that mean we go in early?"

"Only a day or two but the ultimate objective has changed. We are going to head north towards the Baltic once we have broken through.

Monty wants to deny the Russians Denmark. They are moving far faster than we are. Their generals appear even more competitive than ours do."

"So, when do we go?"

"The attack will begin before dawn on the 23rd of March. You and your men will cross the Rhine on the evening of the 21st. You need to be there on the 22nd. Monty wants no chances taking."

"So, four days then?"

He nodded, "That isn't a problem is it?"

"No, we should be up to speed by then."

"You need to take your radio. You can warn us of any problems."

I frowned, "We have not tried the boats laden yet. I was not certain we would need the radio."

"We need it, Tom."

"Right, we'll try it out tomorrow."

He nodded, "I will be back again on the 21st. I will come and see you off."

"Right sir. Well, we had better get on with it then!"

After he had gone I said, "I don't fancy risking our radio while we are practising. Let's take the lorry and see what we can scrounge."

"Sir, you sound just like Fletcher!"

"I know. He is a bad influence."

We drove around the various army camps. There were dozens of them We struck lucky at the camp of the Black Watch. They had a radio they had cannibalised for the workable parts. It was roughly the same size as ours and almost the same weight. I saw the question forming on the Captain's lips and then he saw our shoulder flashes, "I was going to ask a wee stupid question but seeing who you are I will just nod and say, help yerself."

"We appreciate that."

"Are you on this little jaunt too then?"

I nodded, "We'll be with you."

"Good, then I am happier already. I hear, from Intelligence, that there are two German Airborne Divisions ahead of us. We ran into them at Falaise."

"That is useful intel, thanks."

As we loaded the broken radio I reflected that we already knew that. Major Foster had given us a breakdown. The 85th Infantry Division was not a problem but the Heavy anti-tank battalion, 47 Panzer and the Airborne were.

When we compared the two radios there was barely any difference between them. Fletcher could carry the one we had been given and if it received a dousing then there would be no loss. They came back in good humour and I was pleased I had given them leave. There would be no more beer now until we had finished this mission and that would be at the end of the war!

Chapter 11

There was now an urgency to our work. The deadline had been brought forward and the men were competitive. They wanted us to make the advances that Patton had made. It was good that we practised night landings. We realised it would be hard to follow each other. It was Sam White who came up with the solution.

"Sir, if we paint a white line on the back of each dinghy then we will be able to see it but the enemy won't."

We tried it with the spare dinghy and it worked. That would make our passage up the river easier. It was as well we had the broken radio for it took some work to balance it. We had to rearrange Lieutenant Poulson's boat so that Fletcher steered and the Lieutenant paddled. It worked out quite well as Hewitt was about the same build and weight as the Lieutenant. By the 20th we were confident that we could land without having a disaster.

We spent the last day preparing our war faces. We all had the equipment we would need to take. Ashcroft and Betts would operate the mortar. They had just one day at the practice range. It was not enough but it was all that we had. We spent the afternoon of the 20th loading and paddling our dinghies around the lake. We used everything but the real radio. It was not as easy and I estimated it would add an hour to our journey. We would still have time to reach our target. We had our camouflage nets. They would be invaluable.

Major Foster arrived with the latest intelligence. "Patton is racing through Germany. Huge numbers of Germans will be cut off in the Ruhr. Monty is not happy. He and Patton do not get along. He is expecting everything to go smoothly."

I shook my head, "He can wish all he likes but we both know that all it takes is for a German version of us to decide to be belligerent and we could get held up for a week."

He nodded, "You are right. Just do your best." He gave me a sad look, "Tom, don't think I don't appreciate all that you have done for me and our country. Just do me a favour, will you? Keep your head down. Susan told me that you have a wedding planned at the end of this nightmare and I would like to be there. I remember when you were in the Loyal Lancashires. There was something about you even then. I recognised that there was a diamond hiding beneath that roughhewn exterior. Stop going first. There are young lads in your section now. Let them take the chances."

I shook my head, "You don't understand do you, Toppy? It is the older ones who owe it to the young lads to take the risks for them. We have experience. I have lost two young lads because they didn't keep their heads down. When I started in the Commandos I was able to watch others and follow. I learned. These young lads are thrown in at the deep end. The war is nastier now than the last time you fought, on the retreat through Belgium."

He looked aggrieved, "That hurts Tom."

"I know. But it is still the truth and we both know it. Let me run my war that way I have always done it. I will get the job done. I have no intention of standing Susan up. Mum wants grandkids and I am her best shot."

"I know."

"What about the next part? What happens after we are relieved?"

"There will be five jeeps brought to Schermbeck. You will then leapfrog the main column and hold all the crossroads between there and the Baltic. We will have fresh supplies for you. Each time you are relieved there will be more supplies for you."

"That is honest of you, at any rate. You know that fifteen of us are setting out tomorrow but fifteen of us won't reach the Baltic."

He looked at the ground, "You might."

"Honesty, Toppy, you owe us that. Are these lads worth sacrificing so that Monty will get a knighthood or a victory parade? I don't think so. The Russians are almost at Berlin. My lads have dealt with the terror weapon. If Monty dawdled to the Baltic would it make a difference? Only to Monty."

"You have become a cynic, Tom."

"And that comes from the people I have worked with." I shook his hand. "When you were in the Loyal Lancashires I admired you more than you could know. You have changed. You have not become a Colonel Fleming yet but you are damned close. Toppy, look in the mirror."

I did not enjoy hurting him but I was not certain I would ever see him again. The cathedral and the dead who would never come home had affected me. I had to be true to them and true to myself. Once he had gone I gathered my men around me.

"We are on the last leg. The powers that be have great faith in us. When we have held this crossroads we do the same until we reach the Baltic. I am not happy about it and I told the Major so. I want all of us to survive. Do not take risks. You new chaps, you have done well. Two of your comrades died because they kept their heads up instead of ducking. Duck!"

That made them all laugh.

"We all know that our enemies are tricky. If they surrender then search them. If they are wounded then make sure they do not have access to a gun or a grenade. Until we get back to Blighty then do not relax and never think that it is all over. Until we are back in our homes in England, it isn't!"

Our two drivers had been more than helpful. I called them over while the men packed their Bergens. "You lads have done a first-rate job, Tomorrow afternoon we want you to drive us as close as you can to the river. I know it is boggy and there is a good chance that your vehicles could get stuck…"

Private Carstairs held up his hand, "Sir, it is no secret that you are going behind the German lines. I think the two of us can cope with getting two lorries out of some mud! We are honoured to be working with you. When this is all over and I am in the pub with my mates, this will be a story I am proud to tell."

I shook my head, "But what story?"

He nodded at my medals, "That story, sir. We kept our ears open and heard your lads talking about what you did. You are proper soldiers. Me and Harry here, we just drive. You? You make a difference. Don't worry about the lorries. We will get you as close as is humanly possible."

We loaded the three dinghies on one lorry and the men and Bergens went on the other. Carstairs was as good as his word. He drove until the wheels began spinning, "That is it, sir. End of the line."

I saw that we were just a hundred and eighty yards from the river, "And this will do."

We sat and waited for dark. There would be German observers. They would be laughing at the two lorries which managed to get stuck in the boggy ground. As darkness fell the men ran to the river and dropped their bags and equipment. We then manhandled the three dinghies to the Rhine. I said nothing to the two drivers but my handshake was heartfelt. They had saved us time and effort. The mission had more chance of success thanks to two drivers. They were part of the team just as Flight

Lieutenant Ryan and Flight Sergeant Harris had been. We could not have achieved what we did without them.

Our practise paid off and we loaded the boats efficiently and, more importantly, silently. Mine was the lead boat. We had the least weight. The newly acquired mortar was the heaviest item we carried. The current was faster than I had expected. That had been the one thing we could not replicate in the small lake. I steered us diagonally across the river so that we would take advantage of the power of the river and keep us on our way. I glanced back. The other two boats were still on station.

On the far bank, all that I could see was trees. There were Germans there. They were watching the river but, as the river was more than four hundred yards wide at this point, I hoped that we were just a shadow passing downstream. Beaumont was giving the lead with the rhythm. He had them digging in with a beat between each stroke. This was the easy part of the journey. Here the river was wide and the current with us. The Lippe would be narrow and we would be fighting it until we disembarked.

We passed the mooring dock where, in more peaceful times, river barges would have tied up. Now it was just an empty space of water leading to a lock and then the canal which paralleled the Lippe. From the map, I knew that the river was just on the other side. I stopped paddling and used my oar like a rudder to take us to the gap which appeared before us. On the north bank of the Lippe lay Wesel. When the offensive began that would be the southern target of our strike. There were just shadows. As we turned and Beaumont changed the stroke I caught a few words of German. There were sentries on the north bank. I could not see them. There were trees there.

After a few more strokes I saw a fork in the river. I took the right hand one. I risked a glance astern. This was not the place to become separated. The tree line stopped and I felt exposed. Here the river was at its widest. I also suspected that it was quite shallow. The current was not as strong as I had expected and it felt like we were making good time. We had our rhythm and we were heading upstream and were undetected. It did not take long for the small river to narrow. That brought the return of the trees. We had our first danger when we passed under the road and rail bridges. They would have sentries on them. At some point, they would walk across them. I just hoped that they would not be looking down. As we slipped under them I heard, drifting down, the sound of conversation. A glow, like a huge firefly, spiralled down and hissed into the water, twenty feet to our right. It was a cigarette end. Our training had paid off. Our fifteen paddles made not a sound.

Once we were beyond the bridges we then had a couple of tortuous miles where the river twisted and turned through, what I hoped was deserted countryside. I began counting the loops. The first was the largest. When we came to the fourth loop we would disembark and hike the last seven and a half miles to the crossroads. My glances astern told me that, even though they had more weight than we did, the other two boats were keeping up. Just before the last loop, we passed within forty yards of the canal. I heard voices on barges and the sound of engines as the Germans took advantage of the cover of night to move goods up the river. When the offensive began they would be the target of dive bombers.

I was feeling the burn in my shoulders as we paddled up the last loop. I saw the trees, just two hundred and fifty yards away. We had that far to run exposed, and then we would have forest all the way to Schermbeck.

"Beaumont!"

He and White stopped paddling and my paddle guided us to bump into the bank. White and Beaumont leapt ashore and held us close by the two painters. I jumped out with my Colt ready. I saw no one. Davis and Foster began passing the Bergens and weapons to me. I stacked them on the bank. When that was done they stepped out. The three of us took stones which lay on the bank and put them with the paddles at the bottom of the dinghy. Then Beaumont and White punctured the Lucky Lady with their daggers. They pushed her out into the current and she settled lower into the water. She would sink at some point but it would be downstream from where we landed.

I hefted my Bergen and took out my compass. While the other two boats disembarked I waved Davis and Foster towards the woods. It took longer for the others to disembark. They had a radio, a mortar and a Bren gun. They still managed it quickly and their boats were pushed into the current. I could not see the Lucky Lady. Either she had sunk already or was far downstream. I pointed to Bill Hay and he nodded. He was the rear guard. I hurried after Davis and Foster. They were waiting for me at the edge. Davis pointed with his sniper rifle. There was a track. I checked the compass and it was heading in the right direction. I took the lead with Davis at my right shoulder. We set off at a brisk pace. It was not quite a run but it was faster than double time. I wanted to cover the seven and a half miles in under two hours. It had taken us three to reach this point. We had a whole day to hide up before the show began.

This was not the thick forest it had once been. Aeroplanes had dropped bombs and others were shot down to disappear into the forest. This was on the flight path to the Ruhr. Pilots would jettison bombs on the way home and this was the area where stricken birds would crash. Two miles into the forest we saw one such dead bird. It was a Flying Fortress. As we passed I could see that the Germans had stripped her of any metal that they could re-use. The guns had gone, just her name remained, '***Rita Hayworth***'. I could not help but wonder what had happened to the crew. If they had bailed out then they could be prisoners of war somewhere. On the other hand, their bodies could lie within the cannibalised carcass of the bomber.

We had a road to cross close by Drevenback. The village was three hundred yards away but we took no chances. With two men watching to the north with silenced Colts levelled, we sprinted across the road and then continued our woodland walk. I used time as a marker of distance. After an hour I stopped, for we were in a denser section of woods and I risked my torch. I checked the map and compass. In half a mile we would have to leave the woods, albeit briefly, and head across open fields. Farmers had left a strip of trees and hedges as a field boundary. We would have to follow that until we came to the wood near to the Lippe. We were under two miles from our destination.

It was less than half a mile of open ground we had to cover but there was a farmhouse between us and the river. I felt exposed as I led my men at a run across the open ground. I spied the trees ahead and to the north of me. The field had just been ploughed and was not easy to negotiate. Fletcher would be struggling with the radio. When we reached the thin treeline I did not stop but plunged along it. After a hundred yards I stopped to allow the others to catch up. Bill Hay arrived. I held up my thumb and he gave me the okay sign. We had not been seen. I was aware that we were moving more slowly as we came to the last obstacle. It was a farm track which headed south to the river before looping back to the farm which lay on the other side of the woods in which we would be sheltering. It was 0300 hours when we crossed it. I had no doubt the farmer and his family might be preparing to rise but they would not be using the track. Once across we headed into the forest. Inside its canopy of green, we were safe. I slowed us to a walk and we began to search for a campsite. I wanted to avoid paths. The last thing we needed was for a

German to stumble upon us. There was a patch of ground which rose to our left and I began to climb. I found a bare piece of ground behind some wild blackberry bushes. It was a perfect place to hide. In autumn it would be a popular place but there was not even a bud yet. I circled my arm to show that we had arrived.

I pointed to my shoulder and then at Lieutenant Poulson. He was in charge. I tapped Davis on the shoulder and we went back down the slope. I wanted to scout out the crossroads. We reached the edge of the trees and there were open fields. We had a mile of open country to scout. This time there were just two of us. With blackened faces and hands we would be hard to see. Wearing rubber-soled shoes, we were silent. We headed across the fields which, thankfully, had yet to be ploughed. I saw that they had cabbages in them. We were halfway across a field when I heard the vehicle. We stopped and crouched in the middle of the cabbage field. The vehicle was coming from the south and heading north. We now knew where the road was.

The edge of the field was marked with a hedge. It had a few gaps. I poked my head through one and looked south. I saw the river and the bridge. It was guarded. I could not see how many men were there but I saw the shadows of moving men and the barrel of a 20 mm cannon. We did not cross the road. The sentries at the bridge might see our movement. Instead, we ran north using it to shield us from the road. The hedge disappeared at one point and I saw that the road was a wide one. It was the main road. When we heard the sound of a lorry ahead, moving from east to west we dropped to the ground and began to crawl. It took ten minutes to reach the edge of the Wesel Road. We were at the crossroads. We wriggled up until we could peer beneath the bushes. I heard another lorry. I saw its wheels as it headed west. I could not see any guards. It was unprotected. I saw that there were three buildings around the crossroads. All had been hit by either shellfire or bombs. They were wrecked ruins. We could use them. We had seen enough. We retraced our steps and headed back to our camp.

The first hint of grey was in the east as MacLean whistled us in. I saw that the camouflage netting was up. There were fewer German aeroplanes now but all it would take was one and we would be in trouble. I waved over Gordy and Polly. "I have found the crossroads. We can use the wrecked buildings there. I think we can make it a strong point. They have guards at the bridge. I don't know how many. After we have secured the crossroads I will take my team and try to take them out. It will make our job easier."

Gordy nodded, "I have arranged the sentry rota sir. Fletcher has used the radio and told HQ that we are in position. He used a really short burst. If they do have anyone listening they wouldn't have been able to locate us."

"Good, then we get our heads down and wait out this day. As soon as we hear the barrage then we can open fire. With luck, the 1st Commando Brigade will be here by nightfall."

Beaumont brought me a cup of tea. "We could smell the smoke from the farm sir so we thought they wouldn't notice our little stove."

He was probably right and I could not undo it but I would have had just water. Having said that the hot tea was welcome.

"We used the rest of the water to make soup sir and put it in the Thermos. We have turned off the stove now."

I ate some dry rations and washed them down with the tea. I rolled up in a ball and fell asleep. They let me sleep until early afternoon. After I had rinsed out my mouth with water, Bill Hay reported to me. "Not much to be seen, sir. Some American bombers went over and we heard them dropping their load to the east. No sign of Jerry. We heard the sound of a convoy going up the road. We were surprised that they weren't attacked."

"I think they are going to save everything for tomorrow. The barrage will start at about 0300 hours and then the bombers will begin first thing in the morning. One thing you can say about Montgomery is that he is well prepared."

As darkness fell we took down the netting and prepared to leave. We had plenty of time to reach our objective. I wanted to be in position to tackle the bridge as soon as the artillery began. We had the advantage of knowing when it would start. The Germans would hear the shells and wonder what it meant. Their attention would be on the skies and not the ground. It was a merciless war we fought. One moment of inattention could cost you your life.

Davis and I led. We had ironed out the kinks the previous night. We shaved minutes off our journey. We headed diagonally across the last field to the apex of the two hedges. I waved Davis, Hay and Emerson forward. They scrambled through the hedge. If there were any Germans there then they would find and silence them. A few minutes later Davis returned, "All clear sir, and the road looks empty."

I led them through the hedge. I pointed to the nearest building. It faced west. "Gordy, your post. Set up the Bren and the mortar."

"Sir."

I pointed to the building on the east of the road, "Lieutenant Poulson, that is your little home from home. Watch the north and the east."

"Sir."

I took my section to the last building. It was forty yards south of the other two. It looked to have been a cottage. As we entered it I said, "White, you and Foster set up the rifle grenade to cover the road. Davis, go and recce the bridge. I need to know how many Germans are there."

"Sir."

"Beaumont, you and I will make this into a fort."

We scoured the building for anything which could be used for defence. Upstairs I found two mattresses and a bed frame. We used the bed and the chairs to protect us from the east and the south. We placed the mattresses to give us some protection from the north. There were two tables. We placed them so that they would act as emplacements. Our Thompsons would have to be our machine-guns. Finally, we laid out grenades so that they were within reach.

By the time we had finished Davis was back, "One 20 mm, sir, and one MG 42. There are eight men there, sir. There are two sandbagged emplacements on either side of the road. They have a German truck. I think they are using it as sleeping quarters."

"What about the south side of the bridge?"

"Another six men and two MG 42 machine-guns. I think there is a Kubelwagen there but they had disguised it with a camouflage net."

I looked at my watch. It was 2300 hours. "The three of us will leave at 0200 hours. I want to be in position before the bombardment begins. Four thousand artillery pieces should make quite a racket. They won't hear our grenades amongst that lot."

Sam White asked, "What do we do sir?"

"Wait here for us and be ready to give us covering fire if we come back hot."

We were like three interdependent fire points. Hewitt, Gordy and I had done something similar in the Ardennes. There the opposition had been S.S., Tigers and Panthers. I had to hope there was nothing as heavy as that. We just had mortars and a rifle grenade.

Beaumont said, "We'll have something to eat now. It is going to be a hard day ahead of us."

I grabbed my Thompson, "I will go and see how the others are faring. Take charge, Roger."

"Sir."

I ducked out of the back of the building and headed for Lieutenant Poulson. I saw as I approached that they had made it as secure as we had. John Hewitt said, "In here, sir. Duck under this beam!"

They had placed two beams across a partly destroyed wall. There was just enough space to crawl beneath. "How are things?"

"We have cannibalised the upstairs to make this stronger sir."

"I am taking Davis and Beaumont out to see if we can get rid of Jerry at the bridge. We will wait until the barrage starts. Fletcher, get on to HQ and give them the codeword." Just in case the Germans were listening we had been given a set of codewords. '*Jackpot*' meant we had the crossroads. "Then keep listening for traffic when the barrage has lifted."

"Sir."

"You will have to watch the road from the east."

"Yes sir, Bill and John are going out, later on, to set up a few booby traps. There are a couple of trees which Hay reckons he can bring down with a couple of grenades."

"Just make sure they aren't triggered early. Don't set them until the barrage begins."

"Right sir."

I ducked back out and went to see Gordy. Bill Hay was outside he led me through a cunning constructed maze of bushes and obstacles. "It will just slow them up, sir."

"Good." Gordy was having a cigarette. I pointed to the floor, "This is the Alamo. If we get knocked out of our houses we come back here. You are the closest to the advance. Your mortar should have the range to reach the bridge. Until it gets too hot have a spotter outside."

"Right sir. We only have twenty rounds. It was all that we could carry."

"Then you will have to use them judiciously."

"Sir."

"Good luck lads."

I got back to my men. I ate some of the biscuits and drank some water. Once the barrage began we would have little time to eat. Our

Bergens acted as extra defences. We had them in front of our firing position.

"Davis if we can I want you to try to take out the Germans at the southern end of the bridge. Roger and I will use our Colts and our grenades to clear the north end. With luck, most of them will be asleep."

"We could booby trap the bodies and Kubelwagen on the bridge, sir. That would slow them up and give us warning of their advance."

"That is what we will do."

At 0200 I led my two experienced men out of our emplacement. I felt a little guilty leaving my rookies behind but they could not be risked. Beaumont and I had silenced Colts and Davis a silenced rifle. I had my Thompson with me but the silencer on my Colt would disguise the muzzle flash. We did not head down the road but used the field to the east of it. It was open ground. The farmer or whoever had had the house had cultivated it. I guessed he had kept animals there for there were no plough marks and it was covered in grass. As we approached the hedge and trees we could hear the Germans chatting. It sounded like there were just two of them on duty.

Davis slid silently off. He would head to the northern bank of the river. Beaumont and I crawled on our bellies towards the sandbagged position. There were fields behind us but in front of us and along the river were some trees. Most had their leaves but not all. We crawled and took cover behind two of them. The sentries were just twenty feet away. Had it been daylight then they might have seen us. I saw, parked just ahead of the sandbags, the truck. That was thirty feet from us. I tapped Beaumont on the shoulder and then pointed at the grenades festooned on his battle jerkin. He nodded. We waited. This was another reason why I had only brought experienced men. We could wait without making mountains out of the normal noises of the night. We would not worry if the sentry came close to us for we were confident that we could lie still even under an apparent direct stare.

One of the two Germans walked to the middle of the bridge and then returned. He started a conversation with the other guard, "Wilhelm said that he heard on the radio that the Americans have broken through further south. Tanks are heading north."

"Then we will be heading east soon. I am glad we have the truck and enough fuel to reach Munster!"

"What is so good about Munster? That is just closer to Berlin and the Russians will soon be there."

"My uncle is the mayor of Munster. He is high up in the party. I fear that I may need such a friend soon."

"That sounds like disloyal talk."

"Do you think that we can still win?"

"I have heard that the Fuhrer has new weapons being built in Austria. They could turn the tide."

"Perhaps."

Just then a figure climbed from the back of the truck, "When you two ladies have finished disturbing my sleep you can get the kettle on. The next shift would like a brew."

"I am fed up of ground acorns!"

The sergeant laughed, "I have forgotten what real coffee tastes like. I remember the good old days when we first came west! We ate and drank well! You two were probably still at school then! Those Tommies and French knew how to run! Stukas bombing them and our Panzers machine-gunning them. Happy days! Now get the water on!"

The two sentries went to fetch the water while the sergeant put more sticks into the brazier. It flared up. He would have no night vision! They had just lifted the pot of water on to the brazier when the sky was lit up by the barrage. A heartbeat later the sound of the shells erupted. My gun spat three bullets and the three Germans fell. Even as they were falling, the sergeant spilling the water and the brazier, Beaumont was racing across the road. He rolled one grenade under the truck as he hurled the other in the back. I could hear German voices. Beaumont raced back and threw himself next to me. As a head appeared I fired another two bullets in his direction and then took cover. The grenades went off almost simultaneously. The fire from the brazier ignited the fuel and the whole truck lifted in the air and crashed to earth.

I grabbed my Thompson and ran to the bridge. I kept to the left so that I was not highlighted by the fire. The two sentries at the far end were dead thanks to Davis but I knew they had a radio. The barrage was so loud that Beaumont would not have heard me even had I shouted. I just hoped that he would follow me and that Davis would cover us. Two men rose. They were a hundred and forty feet away. Holding the Tommy gun in two hands I sprayed a short burst. The sound was dwarfed by the barrage. I kept running. One of the men I had shot began to rise and was thrown to the ground as Davis hit him. The last two men rose from the Kubelwagen. Beaumont and I fired at the same time and both fell. I saw the radio by the Kubelwagen and I emptied my magazine into it.

Beaumont was already using the dead Germans' grenades to booby trap the Kubelwagen and the bodies. I turned, "Davis, booby trap the north end of the bridge."

As Beaumont worked he nodded to the radio, "Do you think they got a message off?"

"If they did there is nothing we can do about it." I gestured with my thumb at the barrage. "I think that will worry them more than an incident at a bridge." I took one of the MG 42 machine-guns and ammunition canister. "Fetch the other one when you are done."

"Sir."

When I reached the north side of the bridge I saw that the cannon and the machine-gun were both wrecked. "Get back to the house as soon as you have finished. Fetch any weapons you think might be useful."

He held up a box, "I have dropped lucky, sir. Two hundred rounds for my Mauser!"

The MG 42 weighed twenty-five pounds and the ammunition was almost as heavy but I knew that it would add to our firepower. I called out as I approached our fort, "Coming in!" so as to warn White and Foster. I did not think they would be trigger happy but we had been away some time.

I handed them the gun and ammunition. "Set this up where you had the rifle grenade. We have another one, Beaumont is bringing it. I will go and clear a space on the first floor."

The upper floor had been partly demolished but the upper wall to the bottom of the window remained. Crucially, it faced east and would add to Lieutenant Poulson's firepower. I found a half dozen broken roof beams. I laid three of them above the lintel of the window. I found a broken chest of drawers. I hauled it in front of the window and then arranged the last of the beams above it so that the gunner and loader would have some protection. I peered through the window and saw that it had a clear view of the road. I went down the half-demolished stairs and took a section of camouflage netting.

"When Beaumont and Davis get here help them to carry the machine-gun upstairs."

"Sir."

I went back upstairs and risked standing on my defences. I was not certain if the brickwork would hold. I gingerly ascended and, although the wood creaked, it held. I draped the netting down the window. I prised loose a couple of bricks and laid them on the top to secure it. We just needed to disguise the barrel until the Germans were within two thousand feet. That was the range of the MG 42. I heard footsteps as they laboured up with the machine-gun.

"Lay it here and load it."

"Sir!"

"Bridge booby-trapped?"

"They won't stop tanks but infantry or soft-skinned vehicles will get a shock. If nothing else it will give us warning."

"Davis!"

His voice came from downstairs, "Yes sir?"

"I want you and Foster up here with the sniper rifle and this machine-gun. You are our eyes to the east."

"Sir!"

"And Beaumont!"

"Yes sir?"

"Get a brew on, we have earned it!"

While Beaumont went to put on some water to heat up I took the binoculars and went out to look down the road. To the west, I could still hear the sound of the barrage. I had almost tuned it out. I saw nothing down the road. Of course, the Americans were further south and advancing. That would limit the forces they could use to reinforce this area. Gelsenkirchen was just fifteen miles away. If a message had been received it would take them half an hour to must forces. It was now almost 0430. There was no sign of vehicles. They would come north. The barrage would tell them what Monty was up to. They would assume that the defenders would hold out for a short time. We had time. Munster was forty miles to the northeast. They would take even longer to reach us.

Satisfied that there was no one on the way I returned indoors. I handed the glasses to White, "Sam, go outside and keep an eye open for anyone coming up the road."

Beaumont had the tea ready. He handed me my mug and shouted, "Tea's up!"

Foster came down, "Sir, Lance Corporal Davis says he has a good view down the road. Nothing moving."

"Good. As soon as it is dawn and the artillery stops then I expect we will see some movement. Eat while you can."

Beaumont handed me a piece of sausage. "Jerry was cooking this. I have some more for the lads. It is mainly fat but it is spicy. It will fill a hole."

"Thanks, Roger."

It was fatty and it was chewy but it was tasty too.

The barrage stopped shortly before 0700. The sky was much lighter and there was still no sign of the Germans. I took the glasses from Sam and went to look down the road. There was nothing. I moved them from east to west and then a movement caught my eye. There was a vehicle coming up the road. It looked to be less than two miles away. I did not know what kind it was but I knew it had to be German.

They were here!

Chapter 12

"Stand to!" I ran back inside. "No one open fire until I give orders. Davis, how about the road to the east?"

"Nothing yet sir."

"Beaumont, you get on the MG 42 with White. I will use the Thompson."

I used the glasses to peer through the camouflage netting. It was a German column. I saw the black cross on the lead vehicle. It looked to be a 6 Rad 231, German armoured car. It had a 20 mm gun but tyres rather than tracks. I tried to put myself in their position. They knew that the allies had been shelling. They would see the wrecked Kubelwagen and lorry. As there were no British uniforms they would assume that the men had been killed by shells. They would still be cautious but they would be keen to push on to the crossroads. They would be within range when they were at the bridge. I wanted them closer when we opened fire as I wanted the maximum casualties.

When they were just short of the bridge they stopped and I saw the commander of the armoured car scanning the bridge. He was looking for wires. He would not find any. Our booby traps were more subtle. I saw him raise his arm and shout something. Eight men disgorged from the half-track which was following and ran towards the bridge. It was obvious that they were moving the bodies. As they tried to move the first two the grenades exploded and the eight men were thrown to the ground. I saw a couple of them moving but four did not. The hatch was slammed shut and the turret moved around. The booby traps suggested an ambush. The men who were in the half-track kept their heads down. The men who had begun to descend from the lorries climbed back on board. And no bullets came their way. We had posed them a problem. It would take time to solve the problem and that was our task. Delay them.

They had to have radios on board. I could imagine the conversations. The armoured car began to fire into the trees and bushes alongside the river. The half-track joined in. After a few minutes, the armoured car moved forward. We had left the Kubelwagen with its front wing protruding a little from the bridge. The armoured car went to nudge it out of the way. As it toppled backwards it set off another two grenades. Using the glasses I saw that the front tyres on one side were shredded by the shrapnel. The armoured car could still drive. It would, however, move very slowly.

The half-track moved forward as the armoured car reversed out of the way. I hoped that the Sergeant Major and Lieutenant would hold their fire until they heard the sound of a Thompson. That had been the agreed signal. I knew that they would be eager to destroy the Germans.

"White, slip out of the back and, when I give the word, send a grenade into the middle of the bridge. Can you do that?"

"I think so sir, but what about the machine-gun?"

Beaumont said, "Don't worry, White, you'll have time to get back in here and feed the ammo through."

He slipped out of the back and I cocked my Thompson. The half-track was almost level with the lorry. As it drove over the sergeant's body it set off another booby trap. The grenade did little damage to the half-track but the gunner began to fire at the three buildings in which we sheltered. Instinctively we ducked down but the bullets just struck the bricks. They were trying to get a response. The half-track moved up the road towards us. Normally they carried twelve men and eight had been incapacitated. If we could stop the half-track then the road would be blocked and the armoured car would not have a clear field of fire.

They had a gap of forty feet between vehicles. They feared that there were either booby traps or mines. I waited until the half-track was less than fifty yards from the house. I shouted, "Now!"

I aimed my Thompson at the gunner. He was protected from the front but I had a side shot. The grenade landed just behind the second truck. The shrapnel scythed through the open back. Every German gun began firing blindly at the hedges along the side of the road and into the buildings. I fired two short bursts and the gunner slumped. He was hit. As I fired at the driver I heard the crump of the mortar. I stepped out and ran towards the half-track. The MG 42 operated by Beaumont began to chatter. The 20 mm was unable to fire at me because the half-track was in the way. I jammed the Thompson in the driver's visor and emptied the magazine. The bullets bounced around inside making it a charnel house. I took a grenade and, pulling the pin threw it into the open back of the half-track. Even as the last occupants rose I was diving to the ground. The chatter of a Bren gun made the men duck down and then the grenade went off.

The mortar was working its way up the road and the armoured car attempted to get by the half-track. Its shredded tyres did not help.

From above me, I heard Davis shout, "Sir, trucks heading down the road from the east!"

"Deal with them."

I turned and hurled a grenade high into the air. It exploded in the air in front of the armoured car. It did little damage but it takes a brave driver to keep driving with shrapnel flying through the air. I rolled into the house and loaded another magazine.

"White, fire an anti-tank grenade at the armoured car. Use the grenade rifle like a bazooka!"

"Sir!"

The armoured car was moving towards us. Its turret was turning and it fired. It could not lower its gun low enough to hit anything but the wrecked roof. However, the chunks of brick and stone which flew off told us how powerful a weapon it was.

"Any time Sam!"

The grenade flew through the open window at the side and crashed into the side of the armoured car. The range was very close. The armour was thickest at the front and the grenade exploded in the thinner metal at the sides. Fortune favours the brave. White must have hit the fuel tank for we were knocked over by the wall of heat and the concussion as the armoured car was destroyed.

I fired my Thompson at the second truck following the armoured car as the mortar hit the third truck. White fed another belt into the MG 42 and the last of the Germans were driven back over the bridge.

"Can you hold here, Beaumont?"

"Yes sir!"

I ran up the stairs to join Davis and Foster. Lieutenant Poulson now had all his men firing at the advancing column. I could see half-tracks but no armour. "Peter, I'll take over the machine-gun, get your rifle and take out the officers and the NCOs."

"Sir."

He slipped from behind the gun and I lay down where he had been. The infantry had left their vehicles and were running and firing as they advanced towards us. Our changeover and the fact that the gun stopped firing made them think that we were beaten and they rose. I traversed from left to right, firing short bursts. I saw men fall. An officer pointed at our emplacement and then fell back as Davis worked his gun. He was good. Each time he slid the bolt back and aimed the target was as good as dead. They were less than two hundred yards away and the telescopic sight made them seem even closer. The Bren gun was now adding its fire. When Gordy had Ashcroft and Richardson switch their mortar to the east road then the Germans fell back.

"Reload. They will call up for reinforcements." I went back down the stairs.

I looked at my watch. It was just 0900 hours. It would take at least six hours to build a pontoon bridge across the river. The ones who had assaulted across the river in the Buffaloes and Funnies would be hanging on. It would not be until the pontoon was finished that we could really start the push. We could have another ten hours to wait for relief.

"Is that it sir? Will they give up?"

I moved a few of the Mills bombs on to the window ledge next to my right shoulder and peered out of the glassless window, "No Sam, they won't. They tried the fast approach and now they will attempt the slow way. This is where we keep our wits about us. They will not come up the road. They will use the cover from the river. Luckily for us whoever had this house cleared and used the field to the south of us for crops. They only have cover to the edge of it and then we have a hundred and ten yards of killing zone between us."

"How do you know, sir?"

"I paced it out when we headed down to the river. You two make sure the field is where they die. I will watch the road. They can use the hedgerow for cover. If I disappear Beaumont, don't worry. It is because I have gone outside."

"What about the other side of the road, sir?"

"That is the Sergeant Major's domain. Our danger comes if they join up with the men on the east road with these. Then we have trouble."

It took them thirty minutes to plan and then begin their first assault on our strongpoint. I saw another two trucks arrive and disgorge their men over the bridge. They were wary and came over in threes and fours. Our mortar was ominously silent. Gordy had said we had limited ammunition. He would save it until there were enough men to make it worth his while. The first figures in grey began to head up the road but this time they used the hedge for cover. It meant I could not see them. Gordy's team could but he would not waste ammunition. They would wait until they were within the range of the Thompsons.

Beaumont said as he cocked the MG 42, "They are at the edge of the field sir. Here they come!"

I heard the crump of a grenade, "Sir, they are using smoke bombs!"

"I won't be long."

Taking one Mills bomb and my Thompson I slipped through the opening which had been the front door originally. The remnants of the wall around it now afforded protection to Beaumont and White. The Germans were keeping to the east side of the hedge. That was the side I could not see them. As I stepped out I threw myself to the ground and gave a short burst at the grey-clad figures a hundred and thirty yards away. One fell with a large red chest and a second clutched his arm. The others opened fire as they ducked back into the hedgerow. I had an elevated position and I was lying down. Their bullets flew over my head. Then I heard Beaumont's gun as it opened fire. The cries told me that, even firing through smoke, he had hit men. I heard Davis' MG 42 begin as well and the sound of a Bren gun. They were attacking from the east too.

I fired another burst and then, rising, ran towards the hedgerow. I could not see them and that meant they could not see me. I glanced in the field to the south of the house and saw the smoke. To my left, the muzzle of the MG 42 sent bullets into it. So long as the ammunition held out that would be a killing zone. I risked moving down the field side of the hedge. The smoke hid me from the Germans. Then, when I was thirty yards down, I pulled the pin on a Mills bomb and threw it high into the air. I turned and ran back to the house. It exploded in the hedge. I peered through the hedgerow. I saw a couple of bodies.

I raced back into the house. "White, get your grenade rifle." I took the belt from him and continued to feed Beaumont's machine-gun. He was firing blindly into the smoke but he was not using a pattern the Germans could detect. He would have a plan in his head. Sometimes he fired just six or seven bullets and sometimes a longer burst. He fired low and he fired high. There was no pattern.

White shouted, "Where to sir?"

"Go outside and use the grenades to work down the hedge and clear it. Then switch to the trees by the river."

"I can't see them, sir."

"We will spot fall of shot for you. The smoke is clearing a little."

"Sir."

Just then I heard the crump of the mortar. Gordy had to have seen something for the mortar shell exploded to the south of us.

From upstairs Davis shouted, "Sir, they are getting very close to the Lieutenant."

"He will have to hang on. If he heads back to the Alamo then let me know."

"Sir!"

The smoke had cleared considerably and I saw grey bodies littering the field. The closest were about fifty yards away. The wooden and brick defences had meant we had been safe. The camouflage net now had holes in it but it still disguised our exact position.

I heard the grenade rifle as White systematically lobbed his bombs down the hedgerow. The Germans were retreating down the field. Another crump told me Gordy had risked another mortar shell. I grabbed my Tommy gun and slipped out of the door. White was kneeling and using the remnants of a small wall on which to rest his barrel. I risked stepping out into the road. I saw a machine-gun crew carrying a machine-gun. They were rushing up the road. I guessed they were trying to enfilade us. White must have seen them as they began to set up just a hundred yards from us. I aimed at them and began to fire. Two other Germans were behind them and they knelt down and began to fire at me. I concentrated on the machine-gun crew as bullets zipped around me. Then I heard the crump from the mortar and the shell exploded twenty yards behind the two men and the machine-gun crew. A second shell followed a few seconds later and the machine-gun was destroyed.

From inside I heard Beaumont shout, "You are short twenty!"

I watched Sam adjust his aim. He sent a grenade into the air and I heard shouts. Beaumont said, "Bob on! Send another!"

He did so and then a third. He looked at me, "Sir, I only have two shells left. I have another six anti-tank ones."

"Best save them. Well done. Get back inside. I will go and see how Davis is doing."

As I reloaded my Thompson I checked my watch. It was 1100 hours. As I reached the upstairs I saw that the camouflage net lay in shreds. "A little hot, eh Davis?"

"You could say that sir." He pointed. "They have found some dead ground. The hedge hides them from us and from the Lieutenant. They can get to within forty yards of us."

I said, "Get your rifle. You might be able to see them through the hedge. I will go on the machine-gun. How is the ammo holding?"

Foster said, "Half a belt here and then one full belt."

"We will have to go careful then."

We had no targets. There was grey but they were the dead. I saw Davis' barrel traverse the hedge and then it barked. He had taken the silencer off. I saw an arm flail. He reworked the bolt and fired a second time. I saw another movement. "I can see them, sir. I can take care of the ones down this side but the Lieutenant will have to deal with the other side."

"Foster go and fetch White. He has two grenades left. Tell him to come up here."

"Sir!"

As he went I looked up. There was no roof above us. We would be using up our last grenades but if we could drive the Germans back again it would buy us time and time was more valuable than ammunition.

They came back up, "Sam, I want you to send the last two grenades to the other side of the hedge. If you hit the hedge and wall it doesn't matter. The splatter of stones will add to the effect."

"Sir!"

Davis continued to thin the German ranks. His powerful rifle and sight were the best weapon we had at the moment. The first grenade hit the field. The cries I heard told me that he had hit something. He adjusted the barrel and sent his last one to actually hit the hedge and the wall. It was spectacular. I saw men falling and others fleeing.

Then Beaumont shouted, "Sir, they have an armoured car. It is approaching the bridge."

"Sam with me. Tom, keep using the machine-gun. If you fire short bursts you can do it alone."

"Sir!"

As we reached the bottom of the stairs I said, "Use an anti-tank grenade. You will have to be in the lane. I will come with you and cover you. In a perfect world, you will hit the side of the armoured car. The grenade might not penetrate the front armour."

"Sir."

I saw that the armoured car was almost at the bridge. The 20 mm began to fire. The angle of the road and the hedge meant it did not have a good view of us but they could fire at the Alamo. I saw the shells as they gouged holes in the brickwork. Gordy had his men send a mortar shell over. It hit the bridge but the armoured car had passed. The barrel swung around to face us. It was still too far away for White to hit it. He bravely aimed his weapon even as the machine-gun and cannon swung around to aim at the two of us.

Davis shouted, "Sir! They have two Panzer Mark IVs coming down the road!"

Suddenly I heard the roar of rockets. The armoured car lifted in the air and then landed in a blaze of burning fuel. I heard the crew screaming as they burned. Then I heard the sound of Hispano cannons as the flight of Typhoons roared along the river. The hedgerow and tree line were shredded. I saw rockets streak from the second two in the flight and from my left heard the explosions as they hit something. They soared across my eyeline guns firing. Their roar faded and then grew louder. I heard the whoosh of rockets and two more explosions.

Davis shouted, "That's it, sir! The tanks are destroyed!"

The Typhoons roared overhead and gave us a waggle of their wings as they passed.

"Reload. Beaumont cover me."

Taking my Tommy gun I left the house and ran down the lane. The fighters had hit the Germans hard. I heard the MG 42 as Beaumont encouraged the Germans to keep their heads down. I reached the machine-gun destroyed by Gordy. I saw a belt of ammo and I grabbed it. I ran back. Behind me, I heard the crack of bullets as the Germans saw me. I barely made it back to the house.

"Sir! What would your mother say?"

"I trust, Lance Sergeant Beaumont, that she will never learn of it! Foster! I have another belt of ammo for you."

Foster came down, "They are falling back, sir."

I was worried about the other two sections, "Beaumont, take charge. I am going to see how the Lieutenant and the Sergeant Major are coping."

"Sir."

I slipped out of the side door and went first to the Alamo. I had to go along the road to get in at the western side of the house. Gordy and his team had made the east and south a fortress. Gordy was smoking as I entered, "Everything okay, Sarn't Major?"

He nodded, "We were lucky. A few cannon shells hit the wall but that was all. Sorry, we couldn't send more mortar shells over. I didn't want to leave us short."

"How many have we left?"

"Ten."

I looked at my watch. It was 1230. The bridge could be close to completion. "Well if they come in force use them. We should have some relief in four or five hours."

"Sir." He threw his cigarette end out of the window. "The Lieutenant was hit hard. Those tanks got a couple of shots off before the fighters took them out."

I nodded, "Come with me then and we will go and see what the damage is."

We hurried out of the east side and scurried along the road, keeping low. I could hear Davis' rifle as he continued to snipe and to keep down the German heads. When we entered the back of Lieutenant Poulson's emplacement I saw that they had, indeed, been hit. Hewitt was treating Fletcher who had a gashed head. Lieutenant Poulson's left arm was in a sling and the two young soldiers, the big Geordie, George and the diminutive Durham miner, Richardson, lay dead. They had taken the impact of a 75 mm shell. There was a hole in the wall and the Bren was wrecked.

I turned to Gordy, "Bring your team here. We can always fall back to the Alamo."

Gordy nodded sadly. "Sir." He turned to the Lieutenant, "Sorry about that sir. The range was too great for the mortar."

Polly shook his head, "The mortar would have done no damage at that range. At least they knew nothing about it."

"How are you, Fletcher?"

"Just shook up, sir. The two lads took the blast. This was just a bit of flying masonry."

"Then get on the radio and tell headquarters, in plain language, that we need relief."

"Sir."

I turned to Lieutenant Poulson, "If they bring armour or armoured cars then we are in trouble. As soon as you see tanks then head for the Alamo."

Polly nodded and looked at his watch. "In a perfect world the pontoon bridges are up and they are on their way!"

"And how many times has it worked out that way? No, we hang on and try to make life hard. Hewitt, when you have seen to Fletcher nip out and lay a few booby traps." I pointed to the dead Germans just forty yards away. "Take their grenades. I will come out and cover you."

"Sir." He finished applying the dressing and then said, "Right sir."

We went out of the back. I saw the side of our emplacement. When we passed the front I saw the bullet holes. Had they fired at us then that would be Davis and Foster lying covered by their blankets. We moved along the side of the hedgerow. I turned and waved to Davis. Suddenly I saw his rifle muzzle flash and a German with a rifle in his hand fell backwards.

"Best work quick, John." We hurried to the first four bodies. They produced six grenades. They just had rifles. We moved back down the road, Two heads appeared in the distance. They were hidden from Davis by the hedge. I fired a short burst and they disappeared. We edged around the hedge. The field close to Lieutenant Poulson's emplacement had been a vegetable garden and orchard. Many of the trees were destroyed. I saw that the Germans had got to within forty yards of it. The Bren had done sterling work to keep them at bay. I managed to pick up an MP 34 and Hewitt found four more grenades. We walked to the slight rise which was sixty yards from the now wrecked wall of the house and crouched. I nodded to the ground. Hewitt took out his parachute cord. An enemy running towards the house would not see a cord for it would be hidden in the dead ground.

I crawled on my belly. I saw that the other end of the field was another fifty yards away. There were folds and hollows. I saw another eight bodies but I did not risk searching for grenades. As I glanced down the field I saw the flash of a muzzle. I dropped and rolled. The bullets from the MG 42 scythed through the air. I contemplated holding my gun up and returning fire. It would be a waste of bullets. Better to let them think they had killed me.

Hewitt said, "Done sir!"

"Then we crawl back." The German machine-gun fired a second burst. The slight rise in the ground protected us.

We slipped through the hedge and then back into the house. Gordy's team were there and they were shoring up the damage created by the tanks. I handed Lieutenant Poulson the MP 34 and the ammunition.

I took out my whistle. "If I blow this three times, then it is back to the Alamo." They nodded, "Fletcher?"

"ETA 1600 at the earliest sir."

I looked at my watch, it was 1345. It would be a long afternoon. "Good luck, lads."

"And you, sir."

Slipping out of the back I made my way to my team. Beaumont and White had a pan of water boiling. "Everything all right sir?"

I shook my head and told them.

Beaumont nodded, "I am making a brew, sir."

"Give me two for the lads upstairs and I will tell them what the situation is. Sam, you better come upstairs. We will need Davis and his rifle so you can load for Foster."

"Sir." He looked at me sadly, "You know I thought George was indestructible. He was a big chap and as tough and hard as they come."

"We are all mortal, Sam, and a 75 mm shell takes no prisoners!"

I went upstairs and repeated my news. "Davis, you keep on with the rifle. These two will use the machine-gun and Roger and I will man the MG 42 downstairs. Remember, three blasts on the whistle and you get out of there. Leave the gun. It is too heavy to manhandle down the stairs."

Just then we heard the sound of aero engines. They seemed to be coming from the west. I peered up as they came over. It was a squadron of B-26 Marauders. With twin engines and 4,000 pounds of bombs, they could do serious damage. I took out my glasses to see if I could see any anti-aircraft. They flew east, undisturbed. They were almost out of sight when I saw them dropping their bombs. I estimated that they were about forty miles away and there was no major town in that vicinity. They had to be bombing a relief column or a bridge, perhaps both. I went downstairs and heard them returning sometime later.

I pointed to the west, "I am taking that as a sign that the danger is to the east and not the south. Patton and his 3rd Army must have destroyed the Germans in their sector. Unless we get another attack here I will go upstairs and help Davis. You have a watching brief."

"There are still Germans to the south of us, sir. I have seen them moving around."

"This side of the bridge or the other?"

"The far side sir."

"Have you anything to make a charge?"

"You mean blow the bridge?" I nodded, "Sorry sir. Grenades won't do it."

They would come again soon. If they did not then it was all over. I went to the Bergens and took out more Mills bombs. I hung them from my battle jerkin. I made sure that my two magazines, in the Colt and the

Thompson, were full and I drank some water. I hated waiting and not doing anything.

Beaumont seemed to read my mind, "You have done all that you could, sir. There is no point saying what if we had had some explosives. We couldn't have carried any more could we, sir?

"You are right." Just then the ground to the south and east of us erupted. They were shelling us. "Take cover!"

I heard Davis shout, "Get under the stairs!! As Beaumont and I took cover under the table and mattress the other three hurtled down the stairs and White and Foster took shelter there. Davis grabbed the second mattress and pulled it in front of them.

Beaumont shouted, as more shells screamed over, "German 75s and 88s!"

I pushed my hands against my ears to protect them from the concussion. I heard and felt the building being struck. The upstairs had been in a poor state of repair. As the MG 42 tumbled downstairs, along with most of the wall I knew it was totally destroyed. The stairs held but a huge part of the wall crashed into the mattress which sheltered my three men. Beaumont went to move but I dragged him back. He had just been dragged under the table again when the MG 42 disintegrated as huge splinters from a shell demolished it. The air was filled with flying metal. Then, even above the roar of the shelling, I heard the roar of the Napier Sabre engines. The Typhoons were back. They must have gone to refuel and rearm. A few more shells fell and then there was an eerie silence.

The roof and ceiling had gone. Much of it had fallen into the house. Beaumont and I went to the debris-covered mattress. We tore the bigger pieces away together and then began to pull the smaller ones. I shouted, "Davis! Are you hurt!"

No-one replied but, then again, their hearing might have gone. I had shouted but my voice had sounded faint. As the last stones tumbled down we pulled the mattress. Davis' body lay across the two younger soldiers. I turned him over and put my hand to his throat. There was a pulse. He was alive. White looked up at me and his eyes were wide. "Is he alive sir? He threw himself on us to protect us."

"How is Foster?"

Thomas had a gash on the side of his face but he grinned, "I can answer you, sir, so I guess I am alive."

We put Davis into the recovery position. "Sam, go and fetch Hewitt. Foster stay with him. Roger, grab your gun!"

Our Thompsons had been with us under the table. I was pleased now that I had festooned my battle jerkin with grenades. The ones I had placed close by me earlier in the morning were now buried. The door was no longer there and neither was the wall. The table had proved to be stronger than I had thought and it had saved us. We stepped outside but kept in the shelter of the hedge. Smoke and dust hid the road. I glanced behind and saw that Lieutenant Poulson's stronghold had fared better than we had.

I pointed down to the bridge. With the smoke and debris from the shelling still filling the air we could risk getting a little closer. With guns cocked we ran a hundred yards into the smoke. It began to thin and we both dropped to the ground. As a gust of wind Finally, cleared it I began to laugh. Beaumont said, "Sir?"

I pointed and rose, "You didn't need explosives. Jerry did it for us, look!"

One shell had fallen short. The bridge still stood but there was a huge hole in the middle. It would not take any vehicles.

"Let's get back to the stronghold. We have a chance now."

I looked up as the three Typhoons zoomed overhead, heading west. The leader waggled his wings and I raised my arm. As I turned to walk back I saw the extent of the damage. There was half a wall and the stairs left. Davis was awake when we got back in the wrecked house. Hewitt was seeing to his wounds. "You will get a medal for that Davis."

He shrugged, "Instinct, sir!"

"The good news is that the bridge has gone. The bad news is that we have lost the two German machine-guns. How is it up there, John?"

"Not as bad as here. Cuts and bruises; nothing more."

"Right, Davis, take your rifle and go with Hewitt. You will be more use there." I looked at White and Foster, "How about you two? Need a rest?"

"No sir." Sam held up his Thompson. "I am raring to go, sir!"

"Right, off you two go. We will give them a shock when they advance. They will think we are all dead. Find your Bergens and get your grenades, we will need them." Hewitt and Davis headed up the lane.

I looked at my watch. I was 1445. We just had to hang on a little longer. The 1st Commando Brigade and the Black Watch were coming down the road. They would not let us down! I led Beaumont to the east end of the house. We clambered over the wall to the east of the house. The ground fell away from us and there were now craters from the shelling. From the north came the sound of Thompsons and Davis' rifle. Jerry was attacking, they were making the final push.

I turned and waved White and Foster forward. I pointed to the hedge and then to my grenades. They nodded. We ran to the first crater and jumped in. I raised my head. I saw grey. Germans were advancing up the side of the hedge. They were hidden from Lieutenant Poulson's post. They were less than sixty feet from us. I cocked my Thompson. The crack of rifles and the chatter of automatic weapons meant that I could risk speaking.

"On my command, we jump up. We shoot the Germans on this side of the hedge and then I want grenades thrown over the hedge!"

They nodded.

I counted to four in my head and then shouted, "Now!"

I jumped up and aimed at the Germans. They were not looking south. Four Thompsons can deliver powerful firepower. Firing over six hundred rounds a minute we emptied our four magazines in a few seconds. Even as the Germans were dying I was loading another magazine. We ran to the hedge. I dropped my gun and took out a Mills bomb. Pulling my arm back I hurled it high and then pulled the pin on a second. My grenades and those of Beaumont must have cleared the second hedge too. One of Foster's landed in the road. We ducked down and the blast shredded the bushes above our heads. I reached down to take a potato masher from the nearest dead German. I smashed the porcelain and pulled the lanyard. I threw it into the middle of the road. Beaumont and I threw ourselves on top of White and Foster. I heard screams and shouts. We stood and I could now see down the road.

The Germans were being rallied by an officer. Davis' bullet spun him around and when the four of us fired short bursts then the rest fled.

"Grab grenades and then back to the house."

We had no sooner reached it than Ashcroft shouted, "Sir! Germans! And they are coming from the west!"

We were surrounded!

Beyond the Rhine

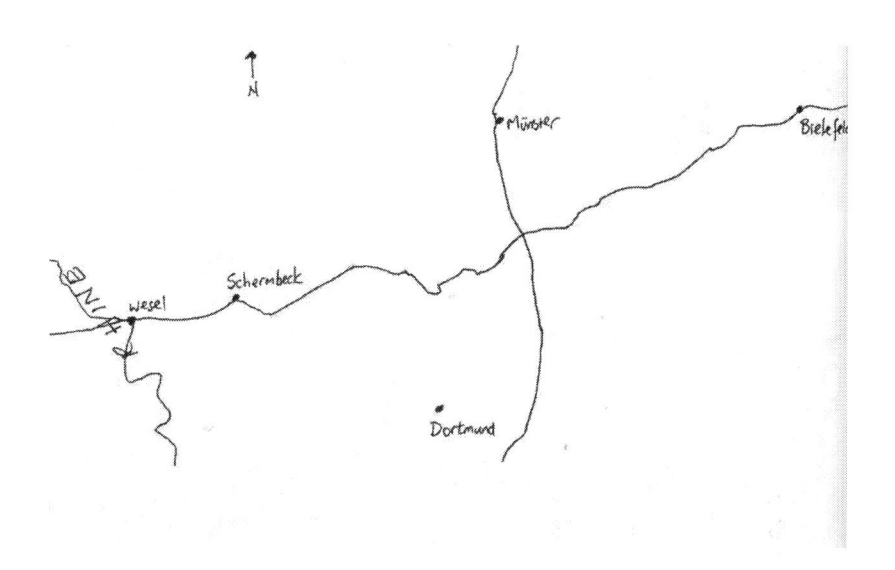

Chapter 13

"Beaumont, Fletcher, Ashcroft, White and Foster, with me."

We ran to the east end of the house. We ran out of the back door and threw ourselves behind the small wall which ran along it.

"Where were they, Ashcroft?"

He pointed along the road to Wesel. "Along there, sir. They were running."

"Then that means our lads are behind them. Hold your fire until I give you the order."

We had the crossroads covered. The bridge was blown and they could not go that way. Soldiers, especially those fleeing, would take the line of least resistance. I had seen it in 1940 when we had raced through the Low Countries. I moved so that I was on the edge of my men. I saw the grey and Ashcroft was right. They were running towards me.

I saw that there were eight men together. A sergeant led them. They still had their weapons. When they were forty feet from me and, as they slowed at the crossroads I stood and fired a burst into the air. I shouted, in German, "Sergeant, surrender. You are surrounded." In English, I said, "Stand and point your weapons at them."

My men rose as one. The sight of five sub machine-guns carried by Commandos had the desired effect. They looked down at the ground despondently. I saw one of them look down the road towards the bridge. "You are welcome to try to run over the bridge, my friend, but your artillery has blown it already. Drop your weapons, sit on the ground and you will live. The war is almost over. Do not be foolish."

The sergeant nodded, "Do as he says! These devils are the Commandos! They must have the ability to fly!"

As they sat I said, "White, Foster, keep them covered, the rest of you disarm them."

As other Germans ran down the road they were greeted by the sight of their comrades sitting in the road with their hands on their heads. I smiled at them and said, "Join your friends."

They all did so except for one Colonel whose hand began to raise his pistol. If I had fired I would have risked killing those who had surrendered. Suddenly Davis' rifle barked and the Colonel gained a third eye. It had a sobering effect. Thoughts of a heroic escape evaporated.

Everyone within sight of the dead Colonel surrendered. I turned and saw Davis leaning on the remains of the upper floor of the stronghold. I waved and he waved back.

It was 1750 hours when the first men of Number 4 Commando marched down the road. The captain who led them looked at the prisoners, there were over three hundred by then, and shook his head, "We were told that some of our chaps were here! We didn't expect this." He turned, "Sergeant, take charge of the prisoners."

The sergeant saluted and grinned, "Yes sir. You know who that is don't you Captain Wilberforce? It is Major Harsker. He is a legend in Number 4 Commando! We could have had a lie in this morning if we had known it was him and his ghosts holding the crossroads."

I laughed, "A great compliment, sergeant, but we were hanging on by our very fingertips." He went off grinning. "Pleased to meet you, Captain Wilberforce, sorry we can't offer you a cup of tea but the neighbours have made rather a mess of the place. We will have to get the decorators in I fear!"

Just then the Typhoons roared overhead. We all looked up to watch them. They would be the final nail in Germany's coffin. There would be no more attacks on the crossroads. A jeep roared up and Captain Wilberforce shouted, "Ten shun!

A brigadier and a colonel got out. The brigadier grinned and walked up to me, "Brigadier Peter Young! I seem to have spent this damned war following you, Major Harsker. First Dieppe, then Sicily and Finally, Normandy!" He held out his hand, "Good job," He nodded to the prisoners, "Yours?"

"Ours!"

"Well, we shall take it from here. Major Foster told me you would be here." He suddenly looked serious. "Did you lose many?"

"Just two sir but that was two too many."

"Quite. I understand you will be ahead of us from now on?"

"Yes sir."

"Your jeeps will not be here until tomorrow. I intend to hold here until then."

"You might want some Royal Engineers sir. Jerry blew up their own bridge."

"Good and tomorrow we should find things a little easier. Operation Varsity begins. Our northern flank should be more secure."

I was tempted to ask what Operation Varsity entailed but I was aware that there were too many men around us. I didn't need to know what it was, just that it would make our life easier, "Yes sir."

"I take it you are a little hungry?"

"We could do with something, sir, yes."

"Things have moved on since Sicily and Normandy, Major. We have hot food following us. Captain Wilberforce see that these chaps are fed first." He turned to Colonel, "Let's go and see what the young Major has left for us to do."

As they drove off I said, "Beaumont, fetch the rest of the lads and then McLean and Richardson. We'll bury them here at the crossroads."

Hot food was courtesy of the Commando cooks who had a trailer. The Brigadier was as good as his word and we ate first. He joined us just as we were wiping our plates dry with some bread. He took his own plate and gestured for me to join him in his jeep.

"I am glad it is one of our own who will be on point but I want you to pace yourself. With air superiority, we can let the R.A.F. do more of the spotting. We just need you and your chaps to be a mile or so ahead of us so that if there is trouble then you can call in the cavalry."

"That suits me, sir. Our backsides have been left out to dry more than enough."

"I know, Major Foster told me about your last two little jaunts into Bavaria and Austria. Very resourceful." He took a couple more mouthfuls. "You know that the plans have changed?" I nodded. "Hamburg is Monty's target."

"It is flatter land there and, to be honest, the fanatics are further south."

"You mean easier?"

"The Germans are never a pushover, sir. I just think that there will be fewer problems going north."

He finished his plate and handed it to his driver, "You have a radio, of course?"

"Yes sir and a good operator."

"Excellent. I will send over my adjutant, Captain Jenkins. He will have the frequencies and call signs. There will be five jeeps for you. You might have to scavenge for fuel but then you are used to that."

"It will be a change, sir, to be vaguely attached to an advance. I am looking forward to it."

"Well, Harsker, I shall just take a quick tour of the chaps. See you in the morning."

Once he had gone we gathered in the garden of the house McLean and Richardson had defended. We found spades and we all dug the graves. I took their identity disks and Gordy their personal papers. After we had laid soil on top of them and planted a rifle in each one topped by their beret, Emerson played last post on his mouth organ. Somehow, it seemed even more haunting than when played on a bugle.

We retired inside. Unlike the others, we had a roof. Captain Jenkins had delivered the information we needed as well as more maps to help us. We had the luxury of an oil lamp. We did not have to sit in the dark. "There are five jeeps. Fred, you will drive one. Lieutenant Poulson, Sergeant Major Barker, Sergeant Hay and myself will drive the others. Fletcher and White, you will be with me. Davis you and Foster will ride with Freddie. Private Betts with the Lieutenant. That leaves Beaumont and Ashcroft with Sergeant Major Barker. Hewitt, you will ride with Sergeant Hay"

They all nodded. We were a team but I had tried to spread the younger ones around.

"Beaumont, take some of the lads out afterwards and see if you can find a couple of machine-guns for the jeeps. Freddie, I doubt they will have full tanks. Take a couple of lads and see if there is any left in the wrecked German trucks. They were just shot up. Even a couple of gallons might help. Roger, we need more grenades for the grenade rifle and shells for the mortar. I doubt we can get a bazooka but we need something." The mortar was our heaviest weapon but the grenade rifle was far more mobile.

Three of them nodded.

"We need to sort out our Bergens. We have travelled in jeeps before now. They are nice little motors but they don't have much room in them. I want the Bergens used as protection for the front of the jeeps. It worked in Antwerp and I see no reason why it shouldn't work now. And if you find any ammo for the Colts or Thompsons then grab it. There will be no friendly quartermaster where we are going."

There were just three of us left around the table. Lieutenant Poulson, Gordy and me, "We have lost six new men. I want to take these four home. Look after them eh? I am going to have Freddie on point. Davis has shown us what he can do with a rifle and he has good eyes. I will be second in the column. Gordy, you will bring up the rear."

"Sir, how do we get ahead of the column? Our jeeps aren't here yet and the brigadier will be heading off first thing."

"We use side roads to get ahead. Besides, there will be some German opposition ahead of us. They will have set up some sort of defensive line."

My foragers came back with more than I had expected. They had two MG 34 machine-guns. They used the same ammunition as the MG 42 and although those two guns had been destroyed we still had their ammunition. Emerson would fit one to his jeep and one to Bill Hay's. Fred had also managed to salvage a large jerrycan of fuel. That would travel with Gordy at the rear. We also acquired another dozen grenades which Beaumont distributed.

Brigadier Young had his men up before dawn. They had a couple of Hobart's Funnies with them; the Sherman tank with the flame thrower called a Crocodile. That would enable them to deal with any strongpoints in Schermbeck just up the road.

As the sun came up we heard the sound of Dakotas. We looked to the west and saw the sky filled with the C-47 and their Horsa gliders. It was the 6th Airborne. We watched the sky to the north of us fill with parachutes as Operation Varsity got underway. Gordy smiled, "A lovely sight that sir. I feel happier knowing that the Paras are to the north of us."

"And I am guessing that means we can head due east. Give me the maps and I will see what the roads are like."

I had studied the maps the night before. "We head for Holterhausen and then Hervest. The furthest I think we can get in half a day is Haltern am See. There is a large lake there and it may be a bottleneck. The Brigadier wants us to keep probing to the north and east along the flank of the Americans."

"It is Yanks to the south of us sir?"

"Yes Lieutenant Poulson, their 16th Corps."

"Then we should have plenty of air support sir and they have armour too."

I pointed to the skies. "I am guessing our armour will be racing to get to those lads. The last time they landed, at Arnhem, they were left isolated for too long. That might explain why we just have two tanks.

Soon the air to the north of us was filled with the crack of small arms fire, the crump of grenades and the occasional heavier sound of an 88. The Brigade was taking Schermbeck. I did not envy them their task. The defenders had had more than twenty-four hours to prepare. I had wondered why no one had come down the road from the north. The Germans were obviously trying to use our crossroads to reinforce the town. We packed everything away and waited, rather forlornly at the crossroads. The support vehicles from the Brigade kept us company. Ambulances brought back the wounded to the temporary hospital which had been erected. The Germans were not going away quietly.

Our five jeeps arrived at 1100 hours. The drivers were part of the Brigade's support companies and, after handing them over, joined their units. It took an hour or so to load the vehicles and fit the two machine-guns. The Brigadier was with his men at the sharp end. I went to see Captain Jenkins, the adjutant, who was with the Headquarters company monitoring the progress.

"How is it going, Captain?"

"Forward elements have linked up with 6th Para, sir. The Brigadier asked if you are ready."

"We are just off now. My aim is to get to Haltern am See by this evening."

"That is sixteen miles."

"I know. If we can we will push on to Selm. We will keep you informed."

"Good luck, sir."

I went back to the jeeps. "Davis, keep a sharp eye open. We hurt Jerry the other day but they are tough soldiers and they might have dug in."

"Don't worry sir, I have had one brush with death. I don't want another. Right, Freddie off we go!"

I drove and White was next to me with his Thompson and grenades at the ready. My Tommy gun was in the back with Fletcher and the radio. We had managed to tie the Bergens in front of us. We had flattened them so that they did not obscure my view. They would not stop much but we had learned to do what we could to preserve our lives.

We passed the wrecked Panzer tanks. The Typhoons had made a mess of them. The sides of the roads were still littered with bodies. Rats, crows and foxes had already begun to feast on them. I saw Sam pale. This was the reality of war. He was a clever man and he had an imagination. That could be us lying there. I saw Davis wave his hand for us to slow as we approached Holterhausen. It was not a large place but it had been demolished. There were many wrecked vehicles there. This was where the Typhoons and Marauders had attacked their reinforcements.

We drove through slowly. Fletcher and White had their guns ready in case of ambush. It was a graveyard of men and vehicles. Once through we speeded up.

We had to drive around a couple of trucks which had been hit in the middle of the road. They had been strafed. Our air superiority had hurt them. There were people in Hervest but they stayed indoors. Wrecked houses lined the road as we drove slowly through.

Scouse said, "Sir, it looks like the war is over eh?"

"Fletcher, we are ten miles from our front lines there will be Germans ahead, we just haven't seen them yet."

The road was rising and I saw the tops of the trees of the forest of Haltern. Davis stopped just two hundred yards from its edge. The other jeeps stopped in the dead ground. We were just a mile from Haltern and that was a couple of miles from Haltern am See. I checked the map as he left his jeep to walk back to us. There was a railway line to the south of us and then the Lippe. Just beyond that was the canal. I took out the binoculars and climbed up on the seat. I saw that a train and its wagons had been hit by an airstrike. I saw no sign of barges on the canal.

"Sir, I don't like the looks of the forest up ahead."

"What can you see?"

"Nothing sir and that is what is worrying me. I didn't expect any opposition in the last two places. They were too exposed but here? This is perfect for an ambush. If our armour tries to come through here then they can use mines and Panzerfausts as well as their 88s to destroy them one by one. The trees are too narrow to allow them through."

He was right, "But we can go through. Fletcher, you take charge of this jeep."

"Sir!"

I circled and pumped my arm three times. My men left their jeeps to join me. "Davis thinks there may be trouble in the woods and I am inclined to agree with him. I am leaving Emerson and Fletcher with the jeeps. The rest you grab your guns and grenades."

"Sir."

" Fred, Scouse, move the jeeps out of range of small arms. Davis, I want you to move to within a hundred and fifty yards of the woods. Find cover and keep watch."

"Right sir."

When my men arrived I said, "We go in two teams. I will take the south side of the road, Lieutenant Poulson the north. Hay, Hewitt, White,

Foster and Beaumont, you are with me. The rest go with the Lieutenant. We go in pairs. White, you are with me. One moves one watches. Get into the woods and let's see if there is any danger there. Let's go."

Hay said, "Foster, you are with me."

I cocked my Thompson and ran across the scrubland to the right of the road. It was undulating. I guessed it had been used for grazing at one time. There was a low wall just forty feet from the road and behind it was lush grass. If we ran into danger then I would leap over the wall. I stopped a hundred yards from the edge of the trees and I knelt. "Sam, I am going to run forty feet and drop. When I wave my arm you come. Cover me while I run. Watch the edge of the wood for movement. If you see any then open fire. It doesn't matter if you don't hit anything, the bullets will warn me quicker than a shout."

"Sir."

I rose and ran. The beauty of my team was that we had done this for years. I was not worrying if Hay and Beaumont were moving when I did; I knew that they were. I kept glancing at the ground and at the wood. I was looking for grey but if the Germans were any good then they would be heavily camouflaged. Suddenly there was a crack from within the woods. I saw a flash and then heard the explosion as an 88 tried to hit the jeeps. I stopped, dived into the long grass and glanced around. Emerson was just moving the last jeep into the dead ground. The shell-covered him and the jeep with soil and stones. Then the machine-guns started.

Sam barely made it. He hurled himself to the ground just as the bullets zipped over my head. We had triggered the ambush. Fletcher would, even now, be on the radio to summon the cavalry. Sam began to rise. "Stay down. They might think they have shot us and we have Davis, remember."

Amidst the cacophony of bullets ahead of us I heard a single shot from behind. The manic noise diminished slightly. A heartbeat later there was a second shot and then I heard just one machine-gun.

"On my count half rise. Give a long burst at the woods from left to right and then drop again. When I shout then zig-zag closer to the woods."

"Sir."

I smiled, "Don't worry. You will do fine." He nodded. To my left, I heard my men returning the German fire. I could still hear Davis' rifle as he picked off visible targets. "Now!"

I stood and, firing from the hip I ran to my left. White rose from my right and sprayed from left to right. When he stopped I ran right and my gun clicked on empty. Bullets zipped to my left. I was now fifty feet from the edge of the wood. I dropped to the ground and, pulling out my Luger, raised it and fired blindly in the direction of the wood. I used half a magazine. That would buy me the time to reload. I holstered the German gun. Lying on my back I reloaded and then rolled six feet to my left. I took out a Mills bomb and pulled the pin. I quickly stood and hurled the grenade high before dropping and shouting, "White, run!" The grenade had a four-second fuse and it exploded in the air.

White dropped next to me. I slowly rose. The smoke was clearing and I could see that I had blown a hole in the camouflage netting. I fired half a magazine and said, "Run!"

We ran the last fifty feet to the wood, firing as we went. There had been a machine-gun position. The gunner and loader lay dead. Each had been shot by Davis. The grenade had scythed through the others. The gun had been wrecked in the explosion. I saw the Germans fleeing through the trees. Then I saw the guns. There were two 88s and a couple of half-tracks with 20 mm cannon. Even as I saw them the two guns traversed towards us.

We had done enough. I blew my whistle three times. "White throw a grenade and then leg it back to the jeep."

I picked up a German grenade. I had found I could throw them further than a Mills bomb. Even when it was in the air I propelled White out of the emplacement and into the open. I saw my other men running back. Hewitt and Hay were helping Beaumont who had been hit. Our two grenades went off. The 20 mm cracked and I heard them hit the trees. It was the trees which saved us. They would have to move closer, now, to the edge of the woods. We kept zig-zagging. White must have glanced behind us for he fell. I turned and ran back. I saw the Germans as they returned to their emplacement. I opened fire and emptied the last of my magazine. I grabbed White's arm and helped him to his feet. I ran towards the road and when I saw the jeeps, I threw myself down into the hollow where Emerson and Fletcher had hidden them.

We were the last to arrive. I saw that Emerson and Beaumont had both been wounded while Betts was limping. He shook his head, "Twisted my ankle, sir."

I nodded, "You can man the gun on the Sergeant Major's jeep. Ashcroft, you are with the Lieutenant."

"Sir."

"Fletcher, did you get a message off?"

"Sir."

"Well tell them that there are at least two 88s and two half-tracks with 20 mm."

"And Panzerfausts." I looked at Lieutenant Poulson. "We were going to grab them but they counterattacked. They had two half-tracks with MG 42 machine-guns. I did not want to risk it."

"You did right. Tell them, Fletcher." I turned to Hewitt. "How are Fred and Roger?"

"Cuts and bruises for Emerson. Beaumont took a bullet in the leg. I have stopped the bleeding but he will need surgery."

I shook my head, "Base hospital for you Roger."

I saw him hang his head, "And that means I won't be there at the end. I so wanted to be there when we Finally, won."

I knew what he meant. None of us enjoyed what we were doing but none of us wanted to shirk our duty. "You never know. You may be back. Make the nurses' lives a misery and say we need you!"

He brightened, "You know I think I will, sir."

"The rest of you load up and then make a defensive line at the edge of the dead ground. Bill, go and fetch Davis. I don't want to risk him. White and Foster, use the grenade rifle to keep their heads down."

"Right sir."

I went to see Fletcher. He had just finished. "They are sending down a couple of Kangaroos and a company, sir. Our orders are to hold. If the light holds they are going to try to bomb it."

I looked up. It was overcast and getting late. It would be unlikely that would happen. I heard the crump of the grenade and then sporadic fire. My four men came racing back.

"Well done Davis."

"I had better make myself a suit sir out of the camouflage netting. I was fortunate there. There was grass as well as rocks and bushes. We won't always be that lucky."

"What did you see through your scope?"

"They look to be in company strength. Just before the Sergeant pulled me back I saw more movement in the woods. They are reinforcing."

"That was to be expected. We had better make ourselves cosy. We will have company soon enough."

It was dark when the two Kangaroos and the lorries arrived with the company of Commandos. The officer saluted. It was the one who had led the advance guard the previous day, "Captain Wilberforce sir. I have brought C Company."

"My men are in a safe place to watch. The woods are a couple of hundred yards away and they have brought up their guns. The next vehicles that move down the road will be destroyed before they can get twenty feet. They have two 88s. It is a company in there."

"Should we try a nighttime attack, sir?"

"We could but they may have booby-trapped the woods. It is what we would do. Let us wait until they have called in the airstrike."

"What if they start to shell us here, sir?"

"In that case, Captain, we will launch an attack. They haven't yet which leads me to think that they are low on HE. I believe the half-tracks are there to protect the 88s and pull them out if we get close. Me and my lads are going to get our heads down. Wake me if there is any movement."

"Sir."

The Captain seemed to know his business. He used the two Kangaroos to anchor the flanks and he had his men dig slit trenches.

We sent Beaumont back in the lorry. The company only had a couple of medics and could do no more than Hewitt had done. The men all bantered with Beaumont as he was carried aboard the lorry. Those who had them gave him letters to post. Fletcher and he were close. I saw them shake hands firmly. They had totally different backgrounds but they got on like brothers. Beaumont would be safe in a hospital for a while but the rest of us could all be dead inside a week. Our farewells were meant. The Vera Lynn song we had sung in Strasbourg suddenly seemed more relevant.

We ate rations and checked our weapons. Emerson went around the jeeps and topped up the tanks. We had the luxury of a company to guard us and we slept well.

I was up before dawn. I went to the slit trenches. There was a sergeant on duty. "Sir!"

"Is it quiet?"

"As the grave, sir. The lads we relieved said there was some noise around midnight and then all quiet."

"That does not bode well for us, Sergeant. The Germans are very good at making traps."

"I know, sir. We helped to clear Walcheren. It was a bugger sir if you'll pardon my French."

"We were just there for the Westkappelle part of the operation and that was bad enough. We lost a couple of good lads there."

"Aye, so did we. That's why I hope they just bomb the bastards in the woods. We have lost enough good men. Jerry has lost! Why don't they surrender?"

I remembered the terror weapons, "Because, Sergeant, the men at the top still think that they can win."

He nodded, "Aye sir and they say that when this is over they will send us to Japan. The Nips are still fighting. We could be fighting until 1950 at this rate, sir."

The thought depressed me beyond belief.

By the time the sun came up my men were all washed, fed and ready to go. Captain Wilberforce was all for attacking the woods. "That would be a mistake Captain. Your men heard them hard at work last night. That means they are making it dangerous for us."

Just then we heard the sound of armour coming up the road. It was the two Sherman Crocodiles leading the lorries with the men of the 1st Commando Brigade. Brigadier Young led them. He stepped out and pointed to the skies. "The R.A.F. are going to help us out this morning. Twelve Typhoons are going to clear the wood before we go in."

I nodded to Captain Wilberforce, "There you are Captain. We can watch the show instead of being part of it."

"Come here, Harsker, let us have a look at the map." Others gathered around but the Brigadier waved them away. "This is to do with your mission in Austria." He jabbed a finger at the mountains in Thuringia. "This is Nordhausen. The Germans have been producing their V-2 rockets at a factory in the mountains to the north of it. It is an underground factory. If you are able Churchill would like you to get there and see if you can capture the blueprints for the rockets and the scientists."

I shook my head, "Impossible. That is two hundred miles away. We were held up just twenty miles from our jump-off point."

He smiled. "That is what I told them. Still, we are heading to Bielefeld. That is less than a hundred miles from our target. Let's see how long it takes us to get there, eh?"

Just then we heard the throaty roar of twelve Typhoons as they screamed in to attack the woods. We were close enough to see how devastating their rockets and cannons were. They tore through the woods. We saw vehicles, guns and ammunition exploding. The noise of the aero engines and the explosions was deafening. The three aeroplanes which had attacked at Schermbeck had been terrifying enough but twelve was horrific. When they peeled away they left a smoking wood with flames flickering within.

I said, "Right lads, mount up!"

The Brigadier said, "Don't be so keen. Captain Wilberforce, take the Kangaroos in first. Major Harsker, your jeeps can follow."

I was not going to argue with a brigadier., "Yes sir."

I slipped behind the wheel. Fletcher and White had their guns at the ready. We had to wait until the two Kangaroos filled up with men. They had two Bren guns at the front. The gunners and driver were protected by steel. I waved Emerson forward as they passed us. It was a sedate pace. We could see little at first because of the huge armoured personnel carriers in front of us. As soon as we entered the wood we saw that nothing could have survived. There were blackened lumps which had been men. There were piles of twisted and contorted metal that had been guns and vehicles. The tyres on the half-tracks were still burning. Then there was the sound of a small explosion. I saw the lad Kangaroo move.

Sam said, "What was that, sir?"

"I am guessing, White, that they laid anti-personnel mines. The Kangaroos are safe but they could have damaged the jeeps."

The explosions lasted for fifty yards and then there was nothing. We came to the clearing where the Germans had bivouacked and the two Kangaroos pulled over. The driver, a cheery sergeant said, "All yours sir! I reckon that is the last of the mines.

Captain Wilberforce pushed his tin lid back and said, "We will be a bit close behind you this time. I have my radio operator tuned in so if you have any bother, sir, we'll be right on it." Our jeeps could move much faster than the Kangaroos.

I waved, "Thanks, Captain. Freddie! Foot down!"

I expected to be held up at Haltern am See. There was water and it was a town. A detour would have added days. However, as we approached I saw neither grey nor guns. I overtook Emerson, "I will go first, Freddie. I don't think your German is up to it."

"No sir!"

I drove cautiously, "Don't point your guns at them and smile. Fletcher, get on the radio and tell them what we are doing."

"Sir."

This was neither France nor Belgium. We were not liberating these people, we were conquering them. There was no band to welcome us. No flags were waved and we were greeted by silence and stares. It was unnerving. It felt as though we were a funeral cortege heading through the town. Perhaps we were and the coffin was Germany itself. This was the surest sign yet that the German people had given up. It was resignation and not resistance on their faces. We were through the town and into the countryside once more.

Fletcher said, "I told them, sir." He shook his head. "That was weird."

Sam said, "Is it always like that sir?"

"I have no idea, Sam. This is the first German town we have liberated."

As we headed east we saw in the distance more bombers as the Allies continued to harass the Germans. Eisenhower was keeping them off balance. We had another, smaller forest through which we had to pass but it was uneventful. We had learned from the first one and drove through cautiously. There was no point in getting too far ahead of C Company. The next town we struck was Lüdinghausen. It was a beautiful little place with three castles and like Haltern am See we were greeted by stares and silence. Perhaps the aeroplanes overhead showed what they might have received.

We hit trouble by Rheda-Wiedenbrück. I had expected it. This was larger than the last two towns and there was a major river, the Emse. They would hold us up if only to prepare more defences deeper in Germany. Freddie was leading and, as we approached the outskirts someone fired from the third storey of what looked like an old school. Freddie spun his wheel and led us into the shelter of what appeared to be a park. There were trees and a wall. It was shelter. Our sudden move took the shooters by surprise but, even so, chips of stone and road surface clattered against the jeeps.

Once inside the shelter of the park I jumped out and grabbed my gun, "Fletcher!"

"On it, sir."

"White, find Foster and get the rifle grenade. I want you to take out the men on top of that building. "

"Sir."

"Bill, get Ashcroft and set up the mortar. Davis, shin up that chestnut tree and tell me what you can see."

"Sir."

"The rest of you get ready to move. Betts, you still have the bad ankle. You guard the jeeps."

"Sir."

White and Foster brought the grenade rifle. "Sir, I think the range is too great sir. It would be a waste of a grenade."

A month ago he would not have spoken up. The rookies were becoming veterans. "Bill, it is up to you two."

He grinned, "I have been looking forward to using this." They set it up behind the wall. The bullets still ricocheted off the wall as they tried to make us move. Davis shouted, "Further down the street sir, two hundred yards away, they have a roadblock and an anti-tank gun."

"Do you have a shot?"

"Yes sir."

"Then make them nervous." I turned to Lieutenant Poulson. "As soon as we have cleared the building take Bill, Freddie and Foster. Clear the building. We will head for the tank trap."

Fletcher said, "They are on their way, sir! The captain says he is less than an hour away."

The first of the mortar shells landed. It was short but it shook the building and I heard cries from those who were sheltering in the lower floors. Bill adjusted it and sent another one. This one hit the parapet and, as part of it fell, some German soldiers were exposed. Gordy fired a burst with his Tommy gun. He missed but it made them duck. The second and third shells were right on the money. Bodies flew over the side.

"Go, Lieutenant!"

They ran at the now wrecked building. There was fire from the anti-tank position in the street but they escaped unscathed. My men knew how to run and use limited cover.

Davis' rifle was still firing. The Germans were trying to locate him but he was outside the range of their sights and rifles. "Get down Davis, you have done enough. Bill, turn the mortar around. You are firing blind but I want six shells laying down as a barrage. Three hundred yards should do it."

"Sir."

"The rest of you with me."

We began to run. We headed to the corner of the street. Two shells had been fired by the time we reached it. As we turned I saw that Bill was short. It was not by much and, as the mortar heated up it had a tendency to send them further. Besides, Bill and his mortar were a distraction. As each shell exploded the defenders took cover. Stones and debris flew through the air and the shells appeared to be creeping ever closer to the defenders. By the fourth shell, we were just a hundred and fifty yards from them. I was using the cover of the doorways and only running when the shells exploded.

The sixth shell hit the barricade. Splinters of wood and metal acted like a giant shotgun and men reeled. We opened fire at sixty paces distance. Our Thompsons fired short bursts. The Germans had rifles. When Lieutenant Poulson and his men joined us it was all over. The survivors surrendered.

I heard the sound of Kangaroos and I sent four men back to bring the jeeps. Captain Wilberforce shook his head, "Very selfish old chap. How about leaving something for us next time?"

"This time isn't over yet, Captain." I pointed to the town. The towers of a castle could be seen. "Unless I miss my guess that is Schloss Rheda. The river runs around it and I think there will be a bridge. They will defend it. You might get your chance yet. Have some of your men guard the prisoners and then follow us."

"Do you want the Kangaroos to go first?"

The jeeps arrived. I shook my head, "Too many high buildings. They can drop a grenade into them and that would be the end of that. We will go first." I turned before I clambered aboard my jeep. "Davis, keep your eyes peeled for men on the roof."

"Yes sir."

"Off you go Emerson."

I got a stiff neck driving the half-mile through the old town. I kept looking up for snipers. Bombers had ruined some fine old buildings but they were close enough to the road to be a serious threat. Davis rifle cracked and a body tumbled from the roof of a two-story building.

Same White shouted, "Grenade!" He sprayed the top of the next building as the grenade exploded in front of Emerson's jeep. The Bergens saved them from injury. Once again Fred's quick reactions had saved us. The twisting road turned and there was the Schloss directly ahead of us on a piece of high ground above the river. Machine-guns and a cannon opened fire. I saw that the road was flanked by woodland. It looked to have been an ornamental one from the nineteenth century. It was cover and we would use it.

"Emerson, into the woods!" I whipped my wheel around and we entered the woods. The castle had a fine position and was on a rock. I was just grateful that they had left the vestiges of a hunting forest. We had shelter. Gordy almost made it without damage but machine-gun bullets shredded his rear tyre and he barely managed to avoid overturning it.

We had done this many times and my men knew what to do. They spread out and took shelter in the trees.

"Get the mortar and the rifle grenade ready!"

The Kangaroos were close behind us. We discovered that they had a serious anti-tank gun when the first Kangaroo was hit by a shell. Two Panzerfaust rockets sped after it and the engine began to pour smoke. As the men began to bail out the machine-guns and rifles from the castle hit four of them. Davis began to fire, seeking the gunners who were hurting our men. I aimed at the gate. I saw muzzle flashes. White and Foster sent a grenade high into the air. It exploded just in front of the men at the gate. The concussion and the shrapnel made their machine-guns stop firing. The anti-tank gun fired at the second Kangaroo which was busy trying to get into cover. It was hit but it was on the side and did little damage.

It was time to evaluate the situation. It was getting late. We had more chance of defeating them in the dark. "Davis and Hewitt, take White and Foster, get as close to the castle as you can. I am guessing that they use the river as a moat. I don't want the bridge damaging."

"Sir."

"Hay and Ashcroft set up the mortar. I want shells inside the castle."

"Sir!"

"Fletcher, get on to the main column. Tell them we have lost a Kangaroo."

"Sir."

"The rest of you I want you to work your way as close as you can to the castle without exposing yourself."

Lieutenant Poulson shouted, "Sir, just there, to the right are some buildings. They have been damaged by bombing but we could use them to shelter."

I glanced to where he pointed. They were forty yards away from the bridge and the road. We might be able to enfilade the gate from there. "Right, lead on MacDuff!, Emerson you are in charge of the vehicles. Betts. You stay with the corporal and help him change the tyre."

Captain Wilberforce had set up his Bren guns and they were firing at the gate. It allowed us to slip through the woods without too much attention being drawn to us. There was a crude bridge to the buildings. It was, literally four long planks. The river was just twenty feet wide but the planks were each only a foot wide. We made it across. When we reached the buildings I saw that they had been in use until they had been bombed. Other than having no roof they were in good repair. I heard a whistle and saw that Davis and Hewitt, along with White and Foster had somehow managed to get on to the first floor of the wrecked building. I held up my thumb.

"Gordy, come with me. Lieutenant see if you can join our intrepid climbers." As we went around the back of the building I saw that it was made of brick and not stone. It was not medieval. The light was fading but, when we turned the corner I saw that the tower and the wall of the castle were stone. I saw brick as well. This castle had been modernised. I saw that there was a double bridge. One went over the River Emse and the other over the moat.

I slid down through the nettles and overgrown undergrowth. We were hidden by the night. I heard the crack of Davis' rifle and heard a scream. He would keep the defenders' heads down. When I reached the river I saw that there was a sort of path which ran along it. I took a chance and followed it. Up ahead, in the fading light, I saw a small footbridge which went over the river. There was a bank and, at the top of it, a low wall. I turned to Gordy, "Let's see if they have any sentries on that bridge. If not then we are in."

"I'm game, sir."

As we moved I heard the sound of mortars, machine-guns and rifles. As we moved around the sound became slightly fainter. The path had not been used in some time and was overgrown. It was harder going than I thought. However, the reward was that we approached slowly and I saw that they had no sentry there. As we neared it, I saw why. There were some of the planks missing. A stray bomb or perhaps poor maintenance had left it almost ruined. However, we could get across. It was only a couple of feet to the water below. As darkness fell we made our way up to the bridge. I slung my Thompson over my back. I would need both hands. I made the sign for Gordy to wait and cover me. That way only one of us would be risked. The light had gone almost entirely and that did not make the crossing any more appealing. I checked the rear of the castle. They had no one watching the walls. It was barely five feet to the water but I knew that these moats were deep. With grenades festooned on my battle jerkin, I would be dragged under if I fell. When I reached the gap I jumped. I made it. I hurried to the other side. I could barely see Gordy and so I whistled.

 I unslung my gun and cocked it. I heard heavy breathing as Gordy emulated my feat. His smoking meant he did not make the jump as smoothly as I had. When he joined me we climbed the bank. In medieval times defenders would have slaughtered anyone doing what we did but the rear of the castle was deserted. When we reached the wall I saw that it was just nine feet high. Gordy stood with his back to the wall and cupped his hands. I ran and jumped into his hand with my right foot. Gordy was a strong man and he boosted me high enough for me to grab the top of the wall. By putting my foot on his head I was able to reach the top.

 I straddled the wall. There was a courtyard. I could see men and weapons. The sound of the battle was louder here. There was a cacophony of noise and confusion. Men ran around. Some were burning documents. There was a brazier and an officer was piling documents into it. I saw that one of the buildings was on fire and men were trying to douse it. In the light of the fire, I saw black uniforms by the gate. They were S.S. That was why they were fighting. Surrender was not an option.

 I reached down as far as I could and Gordy grabbed my hand with his two. He began to walk up the wall. The mortar on the stone was not the best and he found purchase. He joined me. I pointed to the gate. We needed to gain control of the gate but first, we had to reach it unseen. We had the advantage that there was so much noise we would not have to worry about silence. We dropped the eight feet to the ground on the inside. Bill Hay was using the mortar bombs sparingly. He was also moving the mortar for each shell. They were unpredictable. That was as dangerous for us as it was for the Germans. We clambered up the bank. I sprayed a burst at the men burning the documents. If the S.S. wanted documents burned then we needed them to be saved. My burst made some of the Germans turn around. Gordy had me covered and his gun scythed through them. I ran towards the gate. One of Bill's shells hit the building behind me. The concussion threw both Gordy and me to the ground. It probably saved our lives for machine-gun bullets flew over our heads.

I rolled to the right and, while on my back, fired a burst in the direction of the gunner. I stood and began to zig-zag towards the gate. I took a grenade and pulling the pin threw it the forty feet towards the gate. Gordy did the same and we both hit the ground. The two grenades did not reach the gate. They both exploded eight and six feet short. I saw holes appear in the gate. Standing I emptied my gun at the firing platform above the gate and reloaded. I ran at the gate. We had badly damaged it. I shouted, "Hit it together!"

"Sir!"

We threw ourselves at the damaged door. It cracked and flew open throwing us to the ground. If we had not done so then we would have been hit by the bullets from Captain Wilberforce's Bren guns. From the ground we both sprayed the crews of the machine-guns and the 88 mm. Gordy pulled the pin on a grenade and shouted, "Grenade!"

I curled up in a ball, protected by the body of a dead German. The grenade ended the defence of the gate. I stood and waved my arm, "Commandos!"

There was a roar and then Captain Wilberforce led his company across the two narrow bridges and past us. We followed them and I ran to the brazier with the papers. While Captain Wilberforce and his men winkled out the defenders Gordy and I ran to collect as many papers as we could. Many had been burned but we filled a cardboard box with the ones that survived.

"Local knowledge sir?"

I turned around to see Lieutenant Poulson and my men. I smiled, "No Lieutenant. I just followed my nose."

The rest of my men came through the door. The silence told me that resistance had ended. Sam White shook his head, "Well sir, I never thought I would ever assault a medieval castle. If I ever get to teach history I can really bring it to life."

His words made me think, "Anyone hurt?"

Bill Hay shook his head. "We were in cover and they were just using the 88 to destroy armour. They hit another of Captain Wilberforce's lorries. We are all fine and Freddie has replaced the tyre."

"Then go and fetch them, Sam. We might as well have the night in the castle. Who knows there might even be beds."

Hewitt said, "Come on Tom, let's go and find them first!"

Beyond the Rhine

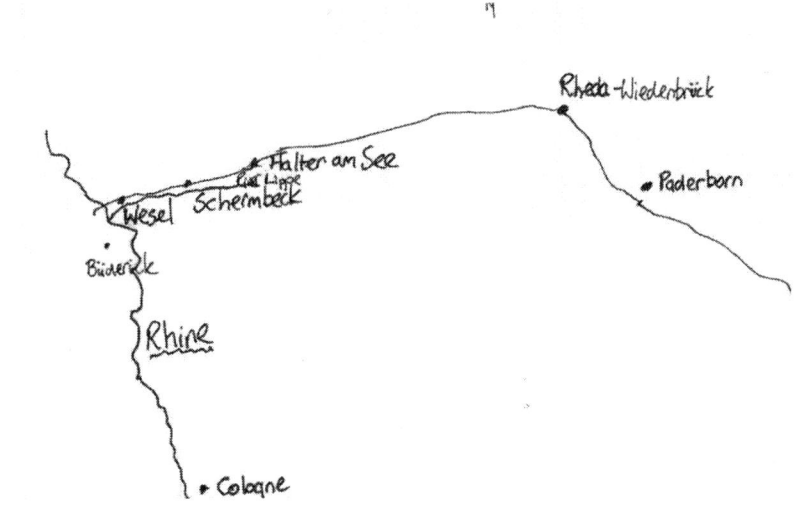

Rheda-Wiedenbrück

Haltern am See

Die Lippe

Wesel *Schermbeck*

Büderick

Paderborn

Rhine

Cologne

Chapter 14

We were a little crowded but Hewitt found us a room with actual beds. We drew cards for them. I lost and was one of the six who slept on the floor. I didn't mind. There were solid walls and, once again, we did not have to do a duty.

I did not get a full night's sleep. I was awoken at 0100 hours when the Brigadier arrived. "Sorry to wake you, Harsker, but those papers you found, McMillan from Intelligence has read them. They talk of death camps to the east of us. They also confirm the secret facility at Nordhausen. They use the word Uranverein." I looked up. "You have heard of it?"

"Yes sir. There were other references to it in Austria and Bavaria. That is the code word for their terror weapon."

"That confirms that we need to get east as soon as we can."

"Sir."

"Anyway, you had better get back to bed."

"Sir, we need armour to back us up, sir. We lost one Kangaroo and almost lost a second. We need some firepower."

"I know. I am working on it. 30 Corps is north of us and they are leading the drive for Hamburg. I have asked if they have a spare unit. Even a couple of Fireflies would be useful."

"Sir."

"I will impress upon the Field Marshal what we need." I turned to go.

Despite my disturbed sleep, I was still up early. Partly that was Gordy's snoring. He had been lucky and drawn a face card which meant he had had a bed. The soft bed and lying on his back meant I slept with a buzz saw above me. I smelled bacon frying. The Germans loved their pork and ham. I had no doubt that the S.S. would have had good supplies of it. I followed my nose and found the kitchen. The Brigadier and his senior officers were there and seated around a table. Brigadier Young grinned, "A true Commando! You sniff out food in your sleep! Jones, a couple of bacon sandwiches for the Major,"

"Thank you, sir and a cup of tea if you have it!"

One of the cooks said, "We have a pot of Sergeant Major tea here sir if you like it that way!"

"Perfect!"

I sat down and saw that they had a map before them. "I have been in touch with Monty. 12 Corps is sending us eight tanks from the Sherwood Rangers Yeomanry. They are Sherman Firefly tanks." He shook his head, "You would have thought that we were using them for a weekend away, the way I had to beg! We will brigade them with Captain Wilberforce's men. You two seem to work well together."

The cook handed me the bacon sandwiches, "Sorry sir, no H.P. sauce."

"I will have to rough it then sergeant." He had soaked the slices of bread in the bacon fat and it ran down my chin as I bit into it. It was the army's way of cooking. I defy anyone in the world to resist the smell of frying bacon and when it was cooked to a crispy crunch like this one then it was the nectar of the gods. The Brigadier handed me a tea towel and I wiped away the grease from my chin. I swallowed and drank some tea. "Sir, he has taken losses."

"I know. We have made good those losses but he was adamant he wanted to be with you."

I ate my sandwich and finished my tea while the Brigadier discussed the next moves with his officers. When I had finished and wiped my hands, he handed me a map. "Here is your new route. We head south and east to Delbrück this means that we can skirt Paderborn. It is a big place and Jerry will defend it. The Black Watch and their armour will attack it and that will protect our flank. The target is Göttingen. I am afraid that the road from there will be more hazardous. It is just thirty-seven miles from there to the secret facility but the roads pass through mountains. The Germans can defend it easily."

I nodded, "I take it the Americans further south, are heading towards it too."

He nodded, "Yes, I am afraid it is a race."

"But surely we are all on the same side, sir."

"You would like to think so wouldn't you? This German technology is going to be a powerful weapon once the war is over. The Russians want it too."

I said nothing. Colonel Reece said, "Look, Major, it doesn't change what we are doing. We need to end German resistance. Our column was always intended to strike into the heart of Germany."

I nodded, thinking about the soldiers I had lost so far, "Yes sir but this haste may cost us soldiers' lives."

"You are correct, Major, but it is what we do."

The Brigadier was right. I nodded and took the map. "Very well sir, we will do our best. Do we have any more fuel or ammo?"

The Brigadier turned to a sergeant who was taking notes, "Williams?"

"There is some fuel here in the castle. We were lucky it didn't get hit in the firefight, sir. It is in the building at the back." I nodded. "What ammo do you need sir?"

"Mortars and .45."

"Mortars you can have but .45 ammo?" He shook his head, "We use Lee Enfields sir and Bren guns, sir."

The Brigadier laughed, "You and your lads are living in the past!"

"And that is why we are still living, sir. Tell me, sergeant, what happened to the German weapons that were captured?"

"In the armoury sir. It is also in the building at the back."

"Then, with your permission sir, we will see what they have."

"Of course!"

I roused my men and took them, via the kitchens, to the armoury. The Brigadier and his officers had left. The cook was preparing the breakfast for the rest of the men. My men were like a plague of locusts. They snaffled whatever the officers had left and then took fresh ones handed to them by the sergeant.

For us, it was like an Aladdin's cave. When my eyes lighted on the eight MP 40 sub machine-guns I knew we had fallen lucky. Using the same ammunition as the MP 34 it could take a 32 round magazine and had a slightly better rate of fire. We took them and all the ammunition we could carry. Lieutenant Poulson discovered a Panzerfaust and four rockets. That would do too. Gordy collected all the spare grenades and we headed out of the Schloss Rheda to our jeeps. It was 0700 when we reached our vehicles. Having lost one of our number we now had more room and we reorganized our equipment. I made sure that every jeep had one of the MP 40 sub-machine-guns. The other three went to Hay, Fletcher and Hewitt.

While we waited for the Fireflies to arrive and for the new men to join Captain Wilberforce I showed my drivers the route and the checkpoints. "It is a short hop to Delbrück. Before that, we just have Amt Rietberg. I think Amt Rieberg will be too small to cause us a problem but that is your job, Davis. You have done a sterling job up to now. Delbrück is another matter. Approach it as though it is defended."

"Where do we bivouac tonight, sir?"

"The powers that be seem to think we can cover a hundred miles today and that Jerry will just let us through. When we get to Göttingen then we have to make a break through enemy lines. Our final objective is another of the German's underground facilities. This one is the biggest that they have."

"And then sir?"

I smiled at Tom Foster, "And then, my keen young friend, with any luck the war will be over and we can stop playing silly buggers!"

Fletcher laughed, "Nah sir, you will miss this too much! You like the excitement."

Shaking my head I said, "I did but after five years it has paled somewhat. A quieter life for me."

Lieutenant Poulson said, "Our Major is getting married as soon as the war is over!"

Fletcher grinned, "A nice girl, sir, I expect."

I nodded, "Well you seemed to think so."

He looked bewildered. He normally had an answer for everything but I had confused him. I saw him wracking his memory. "Me sir?"

"Yes Fletcher, the sergeant WAAF on the radio, the one you thought fancied you, is my fiancée!"

For the first time since I had known him, he looked shocked. My men, of course, thought it was hilarious. Barker said, "Typical of you, Scouse, you try and pinch the major's girl! I am surprised he didn't have you court-martialed."

"But sir I didn't know. I would have said nowt if..."

I held up my hand, "It is not a problem, Scouse, I am certain that Susan would be flattered to know that her voice could inspire such ardour."

Fletcher's embarrassed blushes were spared by the arrival of the tanks. There were only seven of them. We discovered that one had broken down and would be joining them when it was repaired. Now that they had arrived we set off. One night in a bed and bacon sandwiches and hot tea does not sound much but to us, it was as though we had had a leave!

I was right about Amt Rietberg. There were too many side roads around it and it had no defensible features. We raced through. Delbrück was a different proposition. When we were more than a mile and a half away Davis had Emerson stop his jeep. We pulled next to him. Davis was using his telescopic sight as a telescope. I took out my glasses. "Armour sir and infantry dug in."

I peered through my binoculars. He was right. There was a wood. It looked to be half a mile from the town. It looked like a couple of Panzer Mark IVs hull down. As I moved along the edge of the wood I saw the German troops. The last side road we had past had been at Amt Rietberg. It would be a long detour to get around them. Even as I looked I saw the muzzle flash from one of the Panzers.

"Emerson get the hell out of here."

I dropped the binoculars and put the jeep into reverse. Emerson had rammed his into first and whipped it around. The shell exploded just forty feet from us. We were showered with stone and debris. Behind me, I heard Fletcher telling the main column what we had struck. The nearest shelter was a couple of outbuildings three hundred yards away and we drove there. "Everyone all right?"

Sam White said, "A cut above my eye but..."

"Go and see Hewitt, get it sorted!"

The tanks and the lorries rumbled next to us just ten minutes later. I got out of the jeep and climbed up on to the hull of the leading Firefly. "Two Panzers and infantry dug in at the woods. I couldn't give you numbers."

"Anti-tank guns?"

"I would guess yes."

I saw that the Lieutenant was young. He chewed his lip. I turned to Captain Wilberforce, "Have you got ten men I can borrow?"

"Of course, sir, why?"

"I can take half a dozen of my men with grenades and submachine-guns. I have a sniper. If there are anti-tank guns we can take them out so long as the tanks take care of the panzers."

The Lieutenant looked relieved. "I thought if we went in a long line we would divide their fire."

"Sounds good to me Lieutenant." I turned. "Davis, up on this tank with me. Hewitt and Fletcher on the next tank. Emerson and Hay the next tank. You need grenades and your MP 40."

I saw Captain Wilberforce asking for volunteers. He had plenty to choose from. One clambered up behind us. He had a Lee Enfield. I shouted, "Foster, throw me Beaumont's Thompson and three magazines." He passed them up to me and I gave them to the soldier, "Try these. A little extra firepower."

"Thanks, sir."

I looked at the ground. It was a field which had grown crops. They had been picked. It was not flat and there were places where infantry could take shelter. If we had the armour firing to cover us then we might be able to crawl closer and take out their rockets and anti-tank guns.

The Lieutenant disappeared into the turret and we moved off. The Sherman was fast for such a large tank but I knew that the German tank gun was more than capable of brewing a Sherman up. Known as Ronsons for the similarity to cigarette lighters I admired the courage of their crews. The German and British guns had similar ranges. We had the advantage that we would be sending three or four shells at each Panzer. The Lieutenant had guts. The Germans blinked and fired first. The effective range was less than half a mile and they fired at three quarters of a mile. One was aiming at our tank and the shell hit the glacis. I felt the heat from the shell as it soared up into the sky. The second tank had more success. Its shell hit the left front of the tank to our right and it stopped. Its commander came out of the turret and manned the Browning.

A hundred yards later and the young Lieutenant gave the command to fire. All seven guns belched. The smoke was vented close to us and our vision was briefly obscured. When I looked I saw that although we had hit both tanks, one was still firing.

Davis shouted, "Anti-tank gun, about to fire!" Only he had the range and he fired bullet after bullet into the crew. Perhaps he was lucky or just persistent. The shell struck the last tank on the right. The range was too great and it did no damage. All seven guns now fired at the last Panzer. Just before it blew up it managed to score a direct hit, at a thousand yards, on the third tank in the line. It exploded in a ball of fire. The three Commandos crouching behind the turret would have known nothing about it.

Emerson and Hay had jumped off their stricken tank and were now running alongside us. Davis was still firing but we had to get closer. I took out my glasses and saw that there was a line of German infantry, seven pairs of them, and they had Panzerschrecks and Panzerfausts. I saw, behind me, that Captain Wilberforce had his men rushing along in a long skirmish line. We had support. I banged on the turret. The lieutenant's head popped up. "Stop your tanks! They have rocket weapons ahead. Concentrate your fire on the anti-tank gun and have your machine-guns spray Jerry, while we get into position."

"Right sir."

I shouted, "Everyone off and form a skirmish line. Davis, stay here and keep sniping."

"Sir."

I cocked the German machine-guns. We had eight hundred yards to cover. The remaining tanks began sending HE towards the Germans. The ball machine-gun fired and all the commanders manned their Brownings. They had the range and their shells could penetrate armour. However, as with all machine-guns, at the range they were being used they were less than accurate. Some of the rocket launchers would survive. The operators were lying down. The guns, however, were effective at discouraging the Germans from raising their heads. I heard a cheer behind me as one of the two remaining anti-tank guns was hit by the Shermans. It was only a matter of time before they took out the other one.

When we were four hundred yards away I shouted, "Halt!"

I waved the men to the ground and we crawled. It meant that the tanks could continue to shred the tree line and we were almost impossible to hit. We had crawled a hundred and twenty yards when I heard the crump of German mortars. The ground behind us erupted as the shells hit. They would correct and the next salvo would end us. We had two hundred and eighty yards to go. The tanks were now lobbing HE into the woods to silence the mortars. A hundred and fifty yards behind us I saw the line of Commandos. It was time.

I stood, "Commandos! Charge!"

It was hardly the Charge of the Light Brigade. However, we did not have far to run and we had cover. There was a handful of us but we were Commandos and we knew no fear. I began firing the MP 40 in short bursts as I zigged and zagged towards the line of grey. Many of the grey uniforms were soaked in red. I saw a German officer raise his pistol and aim it at me. Davis' bullet threw him to the ground. Another German smashed the porcelain top of his grenade and I shot him even as he pulled the cord. He and the two men next to him disappeared in a red mist. And then we were at the tree line.

"Take cover." We had achieved our objective. The eleven of us who had survived gathered in a half-circle. I changed my magazine and fired at the grey uniforms which were retreating. Then there was a cheer as Captain Wilberforce led his company into the wood. I glanced to my right and saw the five Shermans heading down the road, firing as they went.

I stood and said, "Well done lads! That was bravely done."

The Sergeant who had led Captain Wilberforce's men said, "Should we follow our lads, sir?"

"No Sergeant, we have earned a rest. Let's head back to the lorries. This is not over yet. We still have the town to take."

As we walked back I said to Sergeant Hay, "I don't think we will reach our target today. We will be lucky to get through this wood." I pointed to the shredded bodies lying near to the wrecked 88 mm. "They are fighting for every inch of their country."

Hewitt said, thoughtfully, "To be fair, sir, we would do the same, wouldn't we?"

He was right.

Captain Wilberforce lost nine men all told. When we caught up with them, on the outskirts of Delbrück, I said, "Sorry, Captain. We seem to bring bad luck to you and your men."

He shook his head, "No sir, you just give us something to aspire to. We are getting better."

Bennet, the Commando to whom I had loaned the Tommy gun, held it out, "Here sir."

I shook my head, "Lance Sergeant Beaumont won't need it again. You keep it. It might keep you alive a little longer."

We waited for the main column. The damaged Sherman needed repairs and the other Shermans needed refuelling. We headed for Delbrück. I had the column stop short of the town. The town did not appear to have defences but we had radioed back and I had said that I would take my jeeps in at dusk. Captain Wilberforce needed time to reorganize his men.

"Lieutenant, while you are waiting for your tank have the rest line up half a mile from the edge of the town and elevate your guns as though you are going to fire a salvo at the town."

"Sir, we don't have enough ammunition to do that."

I smiled, "They don't know that, do they?"

As darkness started to fall I led my column of jeeps. Part of me had wanted the German soldiers to have plenty of time to flee the town. Had we followed hot on their heels then they might have been tempted to fight. This way there would be fewer to fight us in the future. Men would desert or simply head home. Others would be dispirited and lower the morale of the units they joined. I remembered the retreat to Dunkirk. We had held together but mainly because we wanted to get back to England.

The Germans were already home. We drove slowly with guns lowered but cocked.

There was not a straight road through the town. It turned and twisted. When we came to the large square I recognised the Rathaus, the German Town Hall. I slowed down for I saw four policemen and a knot of civilians outside the main door. We had seen faces behind windows and doors which had been ajar as we had driven through.

"Sam, take the wheel and Davis, leave the sniper rifle here but bring my MP 40."

"Sir."

"If this goes wrong, Sam, then get the hell back to Captain Wilberforce."

"Sir."

We walked to the policemen and civilians. The policemen were armed but there were five jeeps filled with Commandos holding automatic weapons. I did not think that there would be firing. We stopped in front of them.

I spoke in German. "I am Major Harsker of the Commandos. I am here to accept the surrender of the town."

One of the policemen looked angry and his hand went to his holster. An older chap with a white beard shook his head, "No, Wernher. Let me speak."

The policeman nodded.

I said, "You should thank the Mayor, Wernher, he has just saved your life. Had you drawn your gun then you would be dead." I nodded towards the MP 40 which Davis had pointed at his middle.

"How did you know I was the Mayor?"

"A lucky guess."

"I am Hans Breitling, Mayor of Delbrück. Why should we surrender?"

"Because if you do not then the tanks which are waiting outside the town will open fire to make sure that our soldiers are not shot when we attack. We have lost enough good men already. If anyone is to bleed then it will be Germans."

The Mayor nodded, "A little blunt, Major."

"I speak the truth, Mayor. Do you surrender?"

He looked at his companions and they nodded.

"Good." I turned and shouted, "Fletcher, get on the radio, tell the Brigadier they have surrendered. We will wait here until the forward units arrive."

"Righto, sir."

"A wise decision. The war is lost."

"Sadly, Major, the war has been lost for some time."

Chapter 15

Brigadier Young was happy with the surrender but less happy at the delay. "In that case, sir you need to keep the main column closer to the Shermans and Captain Wilberforce. He has lost too many men and we almost lost a quarter of our tanks today."

"You speak your mind, Major."

"It is how I was brought up, sir."

"Well, you are right. We now have more Kangaroos and the rest of the Sherwood Rangers Yeomanry. We have enough tanks to take on Jerry armour. But tomorrow I want all of us away by dawn. Time is wasting. There are rumours that the Nazis are executing the workers in these factories. They are slave labour. There will be war crimes trials after the war, Tom, and they are trying to hide the evidence. This is not a chase for glory. We are chasing justice. Forget the secret weapons. Intelligence thinks that there are up to 3000 labourers in various camps close to the underground factory."

"You mean we could save them?"

"I confess that I don't know but I want us to make the effort. It is obvious now that we can't reach Nordhausen with the whole column. Let us get as close as we can and then you can make the dash."

"Sir."

I went to my men, "Freddie, how are the jeeps holding up?"

"They are a smashing little motor, sir. We haven't done that many miles yet. How much further do we have to go?"

I gathered them around and told them what I had been told. "So, Freddie, it is about seventy miles or so with the main column and then a push of thirty to forty miles on our own."

"Then they will hold up, sir. That is nothing to these beauties. And we have enough fuel too. The bowser came when you were talking with the Brigadier and we filled five big jerrycans."

"And we have enough ammo. Fletcher, take a couple of the new lads." I took a wad of German money we had recovered from our enemies, "Here is some of the local currency. See what you can buy. I doubt there will be much to be had but buy it, right, don't take it!"

"All right sir, Foster, White, come and have a lesson eh?"

I sat after we had eaten, with Gordy and Lieutenant Poulson. "Do you think we can save any of these workers, sir? I mean, the Germans who run the camps must know we are coming. If they are going to get rid of the evidence then now is the time."

"They are making the V-2 there, Polly. I know we slowed down their production but they are still making them. They will hang on to their workers until the last minute. That is why the Brigadier is sending us alone. The terrain between Göttingen and Nordhausen will take the column a few days to get through. We can do it in one night. We have to try."

"Aye, sir. We have had a tough war but imagine being worked as a slave under a mountain. We know what the S.S. are like. If we save a dozen it will be worth it."

We had made plans and we had prepared. So had the Germans. Paderborn was only fifteen or so miles away from our main column but, as we tried to skirt the town and bypass it we discovered that the Germans had made that impossible. They had tanks dug in at the forest which went from the outskirts of Paderborn south for ten miles. This time the Brigadier was on hand to see for himself.

"Tom, see how close you can get before they open fire."

"If they have any sense sir they will hold their fire and wait for our armour."

"I know but I want you to have a closer look at their defences. You have a good eye for such things. We can all see the tanks. What else do they have?"

"Right. Sam off you trot. Peter, it is you and me. I will drive and you use your eyes."

We slowly drove down the Kleerstrasse. I saw, through the glasses, that when it joined the Alter Hellweg it turned sharply. Their defences were just five hundred yards further on. My plan was simple. I would drive slowly down as though we had not seen their defences and when I reached the Alter Hellweg to throw it around and head back to our lines at top speed.

"Peter, keep up a commentary as we drive. I am watching the road and watching for bullets. You will see far more than I do."

"Sir, I count at least eight tanks. One looks like a Tiger. There are six, no seven 88 mm. It looks like they have one machine-gun for every thirty yards." We were approaching the Alter Hellweg. It was a smaller road than the Kleerstrasse. Even as I prepared to turn they opened fire with machine-guns. The MG 42 had the range. My sudden spin, which I had already started and my acceleration away were all that saved us. As we hurtled north, bullets zipped around us and clanged off the jeep, Davis said, "And one more thing, sir. I saw soil which was freshly turned over."

"Mines."

"That is what I think, sir."

When we reached the Brigadier he shook his head, "Charmed life springs to mind, Major."

I shrugged and told him what we had learned. "Then we call in the Marauders and a Flail."

Colonel Fraser said, "It might be quicker, sir, to just shell a passage. Use mortars and HE."

He gave the order. The airstrike was summoned. The mortars moved forward and, after they were set up, began a creeping barrage which set off the anti-personnel mines. The tanks fired too. I realised that it would make it harder to cross the open ground but that could not be helped. This way we were saving men's lives and that was a price worth paying. The Marauders came in three lines of six. They worked their way through the forest and the roads. As they climbed and circled west the Brigadier gave the order to advance.

The other Commandos did not march. They travelled either in half-tracks or lorries and followed the tanks. The Flail tank went first but, to be honest, there were few mines left. One of the Shermans triggered one but it did little damage. When we reached the Alter Hellweg I saw the devastation caused by the bombers and the Sherman barrage. The Tiger had been totally destroyed and, even though they were hull down, the Mark IV tanks were wrecked. As we passed through the gap and my jeeps once more took point I wondered at the German sacrifice. They had been ordered to slow us down and it begged the question why? Monty's main thrust was to the northeast and yet they had tried to stop our brigade. I began to think the Brigadier was right. They were continuing to produce V-2 rockets. Did one or more of them have the terror weapon?

I let Sam drive for a while. He had been a little put out that I had left him behind. It had been for his own safety. We soon reached the outskirts of Dörenhagen. Although a small place and I was not expecting trouble, Davis made the sign for danger. I took out my glasses and saw that they had a pair of machine-guns behind sandbags. There looked to be about ten soldiers there. I saw an officer's cap. As I focussed the glasses I saw that they were S.S. They were fanatics.

I said, "Sam, pull next to Emerson." When he did so I said, "The Bergens seem to be working. We drive hard at them, side by side. The road is just big enough. With four submachine-guns and driving at top speed, we should break through."

Fletcher said, "I will get a grenade ready too, sir."

The Germans were more than half a mile away. They could have opened fire but I took their reluctance to do as confirmation that they were low on ammo. "Sam, keep the jeep next to Emerson's, it will divide their fire and give us more protection."

"Sir."

I turned and shouted, "Drive through at full speed. Gordy, grenades!"

The road was flat and we began to pick up speed. I cocked my MP 40. The Germans started to fire their machine-guns. They were aiming for Sam and Freddie. The straight road meant that the two drivers could both duck down behind the Bergens which absorbed the bullets. Some struck the jeep itself. The problem with firing at a vehicle coming towards you is that you have to constantly adjust the aim and the MG 42 ended up being a little behind. When we were forty yards away I rose and lifted the Thompson. I rested it on the Bergen. I aimed at the gunner on my side and fired five bullets. I adjusted my aim and fired five at the loader. Fletcher, behind me, was doing the same. Emerson had the harder task for he was on the same side as the machine-gun. The MG 42 on our side stopped firing as the gunner and loader were killed. I finished off the magazine firing at the men who fired their rifles at us.

We crashed through the wooden barrier. Splinters of wood showered us like rain. I heard a crack as Fletcher's grenade went off but the noise was drowned out by the machine-guns of the next three jeeps. "Stop here, White."

I looked around and saw that the attempt to slow us down had failed. I checked our two jeeps. We had no injuries.

"Right Emerson, back on point."

The next forty miles were far harder than we might have expected given the ease with which we had broken through. The sacrifices made at the two woods had allowed the Germans to rally and to organize their forces and make a determined stand. Every small town and village was defended. They had little armour and few guns larger than a machine-gun but, as we trudged along the road, we found ourselves calling up the Shermans, again and again. After the third such halt, the Brigadier assigned Sergeant Dixon and his Sherman Firefly to be part of the scouting group. It made life easier. Emerson spotted the ambush and Sergeant Dixon would drive forward and clear it. We would wait with the prisoners until the column arrived and then we would race off again. It took two such days to reach Kassel.

I had been worried about this place all the way from Schloss Rheda. We were camped at Ahnatal-Weimar. It was a few miles from Kassel. The forty men of the Volkssturm who had been defending the hamlet had held us off for an hour with rifles, grenades and an MG 15. We had had to winkle them out of their houses. Captain Wilberforce had had eight men wounded and one killed. We took just twelve prisoners.

We laagered with our Sherman and Sergeant Dixon asked, "Will it be like this all the way to Berlin sir?"

"Firstly Sergeant I don't think that we will see Berlin and secondly, yes. I expected the S.S. to fight as hard as they did but the ones we fought today were old men and boys. And tomorrow could be even harder." I waved Dixon, Barker and Lieutenant Poulson around the map. Look at this river, the Fulda. What do you see?"

Sergeant Dixon said, "It is only narrow."

I said nothing and Lieutenant Poulson said, "The only crossings are these two bridges in Kassel. They could hold us up there."

"We have to capture those bridges intact. I intend to take them before dawn."

"Sir, they will hear me coming!"

"I know Sergeant Dixon. I intend to use that noise. We will leave at midnight. There is a small road which passes through the forest of Harlehausen. We will park the jeeps there and I will take half of my men. There is a mainline and junction close to Rothenditmold. At 0400 hours, you and Sergeant Major Barker will bring your tank and the jeeps towards the bridge. We should have taken them by the time you get there. The sound of your tank engines will draw every eye and ear to the west and we will use that distraction to take the bridge."

Gordy said, "And if you don't sir?"

"Then, Sergeant Major Barker, you will learn how to write letters of condolence, won't you?" He nodded, grimly. "Get some rest and I will go and tell the Brigadier and Captain Wilberforce what I intend to do."

Brigadier Young was ahead of me. In his command caravan, he and his staff were poring over the map. "Ah Harsker, your ideas would be welcome. What do we do about Kassel eh? The R.A.F. have told us that they are reinforcing it and there is no way around it. There are a couple of bridges there but if they are mined then we will be delayed by days."

"It is the bridges that are the key sir. I was going to take some of my men in before dawn and to try to take and hold one of the bridges. I am certain that they will have them mined. We can't save both of them but if we can save one... The alternative would be to wait for the Engineers. That would add a couple of days to our advance on Göttingen."

"Quite. It is risky Tom."

"If Captain Wilberforce and his company can accompany us then they can follow the Sherman. If they can secure the north end of the bridge then I think we can do it."

He nodded, "And I will get the R.A.F. to launch a dawn strike to support you." He shook my hand, "Good luck, Tom."

"Thanks, sir."

Captain Wilberforce and his men were keen to join us. We left at midnight. We only had four miles to drive. I knew that the sound of the Sherman tank would be heard in Kassel but they would not know from which direction we were coming. There were a number of roads into the town. As I had expected they had kept all their defences for Kassel and we reached the edge of the woods just three miles from Kassel at 0100 hours.

Seven of us would be heading into Kassel. Lieutenant Poulson, Sergeant Hay, Lance Sergeant Hewitt, Lance Corporal Davis, Private Ashcroft and Private White. The others would drive the jeeps. We took no Bergens. Davis had his sniper rifle with a silencer. Hay, Hewitt, Poulson and myself had the silenced Colts and we all had an MP 40. With battle jerkins laden with grenades and blackened faces we left the woods and headed towards the railway lines.

The houses which had been close to the railway line had been obliterated by the American Air Force when they had bombed the busy line. It was eerie walking down a road with the skeletons of houses. Where had the people fled? As we neared the railway line we slowed. To the north of us was a huge marshalling yard. I saw men repairing a length of track. They were still trying to keep the line open. The workers were two hundred yards up the line. We would be hidden... I hoped.

We had more than a hundred and thirty yards to cross but, luckily, there were three places where there was shelter. They looked to be buildings used to store equipment and shelter the railway workers. We would have to cover just twenty yards and then we would have cover. The sound of the hammers on spikes echoed in the night. Watching for a white face turning around we darted across the first four tracks to the cover of some scrubland. We then had two lines to cross but there were four buildings on the other side. They looked to be workers' storage huts. One was partially demolished. Holding my Colt, I darted across. There was no one there although the door of one of the huts was open. The last thirty yards were hidden from the railway workers by a bend in the line.

We could have followed the railway line into Kassel but it was too exposed. We would find it easier to use the cover of back streets. The Germans would have the main roads blocked. The one thing they would not expect would be Commandos raiding. Once we had crossed the lines we ducked into the first alley we saw. It headed in the wrong direction but I knew there would be another quieter street or alley which led to the river. The main road into Kassel was not the one to take. After forty feet we saw another alley and this one paralleled the road we had just taken. The houses were a row of terraced ones. Like the ones on the other side many of them had been destroyed by bombing but the ruins and remains gave us cover and disguised us as we scurried from shelter to shelter.

At the end of the alley, we were at another larger road. Opposite was a smaller one. Davis and I scanned left and right. I could hear a vehicle but it did not seem to be close. I waved my men across. The small road had a few trees. It must have been a pleasant suburb once. I saw wrecked houses and wondered why. I discovered the reason at the end of the road. There had been a factory and it had been bombed. Huge walls teetered without support. Vast parts of it had been laid flat. The good news was that it was abandoned and we could move through it. The bad news was that we would have to creep through it for fear of the noise of feet bringing down brickwork which appeared to say upright when logic said it should have fallen.

There were crates filled with water and mangled machinery littering the site. Whatever they had been making there must have been important for we saw the remains of anti-aircraft batteries. Some had mangled guns there while others had been emptied. Even as we moved through I worked out that it must have happened at some time in the recent past. They would have recycled the metal otherwise. It was a vast site and enabled us to move south by east. I saw that the railway station had also been targeted. It was a ruin. However, the position of the station told me exactly where we were. There were less than two miles to the river. This, however, would be the busier part of town. I looked at my watch. It was 0230. Captain Wilberforce would be bringing his men in under ninety minutes. We had time but we could afford no delays.

As we left the wrecked factory we scrambled over the remains of a large wall. It had hidden the town. It was pitch black. The buildings were, more or less intact. I smelled wood smoke which told me that they were occupied. We dashed across the road. As we did I spied, in the distance, the glow of a cigarette. It was a tiny pinprick of light but that suggested a sentry or perhaps a roadblock. It was not in our way but it was a warning. We walked in the shadows of the buildings. Some were four stories high. When we came to a smaller street which went diagonally, we took it.

It was just in time for I heard the sound of a German truck. It was coming along the road we had just left. We pressed ourselves into the sides of the buildings as the sound of the engine drew closer. I waited for it to pass. Alarmingly it did not. It stopped at the end. We were just thirty yards down the smaller street. If the Germans came down towards us they could not avoid seeing us. I cocked my Colt. I heard the sound of boots landing on the cobbles and orders were shouted. To my relief, the officer ordered them to set up a barricade facing north. I waved my arm and quickly led my men towards the river. Our exit was blocked and Captain Wilberforce would have to negotiate the roadblock. I heard, in the distance, the sound of more trucks. The Germans were preparing their defences while it was dark and our Typhoons and P 51s could not prey upon them. It made it easier for us. Somehow we had slipped inside their cordon.

The streets we passed through were the older part of the town. They were narrow and shadowy. They were perfect for Commandos. I could smell the river ahead. I was able to move with more confidence knowing that their first line of defence lay to the north of us. The second line would be the bridges across the river. It also meant that they would not blow the bridges until their men had escaped across them.

I checked my watch. It had taken us an hour to cover the mile from the wrecked factory. Stealth came at a price- time. We had thirty minutes to be in position. The narrow road we were on had a long bend and then, as it turned back on itself, there was a very short section of road and I saw the river. I led my men towards it. Crouching at the corner I saw that I could see two bridges. One, to my left, was a sturdy one with a good road surface. The second, a hundred yards to my right was a wooden one. There was a sandbagged emplacement there too. It was for foot traffic. If we were to capture a bridge then it had to be the bigger one. I saw sandbags at the end. The barrels of machine-guns protruded. I looked at the other bank. It was hard to see but there looked to be a long barrel there. I could not be certain but it looked like an 88.

To our left was an old building. It ran all the way to the bridge and there were no doors for shelter. We would be seen. That left the river bank itself. It looked to have a sort of promenade. Again there would be no cover. There appeared to be few options. The bridge and the sandbags were eighty yards away. We had but one choice. We would have to get across the road unseen and crawl along the promenade. The old benches would give us a little cover but I did not relish the prospect. I turned and signalled, *'cross the road, lie down, crawl'*. My men nodded.

I made the dash across. Davis would wait until I was hidden before he attempted the run. I lay down next to a bench. I peered across the river. No one was there and I was unseen. I was level with the sandbagged emplacement. If they turned to look down the river then they would see me. I risked crawling to the river. I saw that there were barges there. There was a line of four of them tied up. I climbed down on to one. My rubber-soled shoes made no sound but the boat moved with my weight. The barge was empty. It was riding high in the water. It was a typical barge with a very small walkway around the cabins. I walked down it. Davis joined me. I signalled for him to cover me and I made my way down the line of barges. There were four of them and they made a walkway to the bridge.

When I reached the end of the first one and before I stepped on to the next I waved and Davis followed me. I saw that the rest of my men were descending like black shadows on to the barge. I stepped on to the second and began to walk along it. I felt the boat move. I turned but Davis was still on the other boat. A German soldier appeared from below deck. Before he could shout I shot him in the back. Davis was quick thinking and he quickly clambered on board and slowly lowered the body into the water. It made not a sound. I made my way back to Davis. Bill Hay had joined him.

I pointed to Davis and made the sign to keep watch. I pointed to Bill and signed for him to follow me. I slowly opened the door. A sleepy voice said, "Wilhelm, is that you?"

I stepped into a kitchen and beyond it was another door. I moved towards it. The door opened and a German stood there. I punched him with the butt of my pistol and he fell into my arms. I laid him on the ground and stepped into the sleeping quarters. There were two more Germans asleep.

I tapped one on the shoulder with my silencer and said, in German, "Wake up and do not make a sound!"

Behind me, I heard Bill as he tied the hands and feet of the German I had knocked out. The two Germans opened their eyes and saw the gun. One moved towards his gun. I fired into the pillow next to his head, "Do not be foolish. We are Commandos and we will kill you if we have to."

They both nodded and I saw terror in their eyes.

"Bill come and tie and gag these two."

I covered them while Bill tied them with parachute cord and then gagged them with strips torn from their sheets. When we had finished I saw that there were just fifteen minutes left before the attack.

My men were waiting for us and I led them down the barge to the next one. This time Davis covered the door as we walked along it but we did not disturb anyone. I could now see the defences on the bridge which was above us and just fifty feet away. We would be hidden in the shadows. As we moved down the barges I saw the wires and the explosive charges. They would have to be our priority. Once we were sheltered under the bridge I pointed to Hewitt, Foster and White. I indicated the charges. We would just cut the wires. I doubted that they would be booby-trapped. If they were then we would know nothing about it.

As they did that I signalled to Lieutenant Poulson and Bill Hay. I gestured to the far side of the bridge.

Davis and Bill went to the near side. Davis had the rifle and he aimed it at the men on the far bank of the river. We were in shadow and they were not. They had a brazier and were using it to heat water. Even had they looked their night vision was ruined and they would not have seen us. When daylight came it would be a different matter. We were behind the sandbagged position. The Germans machine-gunners were less than twenty feet from us. We could hear their conversation. I soon realised that these were paratroopers. Cut off from the main unit they had joined in the defence of Kassel. Unlike the despondent soldiers, we had listened to before these were confident and almost arrogant. Their words showed that they thought they were better than the Americans or the British. It was a warning.

I checked my watch. It was 0400. The Sherman would be leading the jeeps, Kangaroos, half-tracks and lorries towards the railway lines. The sound of the huge Ford engine would tell the Germans that someone was coming but it would be some time until they would know the size of the attack. I glanced under the bridge. My three monkeys had climbed to the far side of the bridge. The explosives were almost disarmed. It was 0410 when the field telephone at the bridge rang. I only heard the 'yes sir, right sir and thank you, sir'.

The officer said, "The Tommies are coming down the road. They have armour. We will blow the bridge if they reach our first line of defence. I will go to the other side ready to fire the charges. Sergeant, you are in command."

"Sir, you will wait for us, won't you! Remember the Ardennes. The Americans will have us shot for killing their men if we are caught."

"Do not worry, Sergeant, I will give you time to cross the bridge. When we blow this we stop the British and soon the Fuhrer's new weapons will be unleashed. This is just a temporary setback."

Hewitt, Barker and I had witnessed the slaughter of American prisoners in the Ardennes. These must have been the ones who committed the atrocity. It explained how they had become separated from their unit.

I heard the officer running across the bridge and shouting for his men to stand to. It was though a wasps' nest had been disturbed. Inevitably that was the moment when disaster struck. As they hurried to man the 88 mm one of them must have glanced down. He saw my three men. Even as Davis shot him he was shouting. As the three began to swing back under the bridge I jumped up and fired my Colt at the four men in the sandbagged emplacement. Davis was picking off the men on the far side of the bridge. I heard the distant crack of a seventeen pounder as the Firefly opened fire. Poulson and Hay shot the others and they had the presence of mind to swing around the machine-gun.

Before I could emulate them I heard the sound of a German MP 34 and, as I turned I saw Ashcroft clutch his chest and he fell into the river. Davis killed the man who had slain him. White and Hewitt jumped into the river to save Ashcroft. I had seen the hole in his chest. He was dead.

The field telephone rang and I picked it up. Hay had the MG 42 firing and the crew of the 88 as well as the officer fell. Davis ran to the second MG.

"Allo!"

"The British are about to breach the first line of defence. Tell Oberlieutenant Gruber to blow the bridge."

"Yes sir!"

"Davis swing the machine-gun around. Jerry will be along that road in a moment or two."

"Sir."

I shouted to Lieutenant Poulson, "We are going to get company very soon. It is up to the four of us."

"Where are the other three?"

"Ashcroft is dead."

Billy Hay stood and hurled a grenade across the bridge then he jumped up and ran. I saw what he was intending. The gun crews were all dead but the guns still functioned. Before more men could arrive he ran up to them and dropped two grenades into the 88 mm. Then he turned and ran back. He barely made it before the grenades exploded amongst the ammunition. It was like the biggest firework display I had ever seen. Flying shells and debris filled the air. We buried ourselves in the sandbags. Whoever had ordered the destruction of the bridge would think they had succeeded. When the explosions stopped I looked across and saw that the buildings behind the gun had been set on fire. The flames licked higher and suddenly took hold of the roof. It was an inferno. I saw Lieutenant Poulson swing his gun around to face the north.

All through the explosions and the fire I had heard the Firefly's gun as it drew closer to us. Now that the explosions had stopped I could hear the small arms fire as well as the tank's Browning. Then the Germans appeared. To our left, I saw them streaming across the wooden bridge. They were in range of us but they were not a threat to us. The sixty men who ran down the street were. We opened fire. The two initial bursts hit twelve men and the rest took cover. We used the guns sparingly. We just had to keep them pinned down and Captain Wilberforce and his men would do the rest.

The Germans began to get desperate. Four broke from cover firing their submachine-guns as they ran. Although we hit three one hurled a grenade. It exploded just twenty feet from us. Had we not sheltered behind the sandbags we would have been dead. However, in that moment another twenty ran. By the time we had raised our heads, they were just thirty feet from us. Davis kept his fingers on the trigger of the MG 42. I swung up my MP 40 and opened fire with that. One German took eight bullets but still kept coming. As I clicked on empty I went to draw my Luger when I heard an MP 40 from behind me. It was joined a moment later by a second. That did it. They were broken and they threw down their weapons and shouted, "Surrender! We surrender!"

I turned around and saw a dripping Lance Sergeant Hewitt and Private White with their machine-guns still smoking.

I nodded, "Thanks! We were dead men but for you."

Sam pointed to the river, "We tried to save Stephen sir, but he was already dead."

"And it isn't over yet. White join Hewitt on the MG 42. Davis, sniper time." I gestured towards the small wooden bridge. Eventually, they would realise how few we were and try to retake the bridge we had captured.

Suddenly, to the north of us was a huge explosion. Lieutenant Poulson had a better view of it and he said, "Sir, there was another bridge. They have blown it."

"Then load your weapons and prepare to endure the firestorm when they attack!"

Machine-gun and rifle fire struck our bridge but, just as we could not fire directly at them they could not fire at us either. They would have to change the angle of attack. Davis shot the ones who tried to race across the road to begin to attack us. I went on to the bridge and saw that they were going to use the same method we did. They were going to use the barges. I grabbed four grenades and hurled them as far down the barges as I could. I could only reach the second barge from us. As I recalled it had been empty. I threw three grenades. They hit and exploded in quick succession. The blast hit the four Germans who were attempting to reach us and, more importantly, they destroyed the barge. The superstructure disappeared and then the hull sank into the river.

"Sir, the Sherman!"

I saw the Sherman leading the half-tracks of C Company. I went to the middle of the bridge to wave. It would be ironic if they shot at us.

"Shift the barrier. I want him on the other side as soon as possible!"

I walked backwards and waved Sergeant Dixon towards me. When I saw him nod I held my MP 40 in front of me and headed across the bridge. The fire had burned the wood and was now slowly dying out. The buildings on the far side would have to be demolished but Sergeant Hay's quick thinking had secured the bank for us. When I reached the wall the bricks and stone were still hot. I waved the tank to within a few feet of the wall.

"Sergeant if you use your tank you might be able to push this wall over. It will enable us to see into the rest of the town."

"Righto sir, stand clear."

I walked to the middle of the bridge. The sergeant closed the hatch and swung the gun around to face the rear. Then he reversed a little before engaging the gears and edging forward. He managed to do it delicately. He pushed slowly. At first, I thought he had not done anything and then the whole wall leaned, first towards the tank and then, thankfully, away from the bridge, the tank and me. I clambered up on the back of the tank and stood on the turret. If they had had snipers then we would have been in trouble. As it was, with dawn breaking, I saw the grey uniforms streaming east. They would rally again but not here. We had achieved our objective and it had been paid for by Stephen Ashcroft.

Chapter 16

The Germans who were still trying to get across the river did not cause us many problems but we had to be vigilant. It was 1000 hours before the Brigadier and the rest of the Shermans arrived. There was palpable relief on his face when he saw that the bridge was still intact. While the Shermans crossed to head further into the town he came over to greet us, "Well done Major Harsker, Captain Wilberforce. Were there charges?"

I nodded, "Yes sir and they were going to blow them." I pointed to the north. "They blew that one. The one to the south can be used by men on foot but this is the only one that can be used by vehicles. You might want to get engineers to remove the charges. My men just cut the wires."

"Good thinking. How are you fixed for moving on?"

"We could do sir but we are tired and tired men make mistakes. As far as I could see the Germans were retreating. I think we could continue with the advance."

He shook his head, "There is thick forest ahead and the road twists and turns. It is perfect ambush country. So far we have escaped heavy losses because you have sniffed out trouble. We can wait half a day for you to recover. It will give us time to get the column across this bridge. The exercise will take some time over just one bridge. Take your jeeps and head for Rüsteberg. It is, according to the map, just a mile and half from the outskirts. I intend to make it my headquarters. Get some sleep and then we will send you and your men out again." He must have seen the pained expression on my face, "Tom, what you and your men do saves lives. If I thought you would come to harm then I wouldn't ask this of you."

I nodded, "Sir." He climbed back into his jeep and followed the Shermans. "Right lads, when the jeeps come, get on board. Pack the MG 42s. They may come in handy."

Sam asked, "Sir, what about Ashcroft?"

John Hewitt said, "His body will have been washed downstream, Sam. The river is fast flowing here."

He nodded. He was unhappy but there was little we could do about it. Emerson screeched to a halt, "Where to sir?"

"Head for Rüsteberg. It is just outside the town. We are going to get some sleep and then set off again this afternoon."

He looked around, about to make some comment and then he noticed that one of us was missing, "Ashcroft?"

"Dead."

"Poor little bugger. Reg Deane will be upset. He used to drink in his dad's pub."

Mine was now the only jeep with three of us in it. We followed Emerson. White was also quiet. Fletcher drove and he sensed the mood. "From what Johnno said it was quick, Sam. He would have felt nothing and you showed guts diving into a river with a battle jerkin on."

"I am a good swimmer. I teach swimming at school." I could tell he was just speaking to stop himself thinking about Ashcroft.

Fletcher nodded, "I only learned a month before joining the Commandos. I had to or else I might not have got in and I wanted to be a Commando."

"Are you still glad you joined, Scouse?"

"Are you kidding, sir? It is the best thing to have happened to me. Do you reckon I would have had a posh mate like Beaumont if I had joined a regular outfit? No chance. And the stuff we have done." He shook his head. "I'll never have to stand my corner after the war. I can live off what we have done. The trouble is folks won't believe it. I sometimes don't. And from what the Sarn't Major said about the Ardennes, that was even more unbelievable. How about you sir? Are you going to talk about all the things you have done? I mean you were doing stuff like this long before the rest of us."

"No Fletcher. I shall keep it to myself. I am proud of you all. I will talk of the courage of the men I led but there are too many deaths for me to talk about it with any joy."

White said, "I know what you mean, sir. I have only been in it for five minutes. Like the Sarn't Major says, I am still wet behind the ears but there are now just three of us left from the original draft who joined the section. We trained together. You get closer to people that way. I have no brothers or sisters. Tom and Ralph are like family to me. The others were."

Fletcher drove in silence. We were all lost in our thoughts. The radio operator on the *'Lucky Lady'* had been from Liverpool. He had been called Wacker. We did not know if he was alive or dead. We just knew that *'Lucky Lady'* had been sunk. Wacker was probably dead. We all had someone to mourn.

Rüsteberg was a tiny place. A dozen houses and a church were all that were there. There were people in the houses but they peered from behind curtains. Mum would have called them *'twitchers'*. We found a piece of solid ground on which to park. We laid out camouflage nets for beds and then covered the top of the jeeps with more of it.

"Gordy you are in charge. The lads who went into the attack will need the sleep the most. When the column comes then the rest of you can get your heads down."

Gordy said, almost gently, "You just get some rest, sir. It's time someone else put in a shift."

Normally I would be out like a light but the conversation in the jeep had set my mind going. I was thinking of all those who had died since I had joined up. It was worse than counting sheep. Sheep did not haunt your dreams. Dad had said the same. He had also told me that the one thing that had kept him going was the thought of returning home to Mum. I had Susan. When I was finished in Germany then I would marry her. The last thing I wanted was to be sent halfway around the world to fight for God knows how long. I must have drifted off to sleep for I was woken by Scouse.

"Sir, a cup of tea and some ham."

I sat up, "Ham?"

He grinned, "I went and sweet-talked the lady in the house opposite. I swapped a couple of pans I found for some slices of ham."

"Fletcher!"

He held up his hands, "Sir, she was well happy. Seems the pans and other stuff was taken to make aeroplanes and bombs. I don't think she was a fan of the Fuhrer!"

The ham was delicious. It would have been nicer between two pieces of bread with some cheddar cheese and a smidgen of Coleman's English Mustard but it would do. The tea also had real milk in it rather than powder. As I sipped it I heard the moo which told me that my men had managed to barter for it. It had been inside a cow that morning!

"Have the rest of the column arrived?"

"Captain Wilberforce arrived an hour since and the Brigadier was with him. The rest of the column is still making its way through Kassel."

"I wondered why it was so quiet." I finished the ham and then washed it down with some tea. "How is White?"

"Better since he was able to chat to Betts and Foster. It hit him hard. He's a nice bloke sir. If I had had a teacher like him then who knows what I might have achieved."

"I think Fletcher, that you will do very well for yourself, no matter what happens. You are one of life's survivors."

"I dunno sir. The original section is getting mighty thin on the ground."

"Are you getting twitchy?"

"It's like I can see the end. You know, like one of the runs we did in Falmouth. I know the camp is just around the corner, but can I make it? Will Sergeant Major Deane step out and trip me up and tell me I am too cocky?"

"Scouse, just do what you have done for the last few years and you will get through this."

He nodded, " You are probably right sir. This must be because my oppo got a Blighty one. Lucky bugger."

"You know he would rather be here."

"You have got that right sir."

Lieutenant Poulson arrived, "Sir, the Brigadier wants us."

"Right." I handed my mug to Fletcher, "Thanks for the tea and the ham. They were just what I needed."

"No problem sir, we have to look after you. You are our lucky mascot."

That was a burden I could do without. I followed Lieutenant Poulson. "Emerson managed to scrounge more fuel and we have been given more rations."

"Then things are bound to go wrong soon, Polly."

"Not you too, sir. The lads are all a bit morose. There is only Gordy who is cheerful."

The Brigadier smiled when we entered his caravan. "Coffee, gentlemen? This is the real stuff. An American colonel gave me some beans."

I had enjoyed my cup of tea but the thought of coffee made me nod. Polly shook his head and said, "Sir it would be wasted on me!"

The Brigadier handed me a cup of black coffee. The smell alone was intoxicating. I sipped it as he spoke. "The R.A.F. felt guilty because they didn't manage to attack Kassel for us. Low cloud or something. They have made up for it by harassing the retreating Germans. The roads between here and Göttingen are narrow and they managed to hit a couple of the lead vehicles and then shot up the column of retreating vehicles. I think we can make Göttingen by dark."

"How far is it sir?"

"Less than forty miles."

"But sir we have already taken three days to cover that distance. How can we do forty miles in a few hours?"

"I am giving you four tanks to accompany you. You travel at their speed. They can shunt any vehicles off the road." I nodded and studied the map. "I am assured that they can do twenty-five miles an hour along roads. You and Captain Wilberforce could it in three hours without any stops. Even if the Germans make a stand then four Shermans should be able to shift them."

I nodded, "We will give it a go, sir."

I went back to my men and told them about our mission. They seemed quite happy about it. Sergeant Major Barker said, "Four tanks sir? We have never had that sort of firepower before."

Lieutenant Poulson added a word of warning. "We are going into forested country with hills, twists and turns. They might not have much armour left but they do have anti-tank rockets."

Fletcher nodded, "And that is why we need sharp-eyed Davis here."

The presence of the Shermans inspired a more confident mood amongst my men. White still brooded about Ashcroft but the others had put that thought to the back of their minds. He was not forgotten but he was parked somewhere safe until they could revisit him. I knew that because it was what I would do. I had had my tormented sleep. I would force the image of his broken body falling into the water until I had time to mourn him properly.

I went through the details of our task with Captain Wilberforce. It was as we were talking that the three new Shermans arrived. This time Sergeant Dixon had an officer of his own to lead him. Lieutenant Richard Cunliffe came from Nottingham. He had been promoted from the rank of sergeant and he was a good leader. He knew his men and he knew his vehicles. More importantly, he had studied the maps and knew the problems and issues we would face.

"The Brigadier seems to think that the Sherman is some sort of racing car. The speeds he is talking about are attainable, sir, but that is on the flat and when it is straight."

I held up my hand, "Don't worry, Lieutenant, I am with you. We will do our best but if we have to stop short of Göttingen then we will." I looked at my watch. It was time for us to be moving. "We had better mount up. I will have two jeeps in front of you and the other three behind the tanks. Captain Wilberforce will be behind the jeeps. The roads look narrow. What we cannot afford is for us to be blocked by one of our own broken down vehicles. Let's go."

The two MG 42s we had captured were in the jeeps driven by Sergeant Major Barker and Lieutenant Poulson. The grenades we had liberated were spread out amongst all five jeeps. White was driving. The concentration he would need would make him forget Ashcroft.

The first few miles were easier than I thought. We needed to move two broken down lorries from the roads. That took time as we had to move the jeeps off the road to allow the tanks to act as bulldozers. Once we passed Staufenberg the forest seemed to close in on us and the danger of ambush increased. I used my glasses to look into the forests. I knew that Davis was scanning the road ahead.

"We have covered ten miles in half an hour, sir. We might make it."

I continued scanning the trees. "One step at a time, Fletcher."

The road rose and fell. It twisted and turned. Suddenly, as we turned and began to descend Emerson began reversing towards us and Davis fired his rifle. I heard machine-guns and there was the unmistakable whoosh of a rocket. As Emerson spun his jeep off the road, crashing the rear into a tree, a rocket hit a tree to our left. Davis said, "Ambush sir. They are in the woods to the left and the right at the bottom. They are camouflaged!"

I waved Lieutenant Cunliffe forward, "They have anti-tank guns. Give me and my men ten minutes to get into the woods. When you hear firing bring the cavalry."

"Sir."

"White get the jeep off the road and try to park it better than Emerson did."

"Sir!" Emerson had a hurt look on his face.

"Just teasing Freddie. You did well. Fletcher, get on to the Brigadier and tell him about the hold up." I cupped my hands, "Lieutenant!"

Polly brought the rest of my men.

"There are Germans at the bottom of the slope. Lieutenant take the Sergeant Major and Sergeant Hay, head down the left. I will take Davis, White and Emerson, we will go down the right."

I cocked my MP 40 and headed into the woods. We ran away from the road and, after thirty yards I turned so that we were going down the slope. White kept pace with me. He was eager to get to grips with the Germans. Commandos can move silently. Although we were moving quickly we looked down to ensure that we were not stepping on broken branches. As we neared the bottom Davis tapped my arm and pointed to the left. A hundred or so yards away there were the Germans. They had used some logs to make a barrier. They had, on our side of the road, a machine-gun and a Panzerfaust. I counted twenty men. I could not see the far side of the road. The men on our side obscured them.

I pointed to the sniper rifle and Davis. He nodded and lay behind a tree. He had the silencer on his rifle and the Germans would not know where he was. I waved to the right and led White and Emerson so that we were behind the Germans. I kept my eye on the Germans and saw the German with the Panzerfaust pitch to the ground. The others looked around for the source of the danger. Just then Lieutenant Poulson and my other men opened fire. The fact that they used German weapons appeared to confuse the Germans. They delayed in firing. It allowed us to get to within sixty yards. I waved my men to the ground as Davis continued to pick off key personnel.

As the Germans fired, blindly in Davis' direction we opened fire. We were behind them and our attack took them by surprise. I fired a short burst at the men trying to turn the MG 42. A sergeant was hit by an invisible hand. That would be Davis. Then I heard the crack of a seventeen pounder and the log barrier disappeared in a mass of splinters.

That was enough and their hands came up. We stood and headed towards them. These were not Volkssturm. These were hardened veterans. There were just fifteen survivors. Some had wounds.

"Sergeant Major Barker search them. White, Emerson, go and fetch the jeeps."

I saw that one of them had an MP 40. I held my hand out and said, "Ammunition."

He took out the one clip he had remaining. It spoke volumes. He nodded towards my Commando flash, "Kommando." I nodded. "The Fuhrer was right about you devils. You should all have been shot."

"But we weren't and your Fuhrer and his Third Reich are finished." I waved the tanks forward, "Wait down the road a ways. We will follow with our jeeps when Captain Wilberforce arrives."

This was what the Brigadier had not understood. It was not just the delay in eradicating bottlenecks there was then the problem of prisoners. By the time we rejoined the tanks an hour would have elapsed. We had covered half of the distance but it had taken us two hours. By the time the jeeps had arrived and Captain Wilberforce had taken the prisoners away from us it was almost 1500 hours.

As we overtook the tanks I shouted, "Let's hope there aren't more delays like that."

"Yes sir."

When we finally left the forest we were in farmland and the going was easier. The tanks were able to travel slightly faster and the barrel of Lieutenant Cunliffe's Sherman was just ten feet behind Fletcher's head. The Lieutenant had a good view ahead from his elevated position. It was he who had the first view of Göttingen. "Major Harsker!" I turned. He pointed and shouted, "Göttingen!"

I looked at my watch. It was now 1600 hours. We had managed it before dark. I shouted, "Freddie, stop!"

I clambered out and, taking my map and glasses, climbed up on to the Sherman. Using my binoculars I was able to see the town. It was three miles away and I could see the barrels of guns. It was defended. "Fletcher, get on to the main column. Tell them we are at the outskirts of Göttingen and it is defended. We will get as close as we can."

"Sir."

I turned to the Lieutenant, "The Leine river isn't very large but I am guessing that they will have either destroyed or mined the bridges." I pointed to the map. There is a railway line heading into Göttingen. There are two railway bridges. Let us head up there. It will be straight and there won't be any trains. If we don't have a bridge then the advance stalls here."

"Right sir. You lead?"

"Of course. We are faster and smaller. They might not waste a shell on us. I rejoined my men, "I will lead the way, Freddie."

I directed Sam. We took the next left. It meant we left the shortest route into the small town but we would reach the railway line and that appeared the quickest way in. We were no longer heading to Göttingen, we were keeping it two to three miles to the east of us. Consequently, we did not encounter any more troops. It looked like they were making the Leine the next barrier to our advance. I knew that we were advancing on every front. Italy had been taken and the Eighth Army was heading for the Tyrol. In the north, Montgomery was driving towards the Baltic and, to the south of us Bradley and Patton were heading for Berlin. With the Russians heading west the Germans were being squeezed. They were just slowing the inevitable. Sadly we would lose soldiers while they did so.

We passed the tiny hamlet of Leineberg. The windows were shuttered and the doors closed. The houses looked empty. We followed the road and came to a crossing. There were four railway tracks in two pairs with a gap of ten yards between the pairs. I took out my glasses and saw the two railway bridges. They were about five hundred yards from us.

I shouted, "Lieutenant two tanks on each track. Sergeant Major, you and Sergeant Hay take the far track. Lieutenant Poulson with me. Fletcher tell headquarters that the two railway bridges over the Leine are intact."

"Sir!"

"White, drive as though you are at Brooklands!"

"Sir!"

There was a rough piece of ground between the tracks and White sensibly took that route. We bounced down. There was no chance of firing. The Germans at the bridge saw us. They began to fire. The four Shermans fired their main armament. Five hundred yards was close range for a tank and I saw one of the machine posts disappear as the H.E. from two tanks struck it. The other men fled across the bridge. The tanks' machine-guns spat out and three of the Germans fell into the river. White had reached the river first but he had to stop for there was no bridge in front of us. The riverbank plunged down to the water. As we turned to drive onto the tracks, disaster struck. Cannon shells from a 20 mm tore through the engine and front tyres of our jeep. Even my mechanical wizard would be able to do nothing.

I grabbed White and pulled him behind the shelter of our jeep. Fletcher followed. We lay on the ground as shells tore into the jeep and the radio. The two tanks had seen the cannon and were firing at it. Suddenly it stopped but it was too late for the jeep. I risked rising and peering over the top of the jeep. The Germans were dug in on the other side of the bridge. The cannon had stopped firing and the smoke from our jeep was rising and obscuring us.

"White, Fletcher, grab the Bergens and guns. Head back to Lieutenant Poulson."

"Where you off to sir?"

"I am going to check the bridge out."

I slid down the bank a little and then crawled to the stone piers which rose twenty feet above me. It was a stone bridge and well made. I saw the wires and the explosives. It was set to blow. I shouted, "Down here!"

I took out my wire cutters from my battle jerkin and climbed up to the first charge. I snipped the wires. I realised that it would be hard to reach the charges in the middle of the bridge but, as the river was just ten yards wide at this point if we could take out half of the explosives then any damage might be kept to a minimum. I looked up and saw that there were metal girders under the stone and they had attached the cables and the explosives to them. Holding my wire cutters in my teeth I grabbed the nearest girder and swung up my legs. I worked my way down to the next charge. I held on with one arm and snipped the wires. I put the cutters in my mouth and, pulling my dagger, slashed the tape holding the explosives to the girder. They splashed into the river.

Lieutenant Poulson and Fletcher were on the other two girders. I was halfway across when the Germans tried to fire the explosives. I heard a crackle and nothing happened.

"Back!"

I started to crawl back. No one had begun to clear the explosives on the other bridge. The Lieutenant and Fletcher had almost made it back when the other bridge exploded. The charges had been set to concentrate the damage upwards but, inevitably there was a sideways blast and the concussion made me lose my grip. I fell. The river was just ten yards below me and it broke my fall but the blast had taken the wind from me. I sank and with bent legs, touched bottom. As I came up I involuntarily took in water. My hand broke the surface but I found myself choking. My head popped out of the water. I tried to speak but I could not, I was drowning. I felt myself sinking and there was nothing I could do. I thought it ironical that I would not be killed by a bullet but by falling into the water. I slipped beneath the waves and everything began to go black.

Chapter 17

"Sir! Sir!"

I coughed as someone pressed against my chest. I began to vomit water and I felt as though I was choking.

"Thank God. Get him on his side!" It was Hewitt I could hear. I was still alive. I opened my eyes and looked into his. "You had us worried then sir. When Bill Hay dived in and pulled you out we thought you were dead. It is a good job Bill, here, took that course in resuscitation."

I nodded, not trusting myself to speak.

Bill grinned, "You were a dead weight sir with the grenades and the guns. I was just pleased that the water is only shallow." I tried to rise. "You just lie there, sir. Lieutenant Poulson has taken charge. Jerry has blown a hole in one bridge but we still hold this one. They have anti-tank guns and rockets on the far side. Captain Wilberforce is going to try to cross the river tonight and take them by surprise. Now we know it is shallow they are going to push your jeep into it and use that like a bridge."

I nodded. It was a good plan.

"The column is just fifteen minutes away. We have the bridge."

I lay back. It was what I would have done. Captain Wilberforce had come a long way.

Eventually, they let me get up. There was still sporadic gunfire but Lieutenant Cunliffe was not risking his tanks. Davis had found a spot from which he could snipe at the Germans. I heard a rumble and a splash as the jeep was pushed by my men down the bank and into the river. It flipped on to its back at the bottom. There was a gap of five feet on one side and six on the other. The jeep was submerged but I could see the wheels and the exhaust pipe. Men could walk across it.

Darkness fell as the Brigadier arrived. "Well done Major. Lieutenant Cunliffe told us what you did. I am proud of you."

"Captain Wilberforce will lead a raid over in the next hour. If you send tanks over at the same time we should have our bridgehead."

"You and your men have a rest. Your real mission begins tomorrow. Tonight you are all spectators. The American 3rd Armoured Division took Paderborn and they are now racing ahead of us to the south. We managed to draw their defences away from the Third Herd to stop us. It is likely that the 3rd will reach Nordhausen and the Mittelbau-Dora complex first."

"Then we may not be needed at all?"

"Possibly not but the 3rd Armoured is a huge division. They will move more slowly than you. You might sneak through."

It did not sit well with us to watch while others fought but we obeyed orders. We heard the sounds of small arms fire as Captain Wilberforce led his Commandos up the far bank, under cover of darkness, to take the anti-tank guns and machine-guns by surprise. The first Shermans rumbled and rattled over the railway bridge. We watched as the rest of the armour followed and then the half-tracks and lorries of the rest of the brigade. We heard the sound of the battle as it headed away from the river towards the eastern side of the town. We followed when the last of the lorries had crossed. When we reached the other side we saw that the defenders had been a mixture of paratroopers and Waffen S.S. They had died hard. There were dead Commandos mixed in with their bodies.

We were waved over to the side by a sergeant as we neared the centre of the town. "Brigadier Young says this is your billet for the night." He pointed to a guest house. "We have commandeered this one. The Brigadier reckons you deserve it."

"Thanks, sergeant."

The owner was a pragmatic man. The war was lost but one day tourists would come back. He was smiling and he was helpful. The fact that I spoke German made it easier for us. He had no food but the rooms were clean. The bed linen required washing but when you have slept in a field then any bed linen is a luxury. Fletcher took White and Foster to scrounge. It was an art form. I sat in the lounge of the guest house with my sergeants and Lieutenant Poulson. Emerson and Betts were checking the vehicles.

"First, John, how is Betts' ankle?"

"It is fine sir. He is as fit as he ever was."

"Good, we can afford no lame ducks on this next part of our mission. Any other injuries?"

Gordy said, "You mean apart from you sir?"

"Cheeky, Sarn't Major."

"No sir. Everyone is recovered."

I spread out the map. "We are no longer tied to roads nor to the tanks. We have no radio which means that once we leave here we disappear. Gordy, make sure we have spares of everything. Freddie is going to sort out more fuel for us. We will rearrange the vehicles. Emerson and Davis are a good team. They lead. Gordy you and Bill take Betts. I will have Fletcher and White. That leaves Hewitt and Foster with you, Lieutenant."

"And what exactly do we do when we reach this slave labour factory, sir?"

I turned to Bill, "What we can. Intelligence believes that the S.S. who run these places will attempt to kill all of the workers and then try to destroy the factory. The closer the allies get to the factory the more likely they are to do it. The Americans have a team racing ahead too. We may not be alone."

"Sir, there could be hundreds of guards and they will be well-armed."

"So they will attack us. While they are attacking us they can't slaughter the workers and every hour we can buy brings the Brigadier and his column that little bit closer. He thinks that the Americans may get there before we do."

They understood and we went through the maps identifying where there might be problems and hold ups. Fletcher and his scroungers had done well. We had various bits and bobs of food and we used the guest house kitchen to make an impromptu stew. The vegetables they had scrounged added to the corned beef of our rations and were augmented by a bottle of wheat beer made it a veritable feast.

As we ate Fletcher said, "The locals reckon the war will be over in days sir."

"How do you know that, Fletcher?"

"Sam here, he spoke to them. A couple of the German Fraus took a shine to him. It must be his blue eyes and cute little smile."

Sam blushed, "I just spoke to them politely and they responded."

Gordy lit a cigarette, "So you reckon March 1945 will be when the war ends, sir?"

"No Gordy. Hitler has his Alpenfestung to fall back to."
"What is that sir?"
Sam said, "Alpine fortress."

"That's right. Remember when we were in Austria? That is part of it. Lots of castles and narrow passes. If he gets there it could take months and months to winkle him out."

Gordy shook his head, "I thought it would be too good to be true."

Even as we were eating we heard the sound of gunfire as die hard German soldiers were hunted down. I knew, from what Fletcher had gleaned, that the sheer number of captured Germans was causing a problem. Soldiers who should have been forging east were having to head west and escort the thirty thousand Germans who had been captured to POW camps.

We were not going to take the MG 42 machine-guns. We would rely on our other automatic weapons. The last thing we all did was to strip down and clean our weapons. I sharpened my dagger and I reorganized my Bergen. The Brigadier told us that he was sending out the column of Shermans and Captain Wilberforce's company to probe to the south-east. We hoped it would draw any Germans that way. Then the main column would follow our route northeast towards Waake. We had planned a route which avoided all the major towns between us and our target. It added distance but we would avoid any bottlenecks. What worried me was the lack of radio. We could not call up an airstrike nor for the cavalry to come to rescue us. We were on our own.

The first part of the journey was quiet. We passed through a forest just a mile or so from Göttingen and then we almost stumbled upon the half dozen houses which made up Waake. The road twisted and turned but we were not having to slow up for the Shermans. I suspected that the main column would struggle to make the speed we managed. When we zipped through Seeburg we saw our first civilians. There were some women with young children and, as we sped through the hamlet, they scooped up their young and headed indoors. I took it as a good sign that the Germans were not expecting us to take this route.

I was feeling more confident but I knew we still had many miles to go and the closer we came to the camp and the factory the more soldiers we would find. We turned south and east. Dunderstadt was a bigger place. In fact, it was the last big place we would have to pass.

"Slow down, White." I took out the glasses and scanned the town. There had been factories there and they had been bombed. It was a scene of devastation. The bombing was not recent. There was no sign of smoke but nothing had been rebuilt. "Drive through, slowly. Fletcher, get your gun and a grenade ready." My caution was due to the Nazi flag flying from one of the few buildings which was still standing. I knew that might have been because they did not know the allies were so close but, equally, it could indicate that there were fanatics here.

The roads had not been cleared of rubble. White had to negotiate some quite large pieces. It was as we turned a corner around a half-destroyed church that we saw the German half-track. It had an MG 42 mounted above the driver. The crew had not seen us and were sitting at a table eating. Nearby was a lorry. As they saw us, they reacted. They grabbed weapons and the crew of the half-track hurried back on board. I heard the crack of Davis rifle and the gunner slumped backwards. I cocked the MP 40 and sent a burst at the men trying to get aboard the half-track. Fletcher did the same.

"Foot hard down, Sam!"

As the jeep leapt forward bullets filled the space we had just occupied. I heard Fletcher shout, "Grenade!" as we raced by the half-track. I sprayed the tyres and engine of the truck. We had just passed the end of the German truck when the grenade exploded in the half-track. I heard my men in the other jeeps firing at the Germans. There was another explosion and I turned to see the truck on fire. The Germans now knew there were Commandos in their backyard. I saw a telephone pole. The wire ran to the building with the Nazi flag.

"Stop here. Fletcher, keep them in the building."

I jumped out and tied a pair of German grenades to the telephone pole. The other jeeps pulled next to me. "Keep going. We will follow." They zoomed off. Fletcher fired a burst at the door and the German who had come out to see what was going on jumped back inside. I tied a long piece of parachute cord to the two lanyards and climbed back in. "Drive."

The cord triggered the grenades. We were fifty yards down the road when the grenade brought down the telephone pole and the wire. I had seen no sign of an antenna. I hoped that word of our presence would not spread.

As we raced towards our next waypoint, Bischofferode, I checked the map. We had less than twenty-six miles to go to Mittelbau-Dora. We were making good time. I was, however, worried about the Germans being alerted. I knew we had to turn at Bischofferode. We would head northeast. I could see the mountains already. We were close enough that the road was climbing already. There were also more trees. That was good for it meant we had more cover. Bischofferode was just as quiet as the other small hamlets and I pointed to the road to the left as we passed through. I saw faces behind windows and hoped they did not have a telephone.

We made six miles without seeing a soul. This was an empty part of Germany. Mackenrode was just as small as Bischofferode had been. As we drove through I began to plan for the actual raid on the factory. We had just left the village and were descending down a small road through the forest when Fletcher said, "Stop sir! Sergeant Major Barker has a problem. He has stopped."

I jumped out and, taking my gun, ran back to the stricken jeep. "What is it, Gordy?"

"Puncture sir."

Freddie was already on the job. Sometimes it is easy to change a tyre and sometimes the wheel nuts refuse to come off. So it was that day. The wheel nuts refused to budge. Gordy said, "You lads go on sir. We'll fix it and catch up with you."

"No Gordy. We abandon no-one."

While most of us kept watch Emerson and Gordy struggled with the tyre. "It is a bloody saboteur tyre! I bet it was made in Germany!"

Eventually, after much cursing and swearing, it was changed. By the time we left and continued into the mountains, it was dark. I did not want to risk driving with lights and we could not afford to drive in the dark. That invited an even greater disaster.

Fletcher had sharp eyes. "There sir, to the left of the road down that track. It looks like a building. I can't see any lights or smell smoke."

It was convenient for the track was lined by ancient fruit trees. There was cover. We drove down the farm track slowly. The building was not only deserted, but it was also partly wrecked. It had been a farm. There were outbuildings which looked to have suffered damage too. Fletcher and I jumped out and went to investigate. As we went around the rear, to the wrecked part, I saw the reason. The wing of a Flying Fortress had fallen on the house. Other debris looked to have fallen on the barn and cow byre. I saw that the engine had been removed. This was an old accident but it gave us the chance to have some shelter.

"Put the jeeps around the back. Bring our gear in. Fletcher and I will check out the interior."

There was little in the house. It looked as though it had been stripped of anything worth taking. "Fletcher find somewhere that you can light a fire. We might as well have a brew. I'll go and find water." Sam came in with our Bergens. "White go and check the outbuildings. See what you can find and make sure we are alone."

I saw that the sink had been destroyed and there were the broken ends of pipes. This looked to be an old farm. I went out of the back and saw an old fashioned hand pump. It was stiff but after a few pumps water came out. I went back inside and brought out a couple of dixies to collect the water. I heard Fletcher shout, "We have a fire, sir."

I looked and could detect no light, "Good."

Just then there was a whistle from the barn. It was White. I drew my gun and ran towards the barn. Same had his own Colt out and he gestured towards the upper hay store. He said, "There is someone up there, sir."

"Could it have been an animal?"

"No sir. Smell. That is human."

He was right. It was human sweat. I spoke in German, "We know you are hiding. Come down and I promise that you will not be hurt."

I was greeted by silence.

I repeated myself and again there was nothing. "White nip up the ladder and I will cover you." Although it was dark I could see that there was only one way up and one way down. I held my gun in a two handed grip.

I heard White say, in German, "I can see you! The Major means you no harm. We are English." There was a rustling and hay fell down. I saw a figure rise. I was not even sure if it was human for it looked like a scarecrow with most of the stuffing missing. I saw White helping the figure. I stepped away from the ladder. The man, I could see he was a man from his beard, was wearing striped trousers and a top. He was a prisoner from the slave labour camps.

I holstered my weapon. When he reached the bottom I spoke to him in German, "You are safe now, my friend. We are English Commandos."

His face broke into a smile. I saw that he had no teeth, "English?" I nodded. He grabbed my hand. His fingers were just bone covered with skin. I saw a tattooed number on his forearm. "I am Pál Radnóti."

White had reached the bottom of the ladder. He suddenly started speaking in a language I had never heard before. The man's smile became even broader and he jabbered back in the same language. It was frustrating because none of the words was in the least familiar. Sam turned to me. He is a Hungarian Jew, sir. He escaped from a sub-camp at the Mittelbau-Dora complex. He has been hiding here for four days."

"Come on, let's get him into the main building and get some food inside him. He is a walking corpse."

As we walked in my men all turned. Gordy said, "What the bloody hell is that, sir? I have seen more meat on a sparrow."

"He is one of the slave labourers. Foster, there is some water outside. Go and fetch it in and put it on Fletcher's fire to heat up. This chap needs food."

Hewitt shook his head, "Solid food might kill him, sir. I'll make some soup. We have a little bread left. I will break that up and soak it in the soup. He needs warmth as much as anything. Betts, go and fetch a blanket."

Emerson was smoking a cigarette and the man held out a hand and nodded. Fred lit a second and gave it to him, "You look like you need it. Did Jerry do this to him, sir?"

Sam answered, "Pál is one of the lucky ones. He told me that up to five hundred a month have been dying in the camps. Others were taken away and were never seen again. He thinks that they were murdered and buried in a mass grave."

"Ask him if he worked at the main camp."

There was a conversation and then Sam said, "No sir. He was at a subcamp. The one at Mittelbau-Dora is enormous. There are more than a hundred and fifty guards as well as twenty S.S. He was sent to a smaller one with just two hundred and fifty inmates." Sam pointed north. "It is five miles north of here, sir." Sam shook his head, "I thought we were tough sir but he made it here in this condition. It is nothing short of a miracle."

Foster was adding the bouillon cubes to the soup. I saw Davis adding lumps of corned beef. We had to keep him alive. He might just give us the edge that we needed. "Ask him if he is willing to show us the camp."

Sam looked appalled, "Sir, you can't ask him to go back."

"What is the alternative, White, leave him here? We have a mission to complete. He is better off with us wouldn't you say?"

"You are right sir. Sorry, sir." He turned and spoke to the Hungarian. The man nodded. "Yes sir. He has friends there. His wife and children are dead but his friends and his brother are still in the camp. He said he was worried that they were getting rid of the evidence. He ran because he thought they were going to kill him too. Apparently, they drew lots and he was chosen. They want the world to know what the S.S. did."

"And they will. You and Hewitt look after him. Lieutenant Poulson, let us look at the map. We might be able to work out where this sub-camp is."

As I unfolded it Lieutenant Poulson said, "Aren't we bothering with Mittelbau-Dora then sir?"

"We will get there but this is closer and it sounds to me like they are going to kill the inmates. We might be too late but…"

"You are right sir. How can one human being do that to another?"

"I honestly don't know."

My men fussed around the Hungarian as though he was a newborn. Sam translated their questions and I studied the map. When we looked at the map there were two likely targets: Guidersleben and Woffleben. They were both on the way to Mittelbau-Dora. I pointed at the two places. "We will try these first. From what Pál told us we might already be too late."

"It will be a tricky mission, sir. Some of these slave labourers could get killed in the crossfire."

"Then we will have to be careful."

"And what about this big camp, Mittelbau-Dora, it seems a bigger nut to crack than we first thought."

"You are right. However, rather than speculating, I would rather see the size of the problem first. Although I do have an answer. The Americans. When we get there I will send a jeep with the Hungarian in to find the Americans. The 3rd Armour has the firepower to overcome the opposition."

Lieutenant Poulson nodded and I folded up the map. He said, "You know, sir, I never thought we would end the war like this. I thought it would be like Normandy. There would be a huge push and we would be part of it. We seem to be cut off from it now."

"I know what you mean. Are you still keen to stay in?"

"Yes sir. When I joined up it was just for the duration but I like this man's army. I like the blokes who are in it. The Commandos change the chaps who come in and make them better people, Beaumont, Fletcher, Emerson, even Davis. None of them are the same chaps who joined up. I have no idea what they will do in civvy street but they will be more likely to succeed now. I want to keep on doing that."

"And the others? Gowland, Shepherd, Crowe… the list is a long one."

"That is the part of the job I don't like."

I nodded and stood, "And that is why I am not staying in. Dad stayed in but it was different for him. It was about the flying. When he was in Persia he was like a flying policeman. No, Polly, the next few months, until we beat Adolf, will be my last ones in a uniform."

Before I turned in I spoke with Sam. He confirmed that the sub-camp was at Woffleben. "I think there are thirty S.S. and guards and about two hundred prisoners. They are all men. The women and children were taken away."

"Taken away?"

"Pál seemed to think they were taken away to be executed."

We had a rota to keep watch on the jeeps. When I was woken it was for the 0300 shift. Foster was with me. I went outside and, in the far distance, I could hear gunfire. It carried on the night air. It sounded to be in the west. It highlighted just how far our necks were stuck out. We had wriggled our way well behind the enemy lines. Now we were trapped. There would be no easy way out of this. Even if we did our job we would have to fight our way back to our own lines. Our only hope was the Americans. Ominously I had heard no tanks. The 3rd Armour would not be moving silently. Perhaps they had been held up as we had at Kassel and Rheda. The Brigadier had thought that we would have support. It seemed he was wrong.

We left just after dawn. My men had all donated bits of kit so that Pál was now more warmly dressed. He had eaten soup and some porridge. He looked better for it. Fletcher moved to Emerson's jeep so that Sam could translate for. He could have spoken German but Pál's German was not the best. He had learned it in the camp. We needed the precision of his own language.

I drove the few miles to the subcamp. "White, when we go into action I want you to watch Pál."

"But sir, that will leave you one gun light."

"It can't be helped. Pál is living proof of what the Germans did. He has to testify so that the perpetrators of this horror can be punished. From what he said the Germans are trying to wipe away the evidence of what they have done."

I did not drive fast. Our engines were noisy enough without revving them so that they would be heard. Pál spoke to Sam who said, "Sir, the entrance is half a mile away. It is on the other side of that hill."

Beyond the Rhine

I saw that there was a field close to the trees and the hill. I drove in and parked the jeep next to the stone wall. The others followed me. "Grab your weapons. I am leaving Sam and Pál here. We climb the hill and the camp is on the other side."

I led with Davis and his sniper rifle. I could see the higher peaks beyond us. The camps were all close to the mines where they had hollowed out factories. Pál had described the camp and we had a good idea of what it looked like. The huts for the prisoners were raised from the ground so that the inmates could not tunnel out. There was wire all the way around and four guard towers with machine-guns and, at night, lights. There was a barracks for the guards and a house for the commandant. A generator gave power for the lights. I was not necessarily intending to attack straightaway. I wanted to recce the position. We did not have enough men for a direct assault. When we were just below the crest of the hill we dropped to all fours and crawled.

We moved through the trees and saw, two hundred below us in a cleared bowl of land, the camp. It was as Pál had described it. I saw to the left of us a path which led down. The two hundred feet were almost vertical. It was as though it had been gouged away to reveal the slave camp. I saw that the gates to the camp were open and there were four lorries and a Kubelwagen. Someone was leaving.

Davis tugged at my arm and pointed to the far side of the camp. I took out my glasses. The prisoners were lined up and there were guards with guns. Other prisoners were in a trench digging. Then I felt a chill. It was not a trench. It was a grave. I saw, just behind them a freshly covered pile of earth. There were just eighty or so prisoners left. They were getting rid of the evidence. I saw the Germans setting up a machine-gun.

"Davis, they are going to shoot the prisoners. We will try to stop them. If they line them up to execute them then kill the machine-gunners."

"Sir."

I turned to my men, "Quick, follow me. We have very little time if we are going to save these men."

The path wound down through the trees and followed the top of the cliff. It descended quickly. We should have been more cautious but we had all seen what they were about to do. Pál's words had had an effect on my men. They knew the calibre of the monsters who called themselves men. We moved as fast as was humanly possible. At one point I almost stumbled but managed to grab a tree and stop myself tumbling down the hillside.

When we reached the bottom we were hidden from the camp. There was a wider track with tyre marks. I saw the cut trunks of trees. They had used it for logging. I cocked my gun as we ran along it. I had seen, from the hilltop, that all of the guards appeared to be gathered around the prisoners. The buildings would hide us from the Germans but there was only one gate and that was at the front.

"Lieutenant Poulson, when we get near to the camp take Gordy, Reed and Foster. Position yourselves so that you can shoot through the wire. I will take the rest and go in through the front gate."

"Sir."

As we turned a bend in the track I saw the camp ahead. Polly peeled off with his men and I led the rest. I heard a single gunshot from the camp and then a moment later a shout. As we cleared the building I saw two dead Germans and the others were pointing up to the hillside. Davis had opened fire. German guns sounded. Even as we ran towards the gate I heard the sub machine-guns of my men. They were firing short bursts. With eighty prisoners they could not afford to shoot randomly. Fletcher suddenly fired his MP 40 and a guard tumbled from one of the guard towers. We ran in through the gate. The prisoners were running in all directions and Germans were racing towards us and others to their vehicles.

I stopped by the Kubelwagen and used it to rest my machine-gun. The Germans had not seen us. I fired a short burst and three fell. As soon as I fired they stopped and began to fire at me. My men had taken cover and they began to open fire. These Germans had had an easy war. They had not had to fight. They had been cruelly treating slaves and that showed now. They outnumbered us but they were fighting skilled Commandos. Davis' rifle picked off those who hid and we slew those who tried to rush us. Pál's testimony had hardened us. We would not take prisoners. I fired short steady bursts. Germans broke cover and were shot. We were relentless. I changed my magazine and waved my hand.

When the ones before us had been killed I rose and led my men forward. I could hear Lieutenant Poulson and my other men. They were still firing. Not all the Germans had been killed. As we rounded the corner of the barracks I saw the last of the Germans fall. When I reached the trench, I saw that there were the bodies of five prisoners at the bottom. We had been too late to save them.

"Hewitt, Emerson, Fletcher, go and fetch the jeeps."

"Sir, that leaves just you and Sergeant Hay."

"Don't worry." I pointed, Lieutenant Poulson and Gordy were cutting through the wire. "We won't be alone for long."

They ran off and Bill and I went around the Germans to make sure they weren't playing dead. Sergeant Hay said, as he turned over a dead guard with his toe, "You know sir ten minutes later and they would all be dead."

"I know Bill. It is a sobering thought. If we had driven in then they would have opened fire. Thank God for Davis and his sharp eyes and steady hand."

"These bastards look well fed. I couldn't eat while others were starving."

"You can't compare us with them, Bill." I turned and shouted, in German, "We are British soldiers. You are safe! Come out! Pál Radnóti is with us."

Gradually, in ones and twos, they came out. Lieutenant Poulson and the rest of my men joined me. "We fired as soon as we could but we were still too late for some of them. Are there any left alive?"

"The guards are all dead. Betts and Foster go and search the dead Germans. Take any papers you can find. Fetch their greatcoats and distribute them amongst the prisoners. Bill go into the office and bring anything you find."

"Anything?"

"Evidence of these atrocities."

"I think you just need to show the prisoners sir. That is ample evidence."

"Just search eh?"

"Yes sir."

A knot of prisoners approached me. One said, in English, "Pál is alive, sir?"

"Yes, he is." I waved my arm, "We thought there were two hundred and fifty of you."

He nodded, "There were and then three days ago they began to execute us. They made us dig the graves and then they shot seventy men at a time."

"Why didn't you all try to escape or overpower them?"

He shook his head, "You do not understand, sir, we have lived as slaves for so long that all we know is how to obey orders and we are weak. Two men died while digging the graves."

"Then we will feed you now." I turned, "Lieutenant, Sergeant Major, go and see if there is food. We need to feed these chaps up or they may not last the day."

"We are tougher than we look, sir." The man stood as straight as he could. I saw the effort etched on his face.

Davis walked into the camp. I saw his face as he saw the prisoners close up. He shook his head. It was hard to take in the horror of it. Bill returned. He shook his head, "Nothing sir. They have burned everything."

I looked east. What about the main camp? My plan had been to wait for the Americans. Now I saw that we did not have the luxury of time. The rats were not only leaving the sinking ship they were making sure it sank quickly!

My men gave out the coats from the Germans. I said to the English speaker, "You can tell the others that we are getting food for them. Perhaps if they sat down." I was out of my depth. I needed Hewitt.

Just then I heard the sound of the four jeeps as they approached. When they stopped Pál jumped out and was mobbed by the others. Sam said, "Where are the others, sir?"

I pointed to the graves, "We were too late."

He looked crestfallen, "I thought…"

"I know. It makes it imperative that we get to Mittelbau-Dora."

Chapter 18

With all of my men in the camp, we soon got things organised. The guards had rations and we cooked them to make a watery stew. Hewitt told us that plenty of liquids, porridge and bouillon were what they needed. While it was being prepared he tended to those who needed his skills. It was noon by the time we had the food ready and they were being fed. My men acted as waiters. Davis and Foster stood guard in the watchtowers but I did not expect visitors. The lorries had been there for a quick getaway. Bill found explosives wired to detonate. They were going to destroy the camp.

As they ate I sat with my men. I had run through all the options open to us and I could see only one answer. "We can't afford to wait. We have to get to Mittelbau-Dora. I intend to go tonight. If we recce it in the dark then we can try to stop them executing their prisoners too."

"What about the Americans?"

"I am going to send Emerson and you Lieutenant Poulson, to find them."

"But sir we should be here with you. You can't afford to lose two men. You only have a handful anyway."

"Two men will not make a world of difference Lieutenant but if you and Emerson can bring the 3rd Armour then that will make a real difference. I need an officer to be there. It can't be you, you know that. Hopefully, you will find us alive and the camp intact, if not…"

"And these prisoners sir? What about them?"

"Good point Hewitt. In a perfect world, I would leave you and someone else to care for them but as we all know this world is far from perfect. The Lieutenant is right we need as many men as we can to stop this atrocity happening again. We leave them all the food and hope that Lieutenant Poulson and Emerson can find the tanks. If not then all of this will have been in vain."

I made Emerson and Lieutenant Poulson leave immediately. The sooner they left the sooner they could bring help. One jeep might just be able to sneak around the back roads. We used our spare fuel so that they had enough to search for the elusive American column. Then we sat with the prisoners' leaders, Pál and the English speaker, who we discovered was called Döme and explained what we were going to do. "I am sorry that we will have to leave you to fend for yourselves."

Döme shook his head, "You have given us the chance of life and this morning we had no such prospect. There will be others like us. Even now they may be suffering the same kind of summary executions. You are brave to try but there are so few of you."

"If we did not try then how could we live with ourselves after this war is over? We will leave after dark. We are leaving the German weapons for you. I do not think that the Germans will come but if they do at least you can defend yourselves."

Döme said, "You are a good man. You are all good men."

We knew where the camp was. There were aerial photographs. We had but a few miles to travel. However, that night, as we studied the maps for the last time before setting off we heard the sound of Lancaster engines. It was at least a squadron. We left the barracks and went out to see them and confirm that they were Lancasters. The German anti-aircraft lit them up. When they dropped their bombs I thought, at first, that it was Mittelbau-Dora that they were bombing but then I realised, as the explosions lit up the southeastern sky, that it was Nordhausen. Did this mean the Americans were close? I hoped so. Perhaps my men were already with them! It did not change our plans. We had been too late for at least five of the prisoners here. I would not risk more slaves dying unnecessarily. We would go in. The raid by the bombers delayed our start. There would be vehicles on the roads. Although we were travelling the smallest of country lanes we could not afford to be spotted. It was after midnight when we eventually left.

We shook hands with Döme and Pál. We said nothing. They had been dead men walking and they knew, better than any, that we might not be coming back. There were nine of us in three jeeps. We had left our Bergens at the camp. Our guns, grenades and ammunition, we carried.

We stopped the cars where a forester's track entered the trees. From the aerial photograph, the camp was half a mile through the forest. I had my MP 40 slung over my back and I carried my silenced Colt. Davis was with me. There were animals in the forest. The war had been good for them. There were fewer hunters. Men hunted men and not game. It was, however, unnerving to have a fox dart out in front of you as you walked along the overgrown forest path. As we neared the camp I heard the hum of its generators. There were no lights shining. They might have used them to watch the compound but the air raid had deterred them. The electricity would be needed for the interior lights and the radio. We crawled the last thirty feet to the edge of the forest.

It was when we reached it that I saw another German deterrent. The area between the wire and the forest was mined. I used my glasses to check out the wire. This camp was six times bigger than the one at Woffleben. They had towers at the corners and this time they were manned. They had similar accommodation blocks for the prisoners and a barracks for the guards. Significantly there were vehicles parked close to the gate. It was hard to see in the dark, but I thought I saw the distinctive pile of earth which indicated a fresh, mass grave. I took out my dagger and pointed to the mine-field. Gordy and Bill were next to Davis and me. We slithered forward and used the tip of the dagger to probe for mines.

They must have been buried some time ago for there was no helpful soil spill to show where they were and scrubby grass had hidden the deadly prong on the top. I was four feet in before my dagger touched the metal side of the mine. I slid the dagger around the side and then pulled it back. I carefully peeled back the sod so that the ones behind would see it. I crawled around it and sought another. I found four before we reached the wire. I don't know how many the others found. I turned and waved the rest of my men forward. White crawled carefully over the same ground I had cleared and was followed by Foster.

I had reached the wire first. I was grateful for the black of night. The towers were too far away for them to see us without the aid of lights. The next problem was the wire. Was it electrified? I picked up some grass and threw it at the wire. Nothing happened. I took out my wire cutters. I doubted that the charge if the wire was electrified, would kill me. They did not have enough power and the wire was extensive but I would get a nasty shock. I braced myself as I snipped the first wire. Nothing happened. Fletcher joined me in cutting a hole large enough for us to pass through. Gordy and Bill did the same lower down. Davis kept his gun aimed at the tower. If he saw movement then he would stop the alarm being given.

I was sweating. The minefield and the thought of electrocution had done that. I glanced at my watch. It would be dawn in an hour. We had taken too long. Finally, we snipped the last piece and there was a tunnel through the fence. If they had dogs then it would all be up but we had neither seen nor heard any. Once I was through I stood and levelled my gun at the towers. We had emerged just behind the barracks block. That had been deliberate. The sentries would be more concerned with the inmates. When Fletcher followed me through, I pointed to the barracks. He darted across. No alarm was given and I sent White and Foster to run across in quick succession.

Leaving Davis to follow me I ran to the nearest barracks. There appeared to be two such buildings. There were two doors on our side of the barracks. I pointed to them. Bill and Gordy took out grenades and parachute cord and booby-trapped them. I was about to lead my men around to the front when I heard the sound of a whistle. Was it the alarm? Had they heard us? I heard the sound of men rising. I looked around for shelter. There was none. I pointed to the far side and gestured for Gordy to lead his men there. I took Fletcher, White, Davis and Foster with me. We crawled around to the side and took shelter underneath the building. I could hear voices from above. The Germans were awake.

The floor above us vibrated as the Germans left the barracks. They must have been about to rise. They ran in groups to the slave quarters. I heard them shouting and emaciated skeletons were herded out. My plans had failed. I had hoped to destroy the barracks with their occupants inside. That way the slave labourers would be safe. That would not now happen. The labourers were in the open. I counted at least fifty guards. The only good news was that we remained hidden. I wondered what was going to happen. There were more footsteps above us and six more men stamped down the stairs. As they walked away I saw that they were officers. The prisoners were lined up. If they were handed shovels then we would strike. I wondered if they were simply moving the prisoners. I ruled the idea out as soon as the thought entered my head. They did not have enough lorries. There were over three hundred and fifty prisoners.

The Germans had their backs to us. Suddenly I heard an officer shout, "Open fire!"

Even as the Germans began to fire I had started shooting my Colt. The range was over a hundred and fifty yards but I could not just lie there and watch prisoners being executed. I saw the three officers all fall as Davis and I fired. My men opened fire. As soon as their officers started to fall the guards turned to see where the danger lay. I let rip with the German submachine-gun. I knew that there was a risk of hitting the slaves but we had to stop the Germans. They began to run towards us.

At the same time, I heard feet in the barracks above us. Suddenly the air was torn by the sound of grenades as the men who were still in the hut tried to outflank us by using the rear doors which we had booby-trapped. The explosion sent shrapnel out of the front of the barracks. We were protected by the building. I heard Foster cry out. He had been hit. We could do nothing about that for we were fighting for our lives. The Germans had realised that they outnumbered us and I saw some run towards the other barracks.

I shouted, "Gordy, watch your flank!"

Davis, having shot the sentries in the towers, was now picking off the officers and the sergeants. I saw two of the officers run to the prisoners and dragged five of them to their feet. They walked towards us with human shields. I knew from my conversation with Döme that the prisoners would not try to escape. They had lost their free will.

"Peter!"

"Sir!"

The light was much better now and my sniper fired. One of the officers fell with a third eye. The other ducked behind the five prisoners and they kept advancing towards us. Four of the guards jumped up to take advantage of the human shield. I shot one and Fletcher shot another but now there were three men advancing towards us.

I shouted, "Cover me!"

My men opened fire at the other Germans and I leapt to my feet and ran obliquely across their front. I had taken them by surprise. Bullets zipped around me but I bore a charmed life. I dived to the ground. Dropping my empty MP 40 I drew my Luger. I could see one of the men behind the prisoners. I took aim and squeezed the trigger. My bullet spun him around. His handheld on to one of the prisoners and, as he fell, he dragged the prisoner with him. Davis must have seen a target for he fired and a second German fell. Before the last one could recover I fired three bullets into him. As the others fired at me I rolled, clutching my MP 40. I had, inadvertently flanked the Germans and they were forced to turn to face me. I reloaded while bullets flew above me. White and Fletcher were emptying their guns at the Germans. We were hurting them more than they were hurting us.

Suddenly one of the Germans shot the five prisoners who had been human shields. They were just standing there. For some reason that made me see red. I leapt to my feet and ran towards the Germans who were just forty feet from me. I fired the MP 40 from the hip using short, controlled bursts. I saw one S.S. guard's head explode as two bullets hit him at less than twenty feet distance. My men came to my rescue. They rose from beneath the barracks and charged the Germans. It took the guards by surprise. Even so, it did not all go our way. I saw Betts tumble to the ground with a surprised expression on his face. Bill Hay fell, clutching his left arm.

Gordy Barker roared. It was a primaeval sound and, after emptying his gun he pulled a grenade and hurled it high in the air. My men all dropped to the ground and the grenade exploded in the air. I stood and took one of my grenades. I also threw it high into the air, shouting, Grenade!" As I did so I fell to the ground as the air was filled with pieces of flying metal. Then I stood and began shooting the Germans who had not recovered as quickly as I had. When my gun clicked empty I drew my Luger and, as the guards tried to rise, shot them until that was empty. Finally, I took out my Colt. It still had the silencer attached and I silently fired it until it, too, was empty.

One of the Germans shouted, "Surrender! We surrender!" He shouted in English.

"Watch for tricks! Hewitt, see to Foster, Hay and Betts." I began to reload. I put a fresh magazine in my Colt. I had only one left.

Scouse shouted, "Betts is dead sir. Poor bugger stood no chance."

I reloaded my MP 40. It was my last magazine. I shouted in German to the prisoners. "You are safe now! We are English and the Americans are coming." I saw nods but no one moved. They had truly been damaged by their guards.

"Gordy, Scouse, search the prisoners and make sure that the other Jerries are dead."

"Sir."

I went over to Hewitt who was strapping Foster's leg. "How is he, John?"

"Lucky, the bullet went through the fleshy part of his thigh. He will know he has a wound when it rains."

"And Bill?" I saw that Hay had his left arm held up to his shoulder.

"The bullet creased his collar bone. He will be fine."

I nodded, "Then we were lucky, Lance Sergeant. Poor Betts wasn't but I expected us all to die today."

He shook his head and smiled, "Not today sir."

With my gun reloaded I went over to the prisoners. There were ten of them. Others were wounded. Hewitt would get to them when he could. We had been too late for eighty or so prisoners but we had saved almost two hundred and fifty. I was proud of my men. No one else could have done what they had done. I examined the faces of the guards. They had cruel faces and there was anger on each one of them. We should have shot them there and then but we were British and we didn't do that. Hopefully, they would stand trial for what they had done and then they would be shot legally.

I saw that an Oberlieutenant had survived. He had been shot in the left arm. He glared at me as I approached him, "You will see, Englishman. We were right. The Fuhrer was making the world a better place for us all by killing the Jews! We should have fought together. We would have ruled the world!"

I shook my head, "We would never do as you have done. You disgust me. You will be taken and put in prison. There will be a trial and then you will be shot. Hopefully, I will be there when that happens." I turned and headed back towards my wounded men.

Sam White shouted, "Sir! He has a gun!"

There was a crack and it felt as though a wall had fallen on me. I tried to speak but I could not. I began to fall forwards. My arms would not move to stop me. Machine pistols opened fired but I could not stop my fall. My arms refused to obey me. I hit the ground and saw stars. I lay on the ground and I could not move. My eyes would not open.

I heard, as though from a distance, Fletcher as he shouted for Hewitt, "John! Get to him."

I felt hands on me but it was as though it was someone else's body. I heard Hewitt shout, "Sir, stay with me! Sir, fight! Scouse, stick something in the wound."

I heard more machine-guns. Once more it sounded far away. I seemed to be falling. I remembered going to the dentist when I was a child to have a tooth out and he had used gas. It felt like that. I was going around and around and falling into a deep pit."

The last thing I heard was, "God! I am losing him! Not now!"

It went quiet, and it went black and I felt no pain.

Epilogue

May 8th 1945
It was ironic that I Finally, came out of my coma on VE day. When I awoke I did not know that it was a special day. I just heard sounds. They were the first ones since I had heard, "God! I am losing him! Not now!" I soon discovered that the war was over and I had missed the last month of it. I woke in a hospital in Antwerp. I did not know at the time that was where I was. I opened my eyes and looked at a white ceiling. I thought, perhaps I had died and this was heaven but a pain, shooting up my arm, told me that I was alive. I didn't think that people felt pain in heaven. I turned my head and saw a bed. There was another man there. He was staring at me. He grinned, "I say, chummy is awake! Nurse! Sleeping Beauty has arisen!"

I tried to speak but it came out as a croak.

The man smiled, "Captain Reed, sir. I am due out today and I wondered if you would come to before I left."

A nurse appeared, "Major Harsker. Blink if you can hear me."

I blinked and tried to speak again. I sounded like a frog. She beamed, "Wonderful! Wonderful!"

She fled. Captain Reed said, "There has been someone at your bed every minute for the last three weeks. They will be annoyed that you woke up when they weren't there."

I was going to ask who he meant and then thought better of it. It would only come out as a croak. A door to my right opened. I heard it bang against the wall. I turned and saw Susan and Mum. Susan was crying.

"You are alive and you are awake. They said you would be but…. Oh, Tom!"

She threw her arms around me and began to sob into my chest. Mum held my hand and I saw tears streaming down her face, "My brave, brave boy! I prayed that God would spare you and he did." She squeezed my fingers hard.

Susan lifted her head and kissed me, "You are done with fighting, Tom Harsker! As soon as we can we are going home and we will be married as soon as we can! I have waited long enough."

The nurse came in with a glass of water. "Drink this. You have been on a drip since the last operation."

Susan held the glass so that I could drink. It tasted wonderful. I drained the glass and then tried to speak. "How long have I been here?"

Still holding my hand Mum came around the bed to sit on one side of me while Susan sat on the other. "The best part of four weeks. Today is VE day. The war in Europe is over."

"My men?"

I saw Mum roll her eyes, "I told you, Susan, that would be the first thing he asked. They are well. Lieutenant Poulson said that you lost just one man, someone called Betts. He seemed quite upset. They were here with you until we arrived. They are nice boys and they think the world of you. Such loyalty. You are your father's son."

"But how...?"

"From what I understand the Americans arrived just after you were shot. Your Sergeant, Hewitt, kept you alive until the American doctor could see to you. The bullet had lodged next to your spine. At one time they thought you were going to die. A Major Politho found a doctor who operated on you and took out the bullet. There was nerve damage and you went into a coma. It happened a lot in the Great War. The body shuts down to let you heal. You are healed. It will take some time for you to recuperate but Susan is correct. Your war is over. Major Foster arranged for us to come here and be with you. You have friends in high places. The Americans, Canadians, even the French have all been concerned. I understand the Prime Minister asked after you but forget all that. You are coming home."

I squeezed Mum's hand, "And I think I am ready. I thought I had died. This is the first day of my new life."

Susan kissed me, "When I said we would get married as soon as we get home, I meant it but we shall have your men come to the wedding." She smiled, "Your Sergeant Major Barker said I have someone to tease in your section!"

I laughed. My men were the best and they had served me well. We had survived the war and we could all get on with our lives. I would hang up my uniform and just bring it out on Armistice Day. Then I would remember all the brave men with whom I had served. None of us would ever forget the sacrifice they had made. We would all have to make sure that our lives were worthy of their sacrifice. The world would have to be a better place or it would have been in vain.

The End

Glossary

Abwehr- German Intelligence
AP- Armour Piercing Shell
ATS- Auxiliary Territorial Service- Women's Branch of the British Army during WW2
Bisht- Arab cloak
Bob on- Very accurate (slang) from a plumber's bob
Butchers- Look (Cockney slang Butcher's Hook- Look)
Butties- sandwiches (slang)
Capstan Full Strength- a type of cigarette
Chah- tea (slang)
Comforter- the lining for the helmet; a sort of woollen hat
Conflab- discussion (slang)
Cook-off- when the barrel of a Browning .30 Calibre overheats
Corned dog- Corned Beef (slang)
CP- Command Post
Dhobi- washing (slang from the Hindi word)
Doolally tap- Going mad (slang- from India Deolali- where there was a sanitorium)
Ercs- aircraftsman (slang- from Cockney)
Ewbank- Mechanical carpet cleaner
Fruit salad- medal ribbons (slang)
Full English- English breakfast (bacon, sausage, eggs, fried tomato and black pudding)
Gash- spare (slang)
Gauloise- French cigarette
Gib- Gibraltar (slang)
Glasshouse- Military prison
Goon- Guard in a POW camp (slang)- comes from a 1930's Popeye cartoon
HE – High Explosive shells
Hurries- Hawker Hurricane (slang)
Jankers- field punishment
Jimmy the One- First Lieutenant on a British warship
Kettenhunde - Chained dogs. Nickname for German field police. From the gorget worn around their necks
Killick- leading hand (Navy) (slang)

Kip- sleep (slang)
Legging it- Running for it (slang)
LRDG- Long Range Desert Group (Commandos operating from the desert behind enemy lines.)
Marge- Margarine (butter substitute- slang)
MGB- Motor Gun Boat
Mossy- De Havilland Mosquito (slang) (Mossies- pl.)
Mickey- *'taking the mickey'*, making fun of (slang)
Micks- Irishmen (slang)
MTB- Motor Torpedo Boat
ML- Motor Launch
Narked- annoyed (slang)
Neaters- undiluted naval rum (slang)
Oik- worthless person (slang)
Oppo/oppos- pals/comrades (slang)
Piccadilly Commandos- Prostitutes in London
PLUTO- Pipe Line Under The Ocean
Pom-pom- Quick Firing 2lb (40mm) Maxim cannon
Pongo (es)- soldier (slang)
Potato mashers- German Hand Grenades (slang)
PTI- Physical Training Instructor
QM- Quarter Master (stores)
Recce- Reconnoitre (slang)
SBA- Sick Bay Attendant
Schnellboote -German for E-boat (literally translated as fast boat)
Schtum -keep quiet (German)
Scragging - roughing someone up (slang)
Scrumpy- farm cider
SHAEF-Supreme Headquarters Allied Expeditionary Forces
Shooting brake- an estate car
Shufti- a look (slang)
SOE- Special Operations Executive (agents sent behind enemy lines)
SP- Starting price (slang)- what's going on
SNAFU- Situation Normal All Fucked Up (acronym and slang)
Snug- a small lounge in a pub (slang)
Spiv- A black marketeer/criminal (slang)
Sprogs- children or young soldiers (slang)
Squaddy- ordinary soldier (slang)
Stag- sentry duty (slang)

Stand your corner- get a round of drinks in (slang)
Subbie- Sub-lieutenant (slang)
Suss it out- work out what to do (slang)
Tatties- potatoes (slang)
Thobe- Arab garment
Tiffy- Hawker Typhoon (slang)
Tommy (Atkins)- Ordinary British soldier
Two penn'orth- two pennies worth (slang for opinion)
Wavy Navy- Royal Naval Reserve (slang)
WVS- Women's Voluntary Service

Reference Books used

- The Commando Pocket Manual 1949-45- Christopher Westhorp
- The Second World War Miscellany- Norman Ferguson
- Army Commandos 1940-45- Mike Chappell
- Military Slang- Lee Pemberton
- World War II- Donald Sommerville
- The Historical Atlas of World War II-Swanston and Swanston
- Churchill's Wizards: The British Genius for Deception 1914-1945- Nicholas Rankin
- *https://en.wikipedia.org*

Griff Hosker May 2017

Other books by Griff Hosker

If you enjoyed reading this book, then why not read another one by the author?

Ancient History

The Sword of Cartimandua Series
(Germania and Britannia 50 A.D. – 128 A.D.)
Ulpius Felix- Roman Warrior (prequel)
The Sword of Cartimandua
The Horse Warriors
Invasion Caledonia
Roman Retreat
Revolt of the Red Witch
Druid's Gold
Trajan's Hunters
The Last Frontier
Hero of Rome
Roman Hawk
Roman Treachery
Roman Wall
Roman Courage

The Wolf Warrior series
(Britain in the late 6th Century)
Saxon Dawn
Saxon Revenge
Saxon England
Saxon Blood
Saxon Slayer
Saxon Slaughter
Saxon Bane
Saxon Fall: Rise of the Warlord
Saxon Throne
Saxon Sword

Medieval History

The Dragon Heart Series
Viking Slave
Viking Warrior
Viking Jarl
Viking Kingdom
Viking Wolf
Viking War
Viking Sword
Viking Wrath
Viking Raid
Viking Legend
Viking Vengeance
Viking Dragon
Viking Treasure
Viking Enemy
Viking Witch
Viking Blood
Viking Weregeld
Viking Storm
Viking Warband
Viking Shadow
Viking Legacy
Viking Clan
Viking Bravery

The Norman Genesis Series
Hrolf the Viking
Horseman
The Battle for a Home
Revenge of the Franks
The Land of the Northmen
Ragnvald Hrolfsson
Brothers in Blood
Lord of Rouen
Drekar in the Seine
Duke of Normandy

The Duke and the King

New World Series
Blood on the Blade
Across the Seas
The Savage Wilderness
The Bear and the Wolf

The Reconquista Chronicles
Castilian Knight
El Campeador
Lord of Valencia

The Aelfraed Series
(Britain and Byzantium 1050 A.D. - 1085 A.D.)
Housecarl
Outlaw
Varangian

The Anarchy Series England 1120-1180
English Knight
Knight of the Empress
Northern Knight
Baron of the North
Earl
King Henry's Champion
The King is Dead
Warlord of the North
Enemy at the Gate
The Fallen Crown
Warlord's War
Kingmaker
Henry II
Crusader
The Welsh Marches
Irish War
Poisonous Plots
The Princes' Revolt

Earl Marshal

**Border Knight
1182-1300**
Sword for Hire
Return of the Knight
Baron's War
Magna Carta
Welsh Wars
Henry III
The Bloody Border
Baron's Crusade
Sentinel of the North
War in the West

**Sir John Hawkwood Series
France and Italy 1339- 1387**
Crécy: The Age of the Archer

Lord Edward's Archer
Lord Edward's Archer
King in Waiting
The Archer's Crusade

**Struggle for a Crown
1360- 1485**
Blood on the Crown
To Murder A King
The Throne
King Henry IV
The Road to Agincourt
St Crispin's Day

Tales of the Sword

Modern History

The Napoleonic Horseman Series
Chasseur à Cheval

Napoleon's Guard
British Light Dragoon
Soldier Spy
1808: The Road to Coruña
Talavera
The Lines of Torres Vedras
Bloody Badajoz

The Lucky Jack American Civil War series
Rebel Raiders
Confederate Rangers
The Road to Gettysburg

The British Ace Series
1914
1915 Fokker Scourge
1916 Angels over the Somme
1917 Eagles Fall
1918 We will remember them
From Arctic Snow to Desert Sand
Wings over Persia

Combined Operations series
1940-1945
Commando
Raider
Behind Enemy Lines
Dieppe
Toehold in Europe
Sword Beach
Breakout
The Battle for Antwerp
King Tiger
Beyond the Rhine
Korea
Korean Winter

Other Books
Great Granny's Ghost (Aimed at 9-14-year-old young people)

For more information on all of the books then please visit the author's web site at www.griffhosker.com where there is a link to contact him or visit his Facebook page: GriffHosker at Sword Books

Printed in Great Britain
by Amazon